A Fresh Start in the Countryside

GISELLE ROZZELL

THE CHOIR PRESS

First published in the United Kingdom in 2023 by
The Choir Press

ISBN 978-1-78963-426-6

To Mike, Dan and Vicki for their constant love and support throughout xx

Chapter One

Monday morning came around with a shock to the system, as neither Jodie nor her daughter Amy wanted to get out of bed, yet they would both be late for school. Her alarm went off at 7 am. Within a few seconds she rolled over, placing her legs on the floor, and stretched a few times to get the blood flowing to parts that needed it most. Pulling up the blind, by its cord by the side of the window looking out into the small but tidy garden below, she was pleasantly greeted by the sun beaming towards her. That, in itself, put her in a good waking mood as she went into the bathroom, had a quick shower and dressed, ready for the day ahead, before waking Amy next door. On opening her door Amy was already bolt upright and sitting in bed, chatting away to her two much-loved teddies, one from Jodie, the other from Aunty Sue, her dad's sister.

'Good morning, darling, how are you this morning? It's Monday, so we need to get a move on,' she reminded Amy, with a big smile on her face. She grabbed some clothes from Amy's wardrobe and placed them neatly on her bed. 'Breakfast in five.' She turned to face Amy.

'Thanks, Mum,' she replied, putting her clothes on.

She's a good girl, Jodie thought, *I taught her well how to dress herself*, which was a bonus.

A bowl of porridge and a piece of toast set them both up for the morning ahead. They soon locked up and headed to the car to drop Amy off at the local primary school, where she was greeted by other mums and Amy's class teacher. Before Jodie handed her daughter over, she kissed her goodbye, drawing her into a tight hug, before Mrs Newbury took over with the other classmates in tow. She then jumped back into her trusty car, heading to her local primary school, where she worked as a teaching assistant with children with special needs. She parked up in the staff car park, and walked inside to the staff room, where her red locker was. Taking her bunch of keys out of the rucksack slung over her back, she opened the door, and immediately noticed a note, on the shelf inside the locker, with her name in bold gold-coloured letters written on a white envelope. *What's this?* she thought. She liked surprises; hopefully this was one. She hung her coat on the coat hanger, on the rail above, before she quickly opened the mystery envelope. Much to her surprise it was from her colleague, Jo, wishing her a happy birthday, which she had entirely forgotten, what with all the latest goings on and her move from the farm where she had previously lived with Ralph, her ex; two years before they had gone their separate ways, due to his breakdown after juggling farm life and a newborn overwhelmed him. He had moved, out seeking counselling. *How lovely*, she thought. She continued reading: *meet you later for dinner at 7 tonight; all arrangements made so no need to worry about Amy, we've got this.*

Now that's kindness overload, Jodie thought. She slipped the note into her trouser pocket and headed to Year 1 with a spring in her step. Opening the classroom door she was greeted with a banner overhead, saying "Happy Birthday Mrs Smith", with a pink and red smiley-face helium balloon dangling from the ceiling. Jodie felt touched as she wiped a tear from her eye with the tissue stuck up her sleeve.

'Thank you all so much, it's so kind of you to think of me. I'll remember that for a long time'. She continued, 'We'd better get this morning started.'

Jodie's task was to hear everyone read from the famous Biff and Chip books, all stacked neatly in various boxes. All the books were graded, some with a few words, others a pageful, according to their reading ability. Jodie sat in one corner of the classroom with her list of readers for the morning, whom she called out to sit beside her, all taking turns reading to her for ten minutes, which didn't seem long although long enough for five- to seven-year-olds.

As the day continued, with lunch then play time outside, Jodie was becoming more and more excited about the evening's events which Jo had written about at the start of the day. Jodie, now on her lunch break in the staffroom, took the note out of her pocket. She assumed she would collect Amy from school to take her home, possibly packing an overnight bag as she could be sleeping over that evening; reading between the lines, indicating everything was taken care of, she muttered underneath her breath.

It was fast approaching 3.30 in the afternoon. On hearing the final bell ring, indicating the end of the day, coats on and bags over their shoulders, all the children proceeded out into the front yard where parents and guardians were eagerly waiting for the school gates to open and where they could collect their little live wires! Jodie was finally off duty, so she headed back to the staff room to gather up her belongings from her locker.

'Hi Jodie,' a voice sounded behind her, as she was tapped gently on the shoulder as she stood by her locker. 'All good for later?' her friend Jo asked, as Jodie turned around to see her smiling at her.

'Oh yes, you took me by surprise this morning with the note in my locker! How did you get in without a key?'

'Mum's the word,' Jo continued. 'Your next mission is to go and collect Amy, take her to yours, pack an overnight bag with her PJs and clothes for the morning, and someone will escort her off the premises to her final destination. No need to worry about anything, it's all taken care of. Just enjoy your night, knowing sweet Amy is well catered for and will have a ball.'

'OK, that sounds perfect, thank you,' she said, giving Jo a friendly squeeze on her arm.

'I'll see you in an hour at mine,' she replied.

On that note she headed towards the staff car park to drive to Amy's school, pick her up and take her home, pack her bag as instructed and wait for the next instructions. *Oh, this is getting very exciting,* she thought. *I love surprises and it makes life that much more interesting.* As she drove home, she related the events to Amy, who immediately showed her excitement by shouting 'Yay, I'm going for a sleepover, my first since we moved here, Mummy.' She showed her enthusiasm by clapping her hands and jiggling her little body on her car seat at the back of the car to the music her mum played on Spotify through Bluetooth from her phone.

So far so good, Jodie thought, as she pulled up on the drive by her flat. 'Time is ticking Amy,' her mum made this into a game as she released her from her car seat. 'Come on, let's go inside, have a quick drink then pack an overnight bag as per my instructions,' she smiled at Amy.

The kitchen clock was showing five o'clock when a rat-tat-tat at the front door made her jump out of her skin. She called out to Amy, 'You nearly ready? This could be your driver waiting to take you to the next part of the secret.'

'I'm ready, here I come,' as Amy appeared from behind her bedroom door. 'My bag is packed with my favourite PJs and my teddy to cuddle up to if I get scared in the night.'

Jodie walked towards the front door of her flat, unhooked the chain and opened the door, to see her best friend, Lydia, whom she knew from her days in London. She couldn't believe her eyes as she let out a squeal of excitement. They leant, in kissing one another's cheeks as the French do.

'Hi, gorgeous, I've come to take Amy out for the night and escort her to mine as instructed. And no, we're not going back to London ... I've moved to Winchester with my partner, John, of a year now. We have a little girl, Eliza, who is seven and is very excited to meet your Amy. How about that, then, young lady?'

'Well, you kept that one a secret. I knew nothing about it! Admittedly we've lost contact since I split with Ralph two years ago. I don't know what to say, though congratulations are definitely in order, happy days, as they say!' Jodie swooped her into a huge hug with a clear tear of joy falling down her right cheek. 'We have some catching up to do, later this week perhaps?'

'Definitely,' Lydia responded with a real look of happiness, being clearly slightly overwhelmed by this current meeting.

'Amy love, your chariot awaits you, you can't be late or Cinderella won't be going to the ball. How about that, hey?' Jodie raised her voice with excitement.

Amy soon dashed to see who was at the door and startled her mum by giving her a tight hug, kissing her goodbye and marching out with this strange lady she'd never met; yet Mum assured her she was in safe hands. Amy took Lydia's hand as they walked out of the door, heading to her chariot, as she was told. It wasn't a slightly bigger car than her mum's. Amy formed a picture of a glass chariot on wheels, with windows all around, just as she had heard about once in a bedtime story her mum had read to her.

Chapter Two

With them both safely out of sight, Jodie turned around to concentrate on getting herself ready for her big night, whatever that entailed. She skipped into the kitchen like Amy would, flicked the kettle switch on and took out a green tea bag with lemon, placing it in a mug to calm her anticipated nerves before heading for a quick shower and dressing up for the night ahead. Opening her wardrobe, her eyes fixated on a red block dress she had bought herself before Christmas and not yet worn. She took a brand-new pair of black leggings which would look perfect with her red ankle boots she'd bought a few years ago, keeping her cosy and warm kicking the January blues. Sorted, she exhaled, with a big smile plastered on her face. Now all she needed was a shoulder bag which could house her purse, phone and reading glasses case, not forgetting some tissues, all of which bulked up a bag, leaving little space for anything else.

A quick glance in the mirror: she liked her outfit and felt good about herself, giving her a boost she so needed. A quick glance at her next instructions: she was due to meet others at seven in the Lamb Inn pub in Winchester, being only three miles up the road. *I'd better get my act in gear*, she thought. A quick bit of mat lippy on her lips and she looked the bees' knees, ready for the night ahead, which she was now so excited about; a first in so long she couldn't remember, with her fellow long-lost friends. Dashing downstairs, grabbing her set of keys to lock up the flat, making sure everything was turned off, she headed to the trusty car she'd decided to name Herbie, from the film with the white VW Beetle she loved watching many years ago, only hers was sky blue without the huge headlights coming out of the bonnet of the car and it didn't splutter along as she drove it onto the main road.

Soon she arrived at the Lamb Inn as instructed, parked up, locked her Herbie and marched up with confidence to the front double door entrance, pushing the swing-back door open, noticing a cosy bar in front of her with a handsome barman pulling a pint of beer, she assumed. A few others mingled around the bar, some hitched up on various bar stools.

'Can I help you?' the guy smiled directly at her.

'Oh yes, I'm here on a surprise date with friends, that's all I've been told,' she replied. 'I'm Jodie if that helps' if you have a booking.'

Suddenly she heard a raucous noise coming from the bar. She turned around to see her friend Jo and a few other colleagues spring into life.

'Happy birthday, Jodie, welcome to your mad party date night.' Jo handed her a glass of Bucks Fizz, her favourite party drink, in a flute glass.

'Oh wow,' she beamed from ear to ear, 'now that's a surprise I wasn't expecting.'

'We know, and this is where it all starts!' they replied in unison.

The lamb Inn was one of those nice and cosy, warm-heart-feeling pubs that was local, which many frequented, either in passing or for lunch or an evening meal out. Everyone seemed to know each other, offering advice when needed. It felt like family, especially for those who weren't local or had no family. Jodie fell into that category. It was just her and Amy from now on. She was about to step out into her new life here and start again, meeting new friends for both of them. She'd always had her daughter's best interests at heart since she was born, and more so after seeing Ralph struggling to juggle the farm and home life. She did miss him and prayed he'd get therapy to guide him through this stressful life he led; often wondering how he was and thinking she might pick up the phone or text him, as, after all, he was Amy's father. He must surely miss her, knowing he was just going through a bad patch at the time and needed rescuing. Tomorrow she'd text him. They were still friends for now. She'd concentrate on tonight, pushing that thought from her questioning mind, she decided.

The girls were escorted to a table near the glowing warm fire which had recently had a few logs added to it, lighting up the room with its woody smell which was pleasant. A friendly waitress soon stood by the table asking for drink orders. A bottle of pinot grigio, Jo suggested, all the girls agreeing, and a bottle of still water, she added. Meanwhile they handed round the table menus, perusing their potential orders. Jodie preferred fish or chicken to other meals, so she chose sea bass with dauphinoise potatoes and green beans, a nice healthy option. The others preferred a steak with French fries and peas. The waitress came back with a tray of drinks placed by each one, then took their mains order. No side orders as they all wanted a sweet with a coffee to follow. 'Perfect,' the waitress said, as she went towards the till, punching in their individual orders.

Jo started the conversation by asking Jodie how she was settling into her new job and life in general.

'Things are going really well,' she gestured. 'Amy and I are happy, which is the most important thing, isn't it,' she continued, 'which is all that matters for now, I guess.'

'Any news on Ralph?' Sue asked tentatively, hoping not to push any unwanted buttons.

'Nothing, but I might text him tomorrow as I think we've had long enough to mull over the situation,' she quickly responded.

'Good thinking,' they all replied together, 'you've got this all worked out, we can tell,' they continued.

The waitress soon arrived with all their meals in tow, placing them by each one on the table mats. 'Thank you,' they acknowledged the kind waitress, who looked more at ease as the night drew on.

Each meal looked delicious as they tucked in. 'Ooh, the seabass is beautiful and melts in the mouth, yummy,' Jodie commented first to the others.

'The steaks are perfectly cooked too,' the others responded, fixing their eyes towards Jodie. Within minutes all meals were polished off, and they were ready for the desserts, followed by special coffees. The evening couldn't have got off to a better start; everyone was relaxed and thoroughly enjoying themselves. They soon were devouring the dessert menus after the mains were cleared away. The choices were all to die for, from melting chocolate puddings to mouth-watering sticky toffee pudding with a choice of ice cream or cream. Desserts chosen and suitably delivered followed by coffee floaters, they decided to retire to the nearby lounge on comfy chairs with an oval table in the middle and a pile of red chequered coasters. Another lady, clearly on 'after drinks' duty, soon brought their floaters on a circular tray, placing them by each one on a coaster laid before them. 'Thank you,' they gestured individually as she passed them by.

The night was still young at only 9pm as they were all gathered in a cosy lounge, sipping their coffees and individually wrapped chocolates in silver paper with a picture on top placed on the saucers of their coffees. They chatted away about all and sundry, laughing and joking, making the evening a very jolly memorable birthday treat Jodie wouldn't be forgetting in a long while. She was planning on another get-together in the next few weeks. Whether she could push another sleepover for Amy or possibly take it in turns so no one missed out on social get-togethers had to be discussed between them. She was sure they could come to some arrangement, as they all needed a catch-up after work to let off steam.

Time flew by as 11pm approached and all needed to go home to face the music the following day. Bidding their goodbyes with a French kiss, they picked up their belongings and headed outside to their individual cars.

'I'll pick Amy up in the morning,' she informed Jo with a thumbs-up as she looked back towards her. 'I'll text Lydia once I get home, which she will either read now or later, depending on whether she took advantage of an early night.'

'Perfect,' she replied, waving her goodbye.

———

On driving up to the flat she noticed a light shining through the lounge blind and wondered if she had left a light on before locking up or had forgotten to switch it off. She hoped it was the latter and no one had broken in; imagining the chaos she might find if that happened she put that thought out of her mind and told herself she was just overthinking things. She took her keys out of her bag and turned the key to find that all was well. No damage awaited her; she'd just left the light on, which was a good idea as she wouldn't have to enter a dark flat. She flicked the kettle switch on for a final nightcap of camomile tea before hitting the pillow, as by now she needed her beauty sleep before collecting Amy in the morning. That prompted her to text Lydia her intentions about picking Amy up and hoped all was well.

Sorry it's late, I just got home. Hope Amy will promise to repay you looking after your Lottie. I'll be around at 10am if that's OK. I'm not hungover just tired, lol. She pressed send.

A few seconds later came the jolly reply, *Yes all is well at no. six (the house number). Don't worry, I'll bring her over, we can natter over one of your lush cappuccinos from your fancy machine. Sleep well hun xx.*

'How thoughtful was my lovely friend, where would I be without her,' Jodie said out loud. She finished her tea and got herself ready for bed, checking that all was locked up and all the lights switched off, before walking to her bedroom and changing into her PJs. She lay in bed and turned off her bedside lamp, which was one of those "one touch" with two brightness settings, before descending into a deep slumber.

The next morning, bang on cue, there was a knock at the door. Lydia and Amy waited eagerly on the other side as she peered through the tiny eye hole in the middle of the door, checking to see if it was them or the trusty postie. She quickly opened up, to be greeted by arms stretched out and flung with force into a tight hug around her middle, nearly squeezing her to death; well not quite, but obviously eager to see her mum again.

'Amy love, you OK, had a good time at Lydia's?' She could have said aunt, but hardly anyone said that these days. It seemed so old fashioned, especially when it wasn't really your blood aunt and if Amy forgot to call her aunt she might get told off or something stupid, so she didn't want to start this conversation as it seemed far less confusing.

'Come on in, you two, I'll make us all drinks. Orange for you, Amy, as it is your favourite and coffee for us adults.'

'Perfect,' Lydia replied. 'Oh, and I've brought round one of my jigsaws. I no longer use it; Amy likes this one and seems very good at it, too. She's making big progress in her memory skills and articulation in general,' bringing Amy into a tight hug. Amy was keen to show her mum her jigsaw skills as she promptly sat on the floor and turned the box over, all the pieces flying out into a pile on the wooden floor.

'You start the jigsaw and I'll pour you some orange juice. I'll put it on the dining room table.' Drinks were strictly forbidden on the floor for obvious reasons and Jodie thought it best to start right before a bad habit kicked in. She didn't mind what other mums asked of their children, but Amy wasn't going to fall into any bad habits anytime soon. Amy sensed it was mum's time to catch up, so Jodie clicked the cappuccino button on her coffee machine, hearing and smelling the coffee trickling into the flowery mug underneath, with a dusting of chocolate on top. Lydia was instantly salivating; her cappuccino with pure heavenly delight. After making one for herself she took them over to the small table next to the sofa, then brought out a box of flapjacks to enjoy with their coffees.

Sorted, she mused to herself, with a beam across her face. They soon got chatting about the night out, and how Lydia's evening went with Amy sleeping over. Jodie was confident all had gone to plan as Amy was in general an easy-going child. She had brought her up with the best intentions, teaching her how to behave in front of her friends and adults alike. As with all mums she could only do her best and that she certainly did, as a poorly behaved child wasn't much accepted in today's society; life was hard enough as it was in this current mad climate they lived in with so much unwillingness all over the place. Life had changed so much since Jodie's childhood days. Now you kind of needed to sink or swim and hit rock bottom if you listened to the negative news. A positive attitude these days was a must to keep themselves upbeat and happy.

After a good natter, both Lydia and Jodie needed to get on with their day as a much-needed food shop was required for starters, and so the list went on as usual. They made their farewells. Next on her to-do list was to text Ralph to see how he was doing: she missed him as a good friend and obviously Amy's dad so she thought it was time to see how he was. Perhaps his situation had changed and one day he surely would like to reunite with his girl who he loved so much, but at the time he wasn't coping very well and needed a break. That was then, this was now. On that thought she took out her phone from her pocket, took a deep breath, retrieved his number from her contacts, which she hoped hadn't changed, and clicked the number. *Here goes*, she thought, hoping he'd be surprised to hear from her after a year's break. She was aware he might have hooked up with someone else, even have a new kid, though that seemed unlikely. Ralph was never a chap to fully jump in; he always was cautious about meeting someone. Even though their relationship had grown at a steady pace, no fool rushed in; they both always agreed on that at least.

Chapter Three

Weekends were always welcome; in Jodie's eyes a time to chill, slow the week's pace down by at least two notches, eat favourite food, go out to the local park, breathe in the fresh air, meet up with friends or make new ones; come home, play a few games or do a jigsaw with Amy and just generally relax with snacks in front of the TV. That was her ultimate love of spending a weekend with or without Ralph by her side. OK, here goes. His mobile was ringing, she counted the rings patiently, albeit slightly nervous when he finally picked up. After the third one she heard, 'Hello, who is this please?' Hearing his calming voice, she instantly felt relieved of any pre-stress nerves.

'Ralph, it's me, Jodie. I hope you don't mind my ringing. I just thought it's been a while since we spoke and wondered how life is treating you. I prefer to hear good than not,' she continued.

'Oh Jodie, what a surprise. In fact, I was just thinking the same the other night, just wanted to know how our Amy is doing now. She must be,' he hesitated, 'at least five by now by my simple maths brain.'

'Correct,' Jodie confirmed, 'she is and turning out to be a little beauty, mostly. No big tantrums for the moment,' she added, 'touch wood.'

Suddenly they seemed delighted to hear one another and both spoke at the same time.

'I was wondering if I could see Amy, if that's agreeable to you. Where are you living now, Jodie?'

'Yes, of course, you are her dad, after all, and time has elapsed, so those baby days are well and truly over now. I'm sure you can cope better now, and besides,' she continued, 'I do actually miss our chats once Amy is tucked up in bed. I mean I do like my own company and all that, but once in a while a father-figure chat wouldn't go amiss.'

'OK, let's arrange something. I can come to you if it makes life easier, or vice versa.'

This was indeed going much better than she had first thought. An amicable solution seemed far less hassle than going to a third party, a solicitor or similar, and really much healthier in the long term where a child of this age was concerned.

'So tell me, Ralph, where are you in the country, well I assume you are anyway?'

'I'm in Wolverhampton, near Birmingham, as I finally decided on a career change, away from the lonely farming. As you remember I struggled with it, and so I did a course in carpentry, believe it or not. I was always good at putting woodwork together at school and thereafter at polytechnic college, I just didn't have the opportunity then to develop my skills, so I helped Mum and Dad on their farm. It was fun with all new adventures, growing up with sheep and a few chickens, but I didn't intend to follow it through into adulthood. I just carried on till we met, and the rest is history, as the saying goes. As you age you usually get wiser and I think I realised soon after we had Amy that things were beginning to get on top of me: coping with the farm as Mum and Dad aged, and just having had little Amy, I wanted to spend more time with her, not sorting the daily running of the farm out. I hoped you understood and I have to say you helped get me out of that soul-destroying situation at the time. I would have had a big meltdown had you not stepped in to rescue me, Jodie. I'm sorry it's taken this long for us to communicate again. Can you forgive me, Jodie?' he concluded.

By this time she felt rather emotional and shed a tear, which he fortunately couldn't see. This sounded like a changed Ralph: a side of him she had never seen while they were together. They were still very young then, mid-twenties, with no real idea how their lives were going to pan out. Could this be a reconciliation, she wondered, realising she was jumping too quickly to conclusions.

Back then she'd made the right decision to pack her bags, with Amy in tow, away from the daily stresses they all encountered, as it was blatantly obvious Ralph could no longer cope with the running of the farm and giving his time to Amy, which she so needed and deserved. Jodie saw she'd made a mistake in leaving him to juggle everything whilst she took on her job at school: what was she even thinking of at the time? They were an inexperienced couple yet one of them had to take the lead, and clearly, she had to take the initiative. Following their initial phone conversation, they agreed to meet. She invited Ralph to see her new lodgings, which seemed easier, giving him a nice break from city life, one she was sure he preferred — away from cars, trams and polluted air, full of toxic fumes, smoking out of chimneys from factories, engulfing the skies with black smog, and bad fumes affecting every man and their dog as they walked along the often littered dark and dingy pavements especially at night. This was something she could no longer put up with, having strong feelings about a green plant earth and climate change, which they were all living through, as well as poverty, as prices staggered; people once able to afford basic food were now struggling to make ends meet in today's society. No man, woman or child should have to constantly endure such daily hardships. It was little wonder there were so many mental health issues around the country. There was one crisis after another, the NHS striking here and there, and even ambulance strikes, leaving emergency services in utter chaos; patients suffering the most, with extra-long waiting times, either stuck in ambulances or hospital corridors, waiting to be seen by doctors and nurses. A situation that desperately needed resolving, and fast, before more lives were lost which could have been avoided. *I'm glad I got that off my chest*, she thought, *even if it doesn't resolve anything for now, I think I've had my say on the matter.*

Jodie glanced at the calendar on her phone to sort out a

suitable date for Ralph to come up and see her and Amy. She texted him some dates and waited for his reply. Moments later she read: 'Next weekend Friday night would suit me if that's OK with your plans.'

Checking twice, Jodie agreed, saying she was looking forward to his visit. 'The spare room is already made up. I'll tell Amy, who I'm sure can't wait to see you,' she concluded in her text.

'Thank you, Jodie, I really appreciate that. See you next Friday. Forward me your address which I can add to my satnav.'

Jodie wanted to make his visit a memorable one as she hoped, deep down, that she could reconnect with him in some way, even if just for their daughter's sake. Jodie could settle with that even if there was no further involvement between her and Ralph; she just wished for his father's role to restart in Amy's life, which she so deserved and would surely question more as the years drifted by. Jodie couldn't bear all those questions as to where Amy's dad was and why they didn't live together anymore. This was something that Jodie had never envisaged would happen to her when she had a child, yet these situations cropped up from time to time, especially in the modern society she lived in. At least one positive outcome was that Ralph and Jodie always remained as calm as possible for their daughter's sake. Both had seen the hurt from broken relationships which didn't paint a pretty picture, one that they tried their utmost to avoid.

Amy heard the news that her dad, whom she still remembered, was due to come over and stay. She was excited and asked her mum if she could paint a picture in her next art class, of the three of them together or similar, which Jodie found rather touching, given the fact that Amy had lost connection with her dad all those years ago. Obviously, he must have made a deep impression along the line, which plastered a big beaming smile on Jodie's face. Things didn't turn out as badly as she once thought, back then. She had been conscious of his breakdown and how it might have lasting effects, what with Amy being so young then; however, that proved not to be the case, fortunately for Amy. A huge sigh of relief instantly put her mind at rest concerning what could have been a damaging period in Amy's life.

The days rolled into each other as Friday approached, Amy becoming more and more excited with her dad's imminent visit. Amy drew her image of them being a family again as she completed her painting in class. Amy wanted to keep her painting a secret from her mum, so asked her teacher, Miss Thomas, to keep the painting away from Jodie's inquisitive eyes for now. Amy told Miss Thomas all about her dad and his visit on Friday, telling her about the sheep and chickens her dad had had on the farm she seemed to recall so well, especially when one of the chickens chased her around the yard, much to her amusement and probably a bit scary at times. Miss Thomas enjoyed listening to the children's stories in "share time" once a week, together on a Monday morning, a time when most of the children could still remember the weekend's events. Some were very amusing, making their peers laugh out loud, bringing a cheerfulness to the classroom. There were twenty in the class, which seemed a reasonable number to cope with. Miss Thomas had been appointed a few months after the Christmas break, after accepting her new post at the school, which suited her more. She changed years from third year back to first year, as was often the case: a regular turn around to gain experience in each year.

Jodie's task was to give the spare room a facelift and a quick vac and dust around before Friday, which was fast approaching. This bedroom hadn't been used since they moved from the farm and was generally used as a dumping room, to be sorted at a later date, storing anything from small memorable items her mum had given her, to a few soft furnishings, which included a new duvet and bedding set her mum had given her the previous Christmas, perfect for the spare room, which she was going to make up for Ralph on his arrival.

The room was freshly painted in pale yellow with a window blind in a mid-brown to offer a blackout at night. The duvet was covered in cream with an array of rose flowers printed on top;

underneath was in plain cream, which didn't get seen anyway. A bedside table with two drawers and a one-touch lamp on top added to the pleasant feelgood factor in the room. She stepped back to the bedroom door and was happy with her quick but satisfying makeover which, in effect, took only an hour to complete. Another tick of her satisfied to-do list.

She felt satisfied and pleased with her accomplishment, as she was really hoping for a fresh start with Ralph, as he was Amy's dad. Deep down she still loved Ralph; after all, they had fallen in love and had Amy as a result. Ideally, she would love to rekindle their once so-in-love relationship but for now she could just be satisfied with Ralph's newfound zest for life in his new career and abode. Everyone deserved a second chance at happiness, she couldn't deny that, and he had made that turn around; thinking back, she was proud he had accomplished it. After all, not everyone had the guts to turn full circle. He clearly received some therapy, which must have spurred him on, not wanting to waste any more time of the life that was given to him. *Now that was quite a profound statement, one I have never voiced before*, she thought to herself, showing obvious maturity as she aged and since becoming a mum.

The day had come with Ralph's imminent arrival, which only meant that the weekend was upon them as soon as she woke on Friday morning. Her alarm buzzed into action, telling her it was time to get ready for her day at school, which she was actually looking forward to as her task for the morning was to listen to pupils read, which she always loved; marking their progress in their individual exercise books which the class teacher would peruse when next marking their work. No doubt this was going to be over the weekend, as was often the case for teachers, as there wasn't enough time during school hours.

Jodie jumped out of bed, showered and dressed quickly, enjoying half an hour to herself before opening Amy's door to sort her out. To her surprise Amy was dressed and ready for some breakfast before school.

'Good morning, darling, how are you this morning? It's Friday, which means the weekend starts later.'

Amy, jumping up and down, followed her mum to the kitchen, where Jodie flicked the kettle on to make herself a herbal morning "get you going tea" then sorted their cereal and poured a glass of orange juice for Amy, her preferred drink before school.

'After school we are having a surprise guest to stay, which is all I'm saying for now as I need you to concentrate at school,' she told Amy, who seemed to get the gist as she was keen to get to school. She loved her teacher and her peers. This was the exact response she was looking for as the fewer distractions the better, and at her age Amy didn't really care what happened after school. *That went well,* she thought. Dishes placed by the sink and a bathroom visit made, they were all ready to walk out of the door to the car. Friday was a dinner at school, no packed lunch required, which she was relieved about as she needed to prep last things before Ralph was due at 5pm later that day. At drop-off at Amy's school, a peck on the cheek was sufficient to satisfy Amy as she eagerly marched through the school gates, noticing her friends and pals from other classes. She knew her once-little girl was fast growing up to be a confident fully-in-control girl who knew her own mind. A good step in the right direction, she muttered under her breath. She made her way up and walked boldly into the staff room, unlocking her red locker and placing her coat and bag inside. Grabbing the lanyard, which had a smiley face on her photo, from her bag and slipping it over her head, she proceeded to her assigned class.

'Good morning, Mrs Smith,' they said in unison as she walked into class.

'Good morning, all,' she replied, with "let's get this day started" she wished she could have added, but didn't dare in case of a funny reaction from the class teacher!

All settled down, quickly getting their reading books out to start the long list of readers for Jodie. One by one they were called to sit next to her, to start reading where they had finished on Monday. The idea was that they would take their reading book home and read each night to their parents as their daily homework, which should slowly improve their reading skill to the next level. Some children either forgot to pack their book in their school bag or didn't have the opportunity to read at home for a variety of reasons; which was very common in that day and age. The family was divided or there was a single-parent situation, or it was too much effort from the child's point of view. This was something all teachers faced through the early school years where teaching assistants intervened with much sensitivity, encouraging pupils to read and become more confident as time progressed.

Much to Jodie's relief, the sound of the school bell echoed around the school, meaning lunchtime had finally arrived. The children stood and formed an orderly line by their classroom door, waiting their turn to walk quietly into the dining hall, where all lunch-break supervisors stood to attention, escorting them to form a line in front of the serving hatch. Fish fingers and fries were on Friday's menu, followed by a yummy chocolate brownie with ice cream or a fruit flapjack as an alternative, thus offering something for everyone's taste.

Half an hour later they went outside to play, running around to let off some steam and excess energy, then it was back in an orderly fashion to their individual classes. Today it was Jodie's turn to supervise and she enjoyed giving herself much needed fresh air after being stuck in an overheated classroom, which didn't do anyone good long term. Another bell was rung outside by one of the duty teachers, alerting everyone to attend their classes in the afternoon before home time, which she couldn't wait for. She'd had enough for the week, she wanted to spend quality time with her girl and welcome Ralph to the scene after a year. She felt slightly on edge about this reunion but at the same time was excited for Amy to see her dad again. Jodie wondered how much she remembered him, if she would recognise him after all this time, and she thought she would. Ralph had always tried to play the loving caring dad towards Amy which Jodie often noticed was a blessing. People do change after all; especially after the often trying baby years that everyone, even first-time mums, encountered.

Chapter Four

Friday night came at last, and Ralph was due anytime soon, which suddenly threw her off balance. A zillion thoughts rushed through her brain, which seemed crazy, as she was actually looking forward to seeing him again. Yet the nerves kicked in, followed by doubt, the usual what-ifs and why-nows and what did he really want? Maybe he still had some feelings towards her which secretly she was hoping he did. Would she get together with him again? Actually, she probably would. She at least wished for him to rekindle his relationship with Amy, if nothing else. Amy deserved that, being the adored daughter he had once thought the world of, popping out of Jodie's belly that crisp Monday morning five years ago, much to her relief after all that pushing and panting! She quickly glanced through the bedroom door where Amy's dad would be sleeping, checking that all looked clean and smelled sweet as she placed a scented candle on the windowsill, sending wafts of herbal incense across the entire room. She hoped Ralph wouldn't find it too overpowering, as she loved her tea lights and scented candles, especially when relaxing in a bath, which she hadn't enjoyed for a while.

Amy was currently busy doing a jigsaw in her room, which she often did after school whilst her mum prepared dinner. Tonight would be no different. She'd made a vegetable lasagna, ready for Ralph, remembering it was one of his favourite dishes, with garlic bread on the side. A quick glance at the kitchen clock showed 5.15. Time was ticking, fast approaching Ralph's imminent arrival.

A noise outside in the corridor startled her, as she thought she could hear footsteps outside. Sure enough, the doorbell rang. She became all flustered, looking herself up and down in the mirror hanging on the wall, checking her appearance, then called out to Amy, who by this time was alerted to the ring and popped her head slowly round her bedroom door to see who was there. Jodie unhooked the chain on the door, to find a handsome, casually dressed man holding a perfect multicoloured bunch of flowers in front of her with a gold bow tied neatly around it, a cinnamon-like stick appearing at the top, which added to its elegance.

'Wow,' Jodie immediately exclaimed upon seeing them in front of her. 'They are beautiful,' she added, with a smile beaming on her face. She immediately recognised Ralph even after all those years apart. She had once been in love with the guy, after all, and Amy was the result. She couldn't contain herself, showing her excitement at seeing him standing before her by nearly forgetting her manners and asking him in. She saw Amy, from the corner of her eye, hovering behind the door. Having not seen her dad for at least a year she didn't recognise him. However, she hadn't seen him close-up yet, which might trigger something. She heard her mum welcome this man into their cottage, so Amy assumed her mum felt comfortable with him, and saw the lovely display of flowers, which in itself was reassuring.

'Amy, you can come out now, it's OK, and meet your dad,' she reassured her as Amy quickly wrapped her arms around her mum's legs, protecting them both from any possible harm until she had been properly introduced to Ralph.

'She's a bit shy, which is understandable as she hasn't seen you for so long,' Jodie remarked.

'It is totally understandable,' Ralph continued, making eye contact with Amy. 'Hello Amy,' he gestured, by extending his right hand towards her to shake. 'Remember me, your dad, all those years ago on the farm with the sheep and clucky chickens you used to chase around the yard, then collect the eggs from the coop.'

Amy smiled nervously at her mum, not sure what to say in response. Amy suddenly chuckled, looking straight at her dad.

'Well, that was then, this is now,' Jodie said, looking at Amy. 'Come on through.' She gestured to Ralph, leading the way into the kitchen, pulling out a chair by the small square table in the middle. 'What can I offer you before dinner? Tea, coffee, water or orange juice, which Amy usually has?'

'A cup of tea would suffice for now, perhaps something a little stronger over dinner,' he replied.

'A cup of tea coming up.' She looked at him with a smile that suggested to him she was happy to see him again.

Amy waited for her juice, eyeing Ralph up, eager to show him her room and the jigsaw she had started earlier. She soon walked over to her mum, nudging her to bend down to listen so Amy could ask her a question, which was, could she show him her drawing. Jodie wondered if it was a bit premature to show him her bedroom first, knowing they both needed time to catch up, whilst she was putting the finishing touches to the dinner. Ralph started the conversation by thanking her for letting him come over and also sleep over. He was very grateful for that and to finally meet up with Amy again after all this time.

'I've moved on with my life now, Jodie, and had therapy too, which has helped me move forward, resulting in a career move as well. Mum and Dad had to sell the farm as they were unable to continue living there. They had a change of heart and wanted to call it a day before they got too old and immobile.'

Jodie was surprised but quite understood. They couldn't do everything on their own whilst their son was recovering and naturally, they were worried about his future. They realised that Ralph and Jodie were both still in their twenties and had just had Amy, which was all new to them, and they wanted to support them as much as they could, which seemed very reasonable. They were new grandparents and wanted to spend quality time with the new granddaughter they were so proud of. 'That's all very understandable,' she reassured Ralph.

'Dinner is ready!' She raised her voice towards Amy's

bedroom, in the hope that she would come running into the kitchen at any second.

'Smells lovely,' Ralph affirmed to Jodie, with a big smile on his face.

'Hope it tastes as good,' she replied, looking towards Ralph and noticing Amy standing by her side. 'Go and sit next to Daddy, he won't bite!' she exclaimed, at which Ralph started to laugh, patting the chair next to his.

She started to dish out with a serving spoon and knife, cutting the lasagna into good-sized portions. She opened the oven, retrieving the baking tray with the garlic bread, which she started to slice up into portions; two slices each. They all tucked into their yummy meal, enjoying each other's conversation. She planned on letting Amy get to know her dad now before bedtime then they could finally have some adult time, which included a glass of wine, sitting in the lounge. Amy was showing signs of tiredness after a long school week so a quick bedtime story, read possibly by Ralph if she would let him, would suffice her wishes. They could continue their getting to know one another tomorrow morning, Jodie hoped. She was keen to have some much-needed catch-up with Ralph, hoping the feeling was mutual.

Plan A sorted; she moved swiftly on to Plan B. PJs and a bedtime short story for daughter Amy. 'OK, Amy, choose a short story, perhaps Winnie the Pooh and Piglet, and either Daddy or I will gladly read it in your bedroom,' her mum tried to cajole her into action.

'Erm, Mummy tonight and Daddy tomorrow, please,' Amy whispered to her mum shyly, as Jodie leant down to Amy's level.

'Perfect,' she added, with a wink and a nudge, sitting on Amy's bed.

'It's Winnie the Pooh day today as we celebrate many decades since this humbling story was written, bringing joy and laughter to millions around the world. The book was translated into a lot of languages so that people who couldn't understand English could join in the amusing love and affection shown in all the characters in the book.' She continued to explain simply about the characters in the book. She picked up the picture book, which had a few words on each page, showing Amy the beautiful illustrations and drawings captured inside. 'So we have Winnie the Pooh being the main character, who is well known for his love of honey, as shown here,' she pointed to a large light-brown pot of honey and Pooh dipping his finger into it and licking the yummy runny honey. 'Pooh was a bear dressed in yellow with a napkin tied behind his neck in order to catch any drops of honey or whatever else he ate, being a messy bear but adorable,' she told Amy, which she loved hearing about.

'Sounds very funny and loves his honey,' Amy grimaced with a big smile on her face, turning over the thick page of the picture book. Amy saw a little pink pig named Piglet who was standing beside Pooh, his tiny hand clasping Pooh Bear's chunky hand, which Amy found amusing; she started to chuckle, looking her mum in the eye.

'Piglet is small compared to Pooh and is wearing a little light pink suit around his tiny body,' Jodie explained.

'Isn't he cute,' Amy said, at which she started to giggle with glee, just like Piglet would have done.

This brought a little tear of sheer happiness to Jodie's face. She wiped it away with the back of her hand so that Amy wouldn't notice. As she was reading and explaining the characters and activity going on in the book, she noticed Amy becoming tired as she stifled a yawn. She remarked, 'OK, Amy, I think that's that for tonight, we'll continue the book tomorrow. Perhaps your dad can read you some, if you like,' whereupon she closed the book and put it to one side of her bedside table in the drawer underneath where other favourite books were stored. She bent down, giving Amy a hug, and kissed her on her forehead. She pulled the cord of the window blind and walked to the door. Switching off the light and glancing back at Amy, who was nearly asleep, she closed the door gently behind her. She breathed a sigh of relief and proceeded back into the kitchen to clear up before joining Ralph in the lounge, offering him a glass of wine.

On entering the small kitchen, she noticed the plates had been cleared away and neatly stacked by the sink waiting to be put into the small dishwasher which neatly fitted alongside the kitchen sink. 'Thank you, Ralph,' she muttered under her breath, 'just what I needed.'

Ralph, hearing her return from Amy's room, walked into the kitchen, smiling at her and saying, 'I hope you didn't mind my clearing the plates away. Thanks for making me so welcome tonight, Jodie. I would have stacked the dishwasher but, you know what we men are like, we get it all muddled up, unlike you women who seem to be experts at uniformity and all that, as if something was not quite in its desired place.' He looked at her, laughing.

'Point taken,' she chuckled to Ralph. The tension started to ease somewhat as they relaxed into one another's company. She felt relieved, as she was really enjoying this evening so far. 'A glass of wine, perhaps?' she gestured to Ralph, who nodded yes, feeling equally relaxed.

'A pinot grigio, if that's OK?'

She smiled back at him, seeing his face light up. 'Coming up,' she returned the look. They soon settled into the lounge with their vin blanc on individual coasters on each side of the table. 'Cheers,' she said, holding her glass up towards him. 'To better times ahead, whatever that entails,' she concluded, before they both took a swig of wine.

'And thank you for allowing me into your home and letting me be part of Amy's life again after all this time, it means more than you think,' he added with a smile across his lovely face.

'No problem, Ralph, I'm glad you came, really. Amy needs a dad back in her life while she's still young, before she asks any questions about us.'

The evening started well as they soon settled, relaxing into each other's company. She felt more than happy; things were going as well as she'd hoped, as deep down she admitted to herself that on many occasions she had missed his presence and as a dad to Amy. She always wondered if Amy noticed him missing from their once seemingly happy life together. It didn't feel natural to go it alone, now that Amy had turned five. Could there be any hope of a reconciliation? Was she jumping to conclusions, or was she just wishing on a bright star, placing both hands in a prayer position. 'Stop it,' she muttered under her breath, 'just enjoy the moment, being reunited', so she did exactly that.

They were chatting about everything that had been and gone, Ralph not wanting to dive back into his past life with his minor breakdown after everything clouded around him. He had realised after a few therapy sessions that it was a pointless exercise to keep chewing over the same old thing, knowing that it wasn't going to make him move on in his life anytime soon. The therapist had showed him ways to put all thoughts of despair to the back of his mind, in order to take a positive step forward; it was very hard at the time, so seeing sense in the end had set him free once and for all, he told her, with a big sigh of relief across his once-broken face. It was time to start a fresh move, which meant a career change too, but most of all he couldn't imagine life without his lost daughter Amy; he missed seeing those important milestones whilst she was growing up. That was time no-one could rewind, much as they would like to.

''Top up?'' She lifted her glass, staring into his eyes like a love-sick puppy.

'Why not?' he replied with glee. 'You only live once,' he added, 'thank you, Jodie.'

'No need to thank me, just relax and enjoy,' she smiled, sounding a bit flirty without intending to be. The wine must be to blame, she mused. Ralph was clearly starting to relax more, so it seemed perfect timing for her to delve a little deeper, questioning him on where he thought he stood now, or at least what he wanted in life, where he thought he was heading. She was desperate to understand him more, and also what made him tick, as they say. 'Can I ask you, why did you come yesterday? What was your motive, assuming you obviously wanted to see Amy again, and possibly me?' she chuckled, placing her glass on her coaster.

Ralph started to open up, telling her that he had missed them both and deep down wanted to rekindle their relationship in some way, as life was so precious. He saw that Amy needed him in her life, after making eye contact with her.

She asked about his plans for the weekend and how long he wanted to stay, as she was hoping he would stay a little bit longer.

'I need to be back by Monday morning to start work, so I was hoping I could stay till Sunday afternoon, perhaps have a meal together, then catch the train back to Wolverhampton, if you're OK with that,' he continued, hoping she would say yes.

She looked at him with a smile, which signalled a thumbs-up on her part. 'I'm sure Amy would be over the moon with that. It sounds good to me, as we both have school on Monday. Let's just enjoy the weekend and see how it goes from there. I've made up the spare room for you; there are fresh towels on the bed. I hope you like the décor, as I made an extra effort to perfect it! On that note, I'll see you in the morning at 7 – only joking!' she concluded with humour.

'Good night, Jodie, sleep tight and see you tomorrow.' Ralph got up, stretching his body, enabling him to move with more ease after sitting so long. They put their empty wine glasses by the sink and headed to their separate bedrooms. She was happy and could dream of some flirty moments they had encountered tonight, with no desire so far to allude to anything more. It was early days, after all, having just reunited after all these years. She did miss the cuddles from time to time, being only human, with women's hormones flying back and forth. *Stop this*, she reminded herself, snapping those thoughts out of her mind with a chuckle. Why did life have to be so complicated?

Chapter Five

As morning started to break through, the light seeping through the corners of the window, she knew it was time to get up after having a dreamy night's sleep. Wrapping herself in her fluffy PJs she knocked on Ralph's door, telling him she was going to have a quick shower.

'No worries, Jodie,' he answered.

She then knocked on Amy's door to see how things were with her. As she opened the door Amy looked up, bright-eyed, noticing her mum in her PJs by her door. 'Morning, Mum.'

'I'll just have a quick shower before your dad gets up then I'll start on breakfast,' Jodie told her.

Ten minutes later she was in the kitchen making tea and coffee for whoever wanted it and a herbal tea for Amy. She seemed to like peppermint tea these days, which helped settle any tummy problems; not that Amy had many, but it helped her insides, nonetheless. Her mum was to blame for introducing herbal remedies, which she preferred over the usual tea. That said, she loved her two cups of coffee in the morning as well, which was the sole reason she had invested in a very good coffee machine, which Ralph had helped to fund as a Christmas present one year.

Once they were all seated around the kitchen table, she asked, 'What does everyone fancy doing today? We could go out for lunch later or go to the cinema?' she continued. Amy was the first one to respond.

'Go to the cinema?' She put her hand up, as if she was at school.

Jodie continued, 'What do you think, Dad?' looking at him questioningly.

'I think a cinema outing sounds perfect: some popcorn, my

treat followed by McDonald's if you fancy,' he said enthusiastically.

'I'll see what's on,' she continued, 'sounds like a perfect Saturday to me.' She got up, starting to clear the dishes and stacking them in the dishwasher. She took her phone out and looked up the local Vue cinema, which was advertising a selection of children's movies, and *Frozen* seemed to be a great one, which Amy seemed to like. They agreed on a time to be ready to leave.

After watching *Frozen* they were in need of some food and drink so off they went to McDonald's. As Amy was five, Jodie suggested a Happy Meal with orange juice, with the usual toy included. A McDonald's chicken burger suited the adults, with two cappuccinos, to eat in. Job sorted; they were all happy to tuck in once Ralph had done the honours by bringing it over to their table. All fed and watered, they proceeded back to the car.

'Are we going home now?' Amy asked, feeling a bit weary after the day's activities. 'I want to play with Daddy, perhaps do another jigsaw,' which was her favourite occupation for the moment, reading being next in her top three favourite activities.

'Don't worry, we are all getting too tired to think; we all need some down time together at home. We could also play some board games if you want,' Jodie added.

Back at the flat she asked what drinks everyone wanted: Amy fancied a hot chocolate as her mum had a packet of extra smooth. She flicked the kettle switch on for herbal tea; Ralph just had an ordinary one, taking three mugs from the cupboard. They all sat around the kitchen table discussing which board game they'd like to play, or a picture game with cards, which suited Amy more, given her age. Snakes and ladders was the first choice, followed by several games of snap, with animal cards to match up. They were a family again, which felt wonderful, and Jodie for one didn't want this time to end. Amy was clearly enjoying her dad's company and engaging very well with him, as if no time had passed between them. Things were obviously getting easier as her young years passed by, yet these moments were the most precious ones, which Ralph didn't want to miss out on. The evening was soon closing in and it was Amy's bedtime, which she was definitely ready for as she started to yawn. She went into her room, put her PJs on, had a quick brush of her teeth and a trip to the loo, then she was ready to hit the pillow and dream about today's events.

Adult time resumed shortly, with a glass of wine for both, watching a movie. Jodie flicked through and stopped at the recently shown film with Bill Nighy, whom they both loved as an outstandingly funny and serious actor. *Living* was one neither had seen so this was their time to get comfortable with some popcorn, which Jodie placed in the microwave. Hearing it pop and jump about she was always nervous it would explode from the bag, thinking it can't be that good for the microwave, the smell of the sweet stuff wafting through the room in anticipation. Ping and it was ready to be transferred into a large red bowl she had bought from Tesco some time ago – too big for breakfast yet perfect for snacks and tasty nibbles. They reminded her of French breakfast bowls! She sat on one end of the green sofa and Ralph the other, placing the bowl in the middle for easy snacking. She clicked play on the TV remote to start the film. Seeing Bill Nighy in the starring role brought comfort to both of them, knowing the movie was going to be excellent, expecting nothing less from him. It was only a movie but how could a film be so emotional and mesmerising? It was all how you imagined it in your mind. A pack of tissues was essential as there were sad and touching moments, you couldn't help shedding a tear or two, eyes filling up, sending one trickling down your cheek. The advantage of watching on catch-up was the pause button for bathroom breaks and beverages as you wished. The bottle was soon being emptied into their glasses and, helping themselves to popcorn, occasionally their fingers would touch, both apologising like naughty school children, yet secretly liking the feeling of intimate connections which they had missed over the years apart.

Jodie was aware that they wanted to reconnect with each other but needed to take things at a very slow pace, so as not to rush and spoil what could become a delicate moment. Neither wanted to force anything, so for now they remained the best of friends, knowing that Amy was in the middle of the relationship and didn't deserve to get hurt again. Jodie knew that wouldn't happen, as time had moved on and they were getting older and hopefully wiser. They were aware time was ticking away, with Sunday fast approaching, when goodbyes would have to be said as Ralph was leaving late afternoon to return to his normal life in Wolverhampton.

He'd had the best weekend for as long as he could remember. Meeting Amy after all those years was epic, not forgetting reuniting with Jodie, whom he seemed more relaxed with; a fresh start all round rekindled feelings for one another, sparking some small but definitive flame between the pair of them.

Good vibes, she thought, something she inwardly longed to happen again since she had never fallen out of love with Ralph; it was just his breakdown. She knew neither she nor Ralph could cope with it at the time, as Amy had to come first in every subsequent decision they made to protect her from lasting harm, but fortunately this wasn't the case, they realised, with a huge sigh of relief on both their parts. Jodie was always a very understanding person with lots of empathy to her persona arising from her own experiences growing up. Ralph was very similar, despite his manliness and hanging out with his mates in the pub. Men did that more than women, their roles in life being very different, having different views on life as they knew it. Once you became a parent life changed instantly from the day your child entered the world, solely relying on you for everything. Suddenly your time was put on the back burner, as the saying goes, until much later, in fact twenty years, after which they left the nest and started their own life's journey, having to look after themselves with the good and bad days ahead of them. You never stopped learning in life; kept trying again and again, hopefully rectifying your mistakes, at least if you had any respect for each other, which they had. Everyone was allowed to fall flat on occasion as long as they dusted themselves off to start again, with no judgement. A profound statement but nonetheless a wise one.

After a few drinks and the welcome end to the film they needed some sleep. Ralph suggested a final Sunday lunch out at the local Toby carvery.

'Sounds perfect to me, Amy will love that,' she smiled back at Ralph, lighting up his pale brown eyes with joy.

'Good, I'll book a table for noon tomorrow,' clicking his phone here and there and finally sending his booking. Within a few seconds a ping alerted him to the Toby booking. Sorted. As they both got up, they placed their wine glasses by the sink, switching the lights off everywhere, locked up and headed to their individual bedrooms.

'Good night, sleep tight and don't let any bed bugs bite,' she smiled at Ralph, who laughed back at her.

On Sunday morning Jodie woke up feeling a hint of slight sadness, knowing she had to say goodbye to Ralph. As his departure grew ever closer, Amy would be upset, having spent much-needed one on one time with her dad, which she had really loved, as if they'd never spent time away. Seeing that brought much pleasure and joy to herself, lighting up her face with endless smiles. What's not to like, she chuckled to herself. Wounds were healing, which meant time was indeed a great healer in their world. For now, she wouldn't spoil things by wondering if there could be some future together again, knowing that anything and everything was possible if willingness and love were thrown into the equation; something she relished and thought that possibly Ralph might feel the same way. Time would tell. She had no intention of staying in the flat long-term; as much as she made it a pretty home for herself and Amy, it was just temporary until she knew whether a long-term relationship with Ralph was on the cards. She needed more space, in a house with a lovely garden, possibly with a dog in tow. Jodie had grown up with a dog, a pointer; in her opinion the best breed. They gave out so much love in their personalities and temperament, especially towards children from a very young age. Jodie's dad had fallen in love with pointers on a holiday in Menton, France, when she was thirteen. On returning to the UK, he enquired about local German short-haired pointer breeders and soon picked up a sweet baby girl pup, just nine weeks old, who stole her heart from the start. She cried most of the way home, as leaving her mum and brothers and sisters behind proved to be a big wrench for such a young pup. Jodie remembered holding her in the kennel with the other puppies running around with wire netting all around fixed on wooden panels with a gate opening for easy access. She instantly fell in love with this cute liver and white speckled five-week-old puppy who stole her heart from the start; with a white stripe down the centre of her eyes, looking so cute in her arms as she held her like a baby, her arm underneath her cute bottom supporting her body. They named each puppy once born and hers was named after Trilby, the hat, which was unusual and seemed perfect, so they all agreed to keep the name. Looking back at those childhood days brought great memories for Jodie. From there on she became dog-smitten. She had to be included in every family photo her dad took of Trilby, soon becoming her furry sister as they became inseparable. Jodie pinched herself to bring her back out of her past dreamy moments, knowing she had a few things to sort out before they went out for lunch.

All dressed and ready, they had a little breakfast to tide them over till lunch; with coffee and tea and juice they all were satisfied. Ralph had already packed his weekend bag, ready to be taken to the station by Jodie after their meal. One last check around the house to make sure that he hadn't forgotten anything, and he could then spend his last morning with Amy, playing another game of snakes and ladders, which Amy had perfected over the weekend. She was in her element having great fun with her dad, her new best friend in her life. Ralph clearly enjoyed every moment. Finally, Jodie said, 'Time to clear away, as we need to go to the restaurant for lunch.' Amy didn't need telling twice as she jumped up excitedly for a quick bathroom stop before running downstairs. Coats on, they were all ready to head off in Mum's trusty Polo as she turned the key in the ignition to get her warmed up for the off. She couldn't think of the farewells that followed at the station, no doubt sending them both into meltdown; she just needed to focus on the few hours remaining.

On arrival at the restaurant, they were all agreed on a Sunday roast: chicken, roast potatoes, vegetables, stuffing, with cranberry jelly on the side. Ralph went up to the serving counter, joining the small queue, leaving Jodie with Amy. A lady came over to their table bringing drinks, a final pinot grigio for the road before Ralph started his train journey home; Jodie joined him with another glass. Ralph returned shortly with his plate piled up, letting Jodie join the queue to get hers and a child portion for Amy, which she devoured on her return. Still time for dessert followed by two coffees for the adults. Chocolate brownies for both with vanilla ice cream and two scoops of ice cream with chocolate sauce for Amy, leaving everyone satisfied.

Next stop, the station awaiting Ralph's imminent train on platform two. Jodie didn't want to make a big deal with saying farewells so a tight hug around Ralph's waist sufficed Amy. Jodie kissed him like the French do on either side of the cheek, both secretly wishing for a hug but for now they thought it best not, not knowing how Amy would react later on once Ralph had left. They had all had a fabulous weekend together, leaving them on a high, which in Jodie's opinion was the best place to remain.

'See you both soon.' Ralph shouted as the train moved away from the platform. Jodie couldn't help but shed a tear which she didn't want Amy to see; clearly Ralph had noticed as he finally stared into her eyes, which must have touched him, she convinced herself. The train, nearly out of sight, got smaller and smaller as it started to build up speed departing the station. They headed back to the short stay car park, making their way back to the flat. Jodie needed to catch up on bits of washing and generally tidy up before a new week soon landed, starting all over again.

Sunday was usually an easy day, so Amy was allowed to watch an animated movie of her choice, which was *The Lion King*. She made herself comfortable, curled up on the sofa with the much-loved teddy she had named Ted for short, which Jodie's mum gave her after Amy was born and which she had cuddled ever since. Jodie was happy to continue with her chores, knowing that Amy was occupied for the next two hours. Amy always was an easy-going child and knew how to occupy herself, either with reading a book or doing a jigsaw, which kept her mind stimulated and her in a good mood. Neither Jodie or Ralph could have wished for anything better. They both aimed to be the best parents to Amy, giving her stability at home and at school which proved so far to be working well.

Chapter Six

Monday morning soon came around with the sound of Jodie's alarm by her bed. 'Time to rise and shine and face the day with a smile across our faces,' she muttered to herself. Placing her legs dangling off to the side of the bed, giving a full body stretch, she soon headed to the bathroom for a quick shower. Choosing the clothes for the day she was ready to wake Amy before getting breakfast for them both. She was about to open Amy's door when Amy beat her to it, dressed in the clothes she had laid out the night before.

'Good morning, my lovely, ready for school already!' Jodie remarked, walking towards the kitchen where everything was set out on the table. Amy skipped to the kitchen, seemingly bright and raring to start the new week. She sensed that her dad's visit had lots to do with it; the perfect weekend she had not had in age, if not the only one she fully remembered. This put a huge smile on her face; *a new start in our lives*, she thought. She never planned on staying here long, just a temporary stopover even if things didn't work out with Ralph. She pictured herself living in a small, terraced house with a bit of a garden, enough to have a small dog, perhaps, or a bunny in the interim. She was hoping to inherit some money one day, while obviously not wishing anything terrible to happen to her mum for now. At least she had a vision; many people don't plan that far ahead. That said, life has a habit of changing when you least expect it, and we all have to be ready to adjust in those circumstances.

Coats, hats and bags ready, Jodie grabbed her keys to lock the house up as usual and walked to her trusty car. *Groundhog Day*, she immediately thought, *as each day started the same way. The only difference was that each school day was different; never knowing what was on the agenda made the day more bearable and exciting, giving a vision and a positive spin on things, which was the main thing: a perfect analysis*, she thought. Amy couldn't wait to arrive at the gates to meet up with her classmates and her favourite teachers.

'Good morning, Amy,' some teachers smiled back at her as Amy walked past.

'Good morning, Miss,' followed by their name, Amy replied.

'OK line up nicely, please, before we walk swiftly into class,' the duty teachers chorused together as the children passed them by. 'It's cold out,' they muttered under their breath, rubbing their gloved hands together. They were soon in their classes, waiting to have the morning's register taken by the class teacher. The teacher opened up her register book for that day and started to read the pupils' names in alphabetical order, each replying, 'Yes, miss.'

Ten minutes later the school bell rang, alerting all classes for school assembly in the school hall, which took place each Monday morning. Each class walked in together, sitting on chairs, starting with the youngest class to Year Six. The headmistress, Mrs Harrison, would soon arrive at the front to address the pupils. The school was a C of E school: a Christian emphasis was very much the ethic for the school, despite society being multifaith these days. Jodie was very particular about a Church of England education, as she was a believer back in her day. She naturally only wanted the best start for her daughter; later on, she was free to make up her own mind about life. Mrs Harrison started by welcoming everyone to a new week at school, which she called family: home from home, where they could hopefully relax with each other, supporting one another to form better friendships, where bullying and being unkind would not be tolerated at any level. This was the strong ethos of the school, indeed their motto, which was written on a plaque outside the Head's door for all children to see as they walked past to their classrooms down the corridors.

Mrs Harrison started the assembly with a usual prayer

followed by the music teacher on the piano leading them into a familiar chorus where the words appeared on the overhead screen pulled down from the ceiling. A familiar tune to Graham Kendrick "Shine Jesus Shine", was a much-sung chorus by the school, all clapping whenever they felt it appropriate. Mrs Harrison continued with a short yet thought-provoking "thought for the day" then in a few minutes asking anyone putting their hand up to share what had happened over their weekend, which always proved interesting.

Amy listened very attentively, placing her hand in the air and hoping she'd get picked and asked if anything exciting had happened to her. There was a multiple show of hands as Mrs Harrison turned her head around the hall. Noticing Amy, very eager to announce herself, she was asked to join her at the front and share her weekend's event.

'Amy Smith, lovely to see you this morning and wanting to share your news with the others.' She continued, 'Please tell us.'

Amy, being a bit shy at first, soon overcame it. She eagerly explained, 'We went to the cinema and then had a McDonald's happy meal with my mum and dad.' Everyone began to clap, wanting to know which movie she saw. Amy added, 'We watched *The Lion King* which was awesome.' She nearly started to giggle happily, which everyone found amusing.

'That sounds like a perfect weekend event,' Mrs Harrison replied, with a big smile across her face. 'Thank you, Amy, for sharing that,' as she indicated to her to go back to her seat. 'Time for one more,' looking around for any other eager hands dangling in the air. Sam, from year Three, was next to come forward and share his eventful experience. This time it was a birthday party, again with a McDonald's visit, wearing birthday hats, something which was all too familiar in the younger years and often very trying for parents and other mums. A strong coffee was often needed after such events, most teachers thought, nonetheless an unforgettable experience in their young lives. Usually parents couldn't wait until the party time was over with.

Half an hour later all were back in their class, where they could officially start the new week.

Chapter Seven

Jodie's school day started off with a list of readers, taking a group to a quiet corner of the room to read, ticking them off one by one on her list once they had read to her in turn. Every class had their individual timetables to adhere to. The day progressed with lunch followed by play to let off steam from the morning's learning, then finally home time at 3.45, which everyone eagerly awaited as their learning limits were indeed pushed to the limit, including staff. The further up the school years you went, the harder it became to do homework, therefore the less play they had. Amy needed to enjoy her time being a child and everything that came along with it. Jodie played her part as mum, leaving Ralph to interact during the weekend, or at least that was the plan when he came back to visit, which was becoming more frequent.

Home at last to switch off from school, placing her keys on the hall table, she hung her coat on the coat hook in the hall and placed their hats and bags nearby. Noticing a letter by the front door mat she picked it up and walked into the kitchen, flicked on the kettle for a much-needed cuppa and made Amy a hot chocolate. They sat round the table before they did their own thing, making the most of the time left of the day. After Amy had finished her drink, with a flapjack, she went back into her room, giving her mum some space, and started to amuse herself with a jigsaw.

Jodie put the radio on to listen to Sarah Cox; her daily afternoon programme of mixed music and "name that tune". She picked up the letter again, seeing where it was franked which she couldn't quite recognise, so she put her finger under the seal to open up the envelope. She removed the letter, which was handwritten, noticing it was from Ralph placed a big beam from one side to another of her mouth. It began:

Dear Jodie
 I had to put pen to paper yesterday after safely arriving home, thanking you for the best weekend I've had in ages. Reuniting with our Amy and you, of course, was so special that words fail me to express how privileged I felt. The cinema and McDonald's outing topped it all. I can't believe I missed out on those baby years but seeing Amy so grown-up yet still so young brought it home to me. Please can we do this again soon, as I'd love to be part of your lives. The truth is, Jodie, I've never stopped loving you. I just had a bad patch I had to wriggle out of which required guts to endure or else I would have broken down in a heap. We were still young and new parents then and I think with the farm at the time everything became too much to cope with. I hope you can understand and forgive me. Seeing you again made me realise how much I had missed out on, and you displayed the stronger character so I knew a mother's instinct would soon take over; something I admired about you at the time and still do.

 Take care of yourselves till next time, big hugs to you both
 Love Ralph

She started to wipe away the tears which trickled slowly down her cheeks from awe and surprise, as she reread the letter, holding it in both hands and kissing it in the middle. She was one very happy bunny, quickly looking over her shoulder in case Amy had sneaked out of her bedroom or was standing in the kitchen witnessing her mum in tears, which might have upset her, not understanding they were happy tears. 'A perfect ending to the start of a new week,' she muttered underneath her breath. *The week can only get better*, she thought, her spirits floating on cloud nine.

She made herself another cuppa to digest what she had just read, adding another five minutes to her down time before she thought about dinner in an hour or so. She decided on macci cheese as that was Amy's favourite, and peas, to last her until breakfast. She preferred to make her own meals rather than use shop-bought, depending on how busy or lazy she was unless there were some reduced meals in Tesco, the "yellow label" ones, which saved time and were usually very tasty without any additives. Eating healthily with a few vegetables a day kept any minor ailments at bay was her philosophy in life. On this occasion she had one she had made earlier, which was handy. She had started to heat it up in the microwave when her phone pinged on the table, alerting her to a missed call from her friend Lisa, from London, who she used to hang out with at a local book club she had been a member of a few years ago. She was pleasantly surprised to hear from her, so she quickly sent her a text back, saying she was in the middle of tea and that she'd phone her in an hour after Amy had gone to bed, and she hoped she'd understand. Within a minute her phone pinged again as Lisa replied, *Perfect timing as I'm also getting tea ready. Look forward to catching up later xx.*

Amy soon appeared in the kitchen asking her if dinner was ready yet, which it was, so she started to dish it out and poured an orange juice for Amy. She joined her, as she had worked up an appetite after a long day. A quick jigsaw before bath and PJs on and Amy was ready for her bedtime story as she enjoyed their time together. Lights off at 7, she kissed her goodnight, shut her door, and walked back into the lounge where she could chill on the sofa and catch up on some TV. Her top favourite was *The Repair Shop,* watched by many as it just was brilliant to see all the precious items so lovingly restored, bringing much happiness to their owners. She soon picked up her phone and clicked on the last missed call from Lisa to return her call; after three rings she picked up.

'Jodie,' she answered, 'how lovely to hear from you again. How's life treating you these days?' she continued.

'Couldn't complain,' Jodie replied. 'Even if I did it wouldn't change things much, would it?'

———

'True,' Lisa added, 'life's too short for that, isn't it, Jodie? You just have to adapt to what you've got, I guess,' she remarked, with a definite upbeat approach. 'So, tell me any news and gossip. It's been a while since we spoke, hasn't it?' Lisa added.

'Well, where to begin?' she said, with a hint of a sigh in her voice. 'Lots has happened.'

Lisa remarked that it would probably be better if they met up sometime soon. 'Should we arrange a date now? Nothing like the present,' she concluded.

'OK, I'll look at the calendar, see what dates I'm free and text you later, is that OK, Lisa?' she replied enthusiastically. She proceeded to peruse the calendar, thinking a weekend would probably suit them both better, say Friday to Sunday. She instantly texted her back suggesting the weekend.

Next weekend is perfect, Jodie, thanks.

Friday night it is, chick, see you then. Obviously I'll be in touch with the details later this week, once I've worked them out. Probably hop on an express or train, depending on what's easiest and cheapest.

With that all arranged she could go about the week with a definite purpose; not that she needed one, it was just something to look forward to. A million things were racing through her mind: jobs like strip Ralph's bed and remake it, a quick vac around the flat, dust and tidy. Lisa was a close friend from their school days, one she had always related to very well, easy to talk to and someone she could confide in; all in all, the best she could have on her side when she needed a shoulder to cry or lean on, as they say. Everyone needed a friend like that as life passed us by with the rough and the smooth making you feel more relaxed and generally chilled out. Life wasn't a bed of roses, after all. On that note, glancing at the kitchen clock it was time for bed. She quickly stacked the dishwasher and turned all the lights off, heading to her bedroom, and put on her PJ's which she felt the most relaxed in after work. She went into Ralph's room, breathing in his lingering scent, which sent tingling sensations throughout her body. She thought she'd strip the bed to remake it tomorrow and put the washing machine on before school, trying to be organised as the days ticked on by.

After a good night's sleep, it was back to the old routine, getting ready and out by 8.15 at the very latest. Groundhog Day, she called it, as they soon got into their morning routine. Tuesday was PE for Amy, so there was an extra bag with a clean gym kit to take in. Amy wasn't that keen on PE but enjoyed climbing the bars in the gym hall and playing catch with a ball or playing volleyball with balloons, which soon wore her out, the idea being, of course, to concentrate better later in class. By now, Amy had made many friends from different classes and seemed to have one girl as a close friend. Her name was Lottie, she was seven and in her reading group. Lottie hadn't been round for tea yet but Jodie saw that coming soon; a thing they did at that age, going to one another's houses for tea and then "the sleepover", which some mums liked, others dreaded, especially if there was more than one. They usually pretended to be grown-ups and wanted to burn out their energy till they flopped. Tea usually involved fish fingers, chips and peas or chicken nuggets, in Jodie's day. She didn't think much had changed since then; homemade nuggets rolled in beaten egg with crushed cornflakes, perhaps, being the healthier option if mums could be bothered, if they wanted to go for the easier option. She was holding her breath until Amy asked the question, although she did count herself very lucky as Amy seldom complained and would only choose the good ones to come to hers for tea. That said, things would no doubt change as they grew up; she just had to go with the flow for the time being.

It was Tuesday morning, and she was somewhat relieved that it was her day off. This had recently been arranged in class, giving her a day to catch up with herself and keep the house in good order. She had already made plans and thus was was eager to drop Amy off at her school as soon as possible.

'You're not teaching today, Mum?' Amy asked, as she noticed Jodie was in trousers, not her usual smart self; *that's something a girl of her age wouldn't normally notice*, Jodie thought, *which was rather observant of her. She's bright and will go far in life, my little Amy*, she pondered.

'They're giving me a day off,' she replied with a smile.

'That's nice, Mum, enjoy your day. Bye,' Amy waved as she got out of the car.

Jodie blew a kiss to Amy as she shut the car door. She waited a few minutes to see her walk through the gates before driving out of the car park. She suddenly felt a sense of freedom, yet at the same time odd, having this day to herself. First stop was definitely the coffee shop, which was a bit further up the high street: a friendly bunch the last time she went there.

'Good morning,' a young voice came from the counter directly in front of her. 'What can I get you this morning?' she said, smiling at Jodie.

'A medium-sized cappuccino, please, and a slice of carrot cake, which looks yummy,' she remarked.

'That's £5, please,' then giving her a loyalty card to stamp next time she had a coffee. 'I'll bring it over to your table.'

'Thank you,' she replied. She chose a window seat, as she liked watching people as they walked by, some just meandering along the high street, others whizzing along as if in a hurry; every face told a story. Time to dream and plan the weeks ahead, which she loved; life seemed so hectic, leaving few moments to sit and chill. Lisa's imminent arrival at the weekend was her priority after school, she needed to shop, stock up on food, though meals out were probably going to be on the agenda, which she was looking forward to. She felt a bit cheeky, wondering if she could ring Jo or Sam to ask if Amy could pop over for a bit whilst she and Lisa went to the pub for a drink, having quality time together. She decided to ask Sam at school the next day, knowing she probably wouldn't mind so long as she hadn't any other plans; her daughter Rachel needed a pal too, no doubt. She would promise to return the favour, as mums often did. She was in a good mood so decided to text Lisa.

Good morning, Lisa. Hope it's a good morning your way! I'm just chilling in a cafe on my day off, planning our rendezvous at the weekend. Though a pub night is just us to start off with, hoping my friend can have Amy for a few hours. Bye for now.

A few moments later Lisa fired one back. *I'm good thanks, sounds perfect. Look forward to seeing you both.*

After her much-needed coffee break Jodie jumped back into her car and off she drove to Tesco with her short list which included Lindt chocolate – the red balls wrapped in foil for a cosy snack – and some crisps to snack on with a glass of white vino if she remembered correctly, noting some of Lisa's favourite things.

Opening the flat door, she picked up the post littering the entrance; mostly rubbish, with the odd takeaway menu hidden amongst the pile. One letter caught her attention with an important stamp at the top of the envelope. Looking at it a second time she was thrown about what it could be. Her head suddenly raced, thinking she wasn't up to date on all bills. She quickly opened the envelope, sliding her thumb under the lip, to notice that the letter came from a solicitor. She thought, *what have I done!* She unfolded it and was rather surprised to learn that she had inherited some money from an uncle who had passed away a few years before; she thought this was a bit odd that it had suddenly arisen. Perhaps an account had been forgotten about, which they'd only just discovered. Jodie's dad had died a few years before, leaving her mum to sort out his affairs, which she wasn't very good at when it came to finance. Maths wasn't her strongest subject at school or in later life. The letter read:

Cooper and Sons Ltd
14 High Street
Cheltenham
Telephone 07753496712

Dear Mrs Smith

I am writing this letter to you as it has come to my attention that your late father, Mr John Bird, of 19 Castle Road, Stratford on Avon, has left you a sum of money in his last Will and Testament. We were going through our past papers only to notice this and seeing that an outstanding account had not yet been closed. Your name was on his Will as being the sole beneficiary of the sum, hence the reason for my writing to you.

Please will you contact me on the above number, and I will be happy to discuss this matter further with you.

Yours sincerely
James Brown
Cooper and Sons Ltd

'Well, what a surprise,' she gasped out loud, a pleasant surprise but equally a shock, as she naturally thought everything had been sorted out. *Clearly not*, she concluded. She was dumbstruck, immediately taking her coat off and placing her car keys on the hall table, and going into the kitchen, flicking on the kettle to make a herbal tea, to calm her nerves on hearing this surprising news. 'Wow, I wonder how much it was,' she said out loud. The next thing to do was to ring her mum, as she was sure she wasn't aware of this unexpected news. She pulled out her phone from her pocket, scrolling through her contacts, and clicked on her mum's mobile number. Fortunately, her mum was reasonably savvy with phones, helping her not to lose her memory, by playing word games and suchlike on it. She clicked on the telephone picture to hear it ringing. It took three rings before she heard an old woman's voice, which was her mum answering her call.

49

'Hello,' she said, 'that you, Jodie dear?' reading the number flagged up on her mobile screen. It was one of those large number phones for the hard of hearing as her mum was becoming a little deaf as she aged.

'Yes, Mum, it's me. How are you these days? I hope I haven't interrupted your morning, only I've just come home to find an unusual letter in the hall from my trusty postie. On closer inspection it was from a solicitor, regarding a sum of money they found in Dad's Will after all these years. Ring any bells with you, Mum?'

Silence, as she assumed her mum was equally stunned, after all these years thinking all affairs had been sorted out. 'Mum, are you still there, are you OK?' she asked, as everything went suddenly quiet.

'Well, I never,' she reacted. 'Like you, I thought this was sorted out long ago. I guess they clearly must have found something when having a clear out!' Dot, her mum, replied with a hint of laughter, although it wasn't really funny, just odd. 'I can't remember after all these years, if I'm honest, but I've heard these things happen from time to time. OK, dear, I'll leave it in your capable hands to ring them and start the interesting detective work, "Madame Poirot", I'm all ears, as they say these days.' Dot hung up, feeling somewhat uplifted.

Jodie flicked the kettle on for another cuppa, this time green tea with a hint of lemon, before she embarked on ringing the solicitor as suggested, hoping to shed some light on this finding. She tapped in the number and pressed the button, which soon started to ring. She waited patiently until a young-sounding lady picked up, going through the usual greeting of 'Good morning, Cooper and Sons, may I help you?'

Hearing her pleasant-sounding voice with a delectable accent she felt at ease and confident enough to continue. It was quite calming to hear a pleasant voice on the end of a phone. The recipient was made to feel at ease before the conversation continued; a sign of a good receptionist, in her opinion, as she took a sip of her soon cooled-down tea.

She started to explain how she had felt on seeing the letter; initially feeling nervous and surprised, reading through the letter twice before understanding that she was the recipient of some money from her late father. At first she wondered how this could have happened after a few years, thinking there was a mistake; but clearly not, as a solicitor would never lie. She assumed they were legit from looking at the embossed header printed at the top of the letter.

'I see,' the receptionist said. 'I'll put you through to Mr Brown, who will no doubt clarify your findings. I've just taken the file in question to him, which he knows he will be pursuing this morning. From time to time, we go through older files, making sure nothing is outstanding before we incinerate them. On seeing your father's, it came to our attention that there was something which needed our immediate attention. Putting you through now, Mrs Smith.'

A few musical notes of what sounded like Enya playing in the background before a well-spoken male voice picked up. 'Mrs Smith, thank you for getting in touch so soon. I hope my letter didn't alarm you too much as there really isn't anything to be alarmed about, just a little unusual surprise in store for you by which I, too, was rather taken aback. I have since been in contact with your mother, I assume, Mrs Ramsey of 19 Castle Road. I wrote her a letter detailing our findings, which was only sent out yesterday, as, my receptionist informs me, was yours. I take it she hasn't yet received it or not replied. Anyway, we can go through the initial findings when we meet in person next week, as I know you would like this problem to be solved as soon as possible, as indeed do we.'

'Yes, thank you, I would appreciate that and yes, I could arrange to come in next week. I just need 24 hours' notice, as I have a daughter at school to arrange to pick up and I need to rearrange my work, which shouldn't be a problem,' she added, optimistically.

'Perfect,' Mr Brown replied. 'I'll ask Sally, my receptionist, to book you in next week when we can chat further regarding this matter. I'll transfer you unless you have any further questions before we meet. Please bring some proof of identity as well as an original death certificate for your late father, if you have one, which would make things a lot smoother, and account details to where I can transfer the sum in question. On that note, I'll see you next week, Mrs Smith.'

More of the same music sounded before Sally, the young, spritely receptionist, picked up. 'Looking at his diary, would next Wednesday be suitable at eleven o'clock? Or is that too short notice? I can do Friday if you prefer, at the same time.'

Jodie had to think quickly, then realised that Wednesday would be better, being her day off, so she could ask one of the mums to take Amy after school and she would obviously reciprocate.

She ended the call feeling more at ease and even looking forward to their meeting, which involved an hour's car journey at the most. She pulled up the calendar on her phone, which was where most people stored their appointments these days as it was the age and rage of technology. She set it as a reminder for early next week. Next on her to-do list was to ring a friend to arrange cover for Amy to go round after school, preferably one of Amy's best friends and a mum that she got on well with; Jo or Sam sprang to mind. Lottie, who was Amy's best friend, and her mum Sam came to mind when she had to arrange cover for Amy that day, so she decided to click on her number and ask if next Wednesday would suit her. She thought it best to give her advance notice rather than wait until the next day, seeing her at Amy's school.

'Oh, hi Jodie, how's things?' Sam asked, answering her call.

'Great thanks,' Jodie quickly replied. 'I've got a favour to ask; a bit of a last-minute development my end, like things are in our world!'

'Ok,' Sam interjected with enthusiasm, 'I'm all ears!'

Jodie took a deep breath and started explaining the letter she'd found on her doormat and that it was a complete shock to hear from the solicitors as she thought all had been resolved at the time of her dad's death, though clearly that was not the case. 'They want me to see the solicitor, which has been arranged for next week, Wednesday, which is my day off, so I wondered if you could take Amy after school. She would love to play with your Lottie, as they seem besties, which is great.' Jodie felt a bit nervous as she awaited her response, hoping she'd say yes, knowing that she would repay her by having Lotti the week after.

'Just checking the calendar, which is empty that day, so yes, that's fine, Jodie,' Sam replied.

'Oh, thank you so much, Sam, I really appreciate it,' feeling quite relieved as she needed to find out what was going on. 'We'll finalise arrangements before this weekend, hopefully it shouldn't take me long to get there and back, as it's just an hour's drive,' she added.

'Bye for now,' they said in unison before ending the call.

The next morning, she woke up feeling refreshed despite the initial surprise of the solicitor's letter.

At least she had dealt with the initial situation by making an appointment to find out more details of the unexpected inheritance. She had contacted Sam, whose daughter Lotti was besties with Amy, and they would have tea together next Wednesday while Jodie saw the solicitor. It felt like a detective story to be unravelled, which initially flummoxed Jodie and her mum Dot. She had to put this to the back of her mind to get herself and Amy ready for school. 'Groundhog Day recommences till the weekend again,' she muttered to herself!

Thursday was show and tell day for Amy, which she always looked forward to. Today she wanted to bring in her cuddly fawn-coloured teddy bear she loved to sleep with, to give her comfort if she had a bad day at school, or generally needed a fur baby hug. Amy thought everyone should have a teddy to snuggle up to, age being no barrier. 'May I take Teddy to class today, Mum" Amy asked, running into the kitchen.

'Yes, of course, darling, something lovely to show the others.'

'Yippee!' Amy skipped around the kitchen. Jodie was dreamily transported to her childhood days, collecting teddies and lining them up sitting on her bedroom carpet, bringing out the plastic cups and teapot so they could share a tea party, as little girls of a certain age did as part of growing up. Oh, to be a child again, she thought, *with no responsibility, something that gets too much once we become grown-ups*.

On arrival at Amy's school gates Lottie was waving vicariously at Amy, clearly excited to see her, followed by her mum Sam, who came up to Jodie, quickly giving a thumbs up indicating all was OK for Friday week, before she had to dash off to her school or else she'd be marked late. Her phone pinged with a text from Sam telling her not to worry, all would be fine, adding a smiley face at the end. She promptly sent one back with *TY*. The day soon flew by with the usual routines and fortunately nothing out of the ordinary happened in her class, which was always welcome. She didn't need any extra dramas as the impending solicitor's appointment was enough to keep her occupied out of school hours and she tried to push it to the back of her mind. Work and home life were, after all, two separate things which would interfere with her school day if she let it, which she tried not to do as she was only human like everyone else. The sound of the school bell brought her back to earth, indicating it was lunchtime. It was her day off from playground duty so she headed back to the staffroom to her locker get her packed lunch, which consisted of a tuna and cucumber sandwich on granary bread which was healthier, and a banana to balance it off. Amy had a school dinner today, usually once a week, which helped her mum with less cooking once home. Time after school usually consisted of reading and any other homework the class teacher set before the bedtime routine, by which time Amy was ready for some shuteye. Time to chill and relax with one of her herbal teas. She chose peppermint tea this time to soothe the tummy of any tension and stress, which always worked a treat. She sat down in her lounge, and pulled out her phone to see if there were any important messages or emails which she needed to deal with; nothing except one text from Ralph. She hadn't heard from him in the last few weeks, so this put a huge smile on her face. She did miss him and was always pleased to hear his news.

Hi Jodie, it's me. Sorry I haven't been in touch recently as I have had a deadline to meet with lots of work coming in which is good, but tiring to, giving little time for anything else really.

Hi there, Ralph, good to hear from you, I'm the same, had lots going on, life just passes us by, doesn't it. I'll ring you tomorrow as I had an important surprise letter yesterday which I now urgently need to deal with. Don't worry, all is well, just some money owed to me from Dad's Will which I thought had all been finalised but clearly hadn't, so I need to make a trip to the solicitors in question. I've got cover for Amy so no need for concern there, all is well in my soul as they say.

Oh, wow, now that's a turn up for the books, to coin a phrase. Hope all goes well, ring me once you're back home or if you need an ear, I'm here Jodie xx

'He loves me,' she spoke out loud, or at least he cares, which always sounded positive coming from Ralph who, deep down, had a caring nature which she loved about him. He's definitely moved on after his initial meltdown, she admitted to herself.

The days flew by and finally the working week came to an end. Friday was here at last despite having nothing pre-planned. It was time to wind down and relax and face any situations, preferably good ones, which came her way. She liked to get all Amy's homework done after school so they could do something exciting together, building up precious memories in her young life so far. Amy always enjoyed the outdoors and nature, especially if it was warm outside, or having a friend over to play. Perhaps a walk in the local arboretum would be lovely, seeing the ducks on the lake and going on the swings which all children enjoyed in the sunshine.

Saturday morning was usually taken up by cleaning Daisy the bunny's cage out, which she enjoyed doing with Amy, as having a pet to care for was important in her young life, learning new skills. Daisy was a white and fawn-coloured bunny with long ears, who loved being stroked, munching on her carrot or lettuce. Jodie and Amy took great pleasure in watching her and it gave them both pure enjoyment; a therapeutic time, sending calming vibes throughout their souls. She had bought Amy a lovely ash wood hutch from the local pet shop, a straw and a water holder with a rust-coloured circular food bowl did the job for any happy bunny, giving Amy hours of pleasure. Jodie loved seeing the laughter, chuckles and smiles on her glowing face, sending happy vibes throughout her body, knowing that she had fulfilled her daughter's wishes and dreams, which were all so real to her now six-year-old girl.

Suddenly out of the blue, Amy said, 'Mum, I miss Dad, can we see him again soon?'

Jodie was taken aback, as this was the first time she had mentioned her dad again. It sparked happy goose pimples down her arms. Ralph had obviously left a lasting impression on Amy which was lovely, as she really hoped they could find that connection and could one day become a happy family again, reunited in love. Jodie couldn't have wished this more for herself and Ralph.

'OK, I could ring him if you like and see if we could arrange a meet up soon, how about that, darling?'

Amy's response was clear as she performed a skip and a jump whilst they were meandering around the arboretum that afternoon.

'Nothing like the present. I will ring him now, shall I?' She removed her mobile phone from her coat zip pocket and clicked on his number in her recent contacts … just four rings and he picked up.

'Jodie, lovely to hear from you. Funny, I was just thinking of you and wondering how Amy was doing,' he uttered at the other end.

'Well, we are in the arboretum. Amy had just asked about you and said how she misses you, which I thought was so sweet of her, and she would like to see you again soon, if that's possible.'

'Sounds good to me, got any ideas when, Jodie? I've got nothing planned this weekend. I could come to you if that suits you both? It's a bit short notice but I could pop on the train later and stay over like last time then return Sunday after lunch, my shout,' Ralph added, sounding enthusiastic.

'Oh wow, that is spontaneous. I think Amy won't say no and I'm OK with it too. Nothing like a spontaneous move, Ralph, is there? The spare bedroom is all ready.'

'OK, I'm at home now so I can pack a bag and hop on the next available train which, looking at the timetable, is in an hour, and it's direct so tell Amy I'll be there soon.'

Sunday couldn't come quick enough for Amy. She was getting over-excited about seeing her dad again, hoping he would bring her a little surprise, as dads sometimes do. She raced to her bedroom, closed the door and brought out her sketchbook. She kept it under her bed with her light blue Nemo pencil case holding lots of coloured crayons and pencils. She liked drawing and painting, as her art teacher had informed Jodie once at a recent parents' evening.

Knock, knock, came a sound at the door as Jodie was about to tell Amy that tea was ready. 'What are you up to in there, darling, anything I should know about?' she asked with a giggle.

'It's a surprise for Dad tomorrow when he comes, Mum. I can't say anything, don't worry.'

Jodie shouted back quietly, 'Ok, mum's the word, meaning I won't tell anyone, Amy. See you in five in the kitchen for tea, OK?' Jodie added with humour.

'I'll be there,' Amy replied.

Chapter Eight

Amy wanted to get an early night as she knew her dad would be there in the morning, so she took herself to her room, put her PJs on, brushed her teeth in the bathroom, glaring afterwards in the mirror over the sink checking she'd done a good job, and feeling satisfied with herself, promptly went back to her room and called out to her mum, 'I'm in bed, can you come and give me a kiss now?'

Jodie was there in a flash as she had stuff to sort out before Ralph turned up later, unbeknown to Amy. She knew she would be delighted to see him at the breakfast table on Sunday morning. She closed her door afterwards and went back into the kitchen to tidy up. Her phone suddenly pinged on the kitchen top; seeing it was Ralph she checked his message.

I managed to get a direct train to arrive at nine o'clock at the station. I'll get an Uber to yours, as Amy's probably in bed now. X

Great, I've just kissed Amy goodnight, so an Uber sounds perfect, Ralph, safe journey see you soon X

Jodie gave a chuckle as she carried on wiping the kitchen tops and table, generally making the place look spotless, as if royalty was about to make its presence. She took pride and joy in making her cottage look presentable, whether guests were coming or not. She thought making the extra effort would make her guests feel more at home, lighting up a scented candle in a few places in the lounge, adding to the welcoming ambiance. Once having put the finishing touches she took a few steps back to admire her efforts. She kept checking the time on her phone, knowing it wouldn't be long now before Ralph arrived. Having glanced in his room, checking all was ready, she headed back into the lounge and plumped up a few new cushions she had bought the other week from Tesco. Job sorted, she could now sit down and relax before Ralph arrived.

She had half an hour to herself before he would finally arrive so she thought she'd make herself a camomile tea, as they would be going to bed later, once he'd arrived, before all the excitement started in the morning once Amy woke up to see her dad.

A knock on the door instead of a ring of the bell, so as not to wake Amy up; she promptly opened it and was greeted by a medium height, handsome, in her eyes, man, holding a lovely bunch of pink carnations wrapped in cellophane with a red ribbon around it tied in a bow. She couldn't hide her excitement on seeing them saying, 'Are those for me? They are gorgeous, Ralph, thank you,' as they each leaned in, giving one another a French kiss on the cheek. She had shivers down her spine, rushing all over her, as she was so taken aback by the flowers.

'Of course they are for you, silly. Thank you for having me back at such short notice. It's lovely to see you again, Jodie. I've missed you if I'm honest, life just isn't the same without you and my Amy. Can we start again?' almost pleading, with a soppy-eyed look towards her.

She was completely taken by surprise at his impromptu remark, and his suggestion, which sent flutters in her tummy with delight. She couldn't agree with him more, as the feeling was mutual. Life was indeed too short to mess about in this situation, where clearly there was a spark between them, and Amy certainly showed clear signs of willingness for her mum and dad to reunite. After all, Amy was still so young, and neither she nor Ralph wanted any revenge later as she grew up to be a teenager. Others might be hurtful, saying nasty spiteful things behind her back, questioning why Amy's parents weren't together, resulting in all parties being deeply hurt and offended. Neither Ralph nor Jodie could face this over time as Amy grew to become a responsible adult. *Could this be the weekend where our relationship steps up to the next level*, she thought, feeling cautious; taking a huge leap of faith forward where mistakes could be made. Neither of them could really afford to mess up again, for the sake of their daughter. That said, Ralph couldn't be blamed for his breakdown, as it could happen to anyone in any walk of life. She was the one who had helped him pick himself up again and Ralph saw that he needed professional help, as in counselling therapy, which often helped in these tricky, temporary situations. Fortunately for Ralph he had come out the other side a much happier and more relaxed person; he could move forward, initiating a career move, doing something he had always enjoyed from college days. He was just a bit confused at the time; they were quite young parents, with no real knowledge of how life was about to change literally from one day to the next. They received little support from either set of parents, which was something neither she nor Ralph ever wished to repeat. *Lessons had indeed been learnt so it was time for him to step out of his comfort zone and to move on*, she thought, *and man up and face the music.*

'Come in, take your coat off and put your bag down and make yourself at home,' she said, opening the door further to let him in. 'I'll put the kettle on as I'm sure you're parched,' adding, 'one tea coming up,' then briskly walked into the kitchen with a beam across her face. Ralph took a seat on the sofa whilst waiting for his tea, which she swiftly brought in with a small plate of Hobnobs, to see them through before bedtime.

'So how have things been here, Jodie? Anything new since we met up last?' Ralph asked, looking into her eyes gleefully.

She didn't wish to explain about the solicitor's letter for now, as it seemed boring and uneventful for this time of night, instead she just replied with, 'Same old day in, day out, run of the mill school stuff really, nothing to get too excited about. That's life, isn't it, until the weekend, where we liven things up a bit, I guess!' she concluded with a chuckle.

'Yes, I know what you mean, I've been so busy making things for clients I've hardly had time to stop for a lunch break. I enjoy it but it's just a stop gap for now. I'm thinking I'd like to move back closer to you and Amy, if you agree to that, Jodie. Obviously initially I'd get my own place to start with and we can take things from there. My contract is coming to an end soon anyway, so it's a good time to have a rethink; I prefer the countryside rather than the rush of city life.'

'Sounds like a perfect plan, leaving city life behind you; I love it out here. I was never a city girl; it's OK for holidays being a tourist for a while, but actually, moving and living in an often smog-filled city doesn't quite tick all those boxes any more for me and a young child. We live in a changing world, where climate change has impacted us so much.' *Lecture over for tonight,* she thought, as they both needed their beauty sleep before all the drama kicked off in the morning where Amy was concerned.

'I'm sure we won't get much time for ourselves tomorrow, but I've booked a table for lunch at Toby's again, as Amy seemed to enjoy it there, before I need to go back home in the afternoon.'

'Perfect,' she smiled back at him, 'perhaps we can walk in the arboretum so that Amy can run around and let off steam, as the forecast is for sunny weather tomorrow, which always helps.' Within a few minutes they bade each other goodnight and went their separate ways.

The Sunday morning sun shone through her window as she pulled up her blind, seeing a hint of spring, as daffodil bulbs were starting to sprout with some yellow and white colours emerging. It was always a pleasant time of year as flowers and bulbs began to grow, lifting the blues after Christmas and January, when everyone seemed slow and dull, often due to the dark, dull cloudy days. Spring was a time when the days were getting lighter before March, when clocks would once again go forward to summertime, loved by all. She quickly showered before Ralph used the bathroom and hopefully before Amy emerged, soon to be surprised to see her dad downstairs sitting at the breakfast table. She was looking forward to her reaction, one of complete surprise and joy, she guessed.

She started to get the breakfast dishes and mugs out and placed them on the kitchen table, ready for the onslaught and temporary mayhem after Amy dashed through the door to find her dad waiting to be engulfed by her huge hug and kisses. Well, that was how she envisaged it. Breakfast all nicely laid out on the table, she called out, 'Breakfast is ready!' which sparked an initial interest as she saw Ralph's door creep open. He rushed towards the kitchen, where Jodie placed her right finger to her lip, indicating, ssh, she's coming, so Ralph could take his place at the table.

As soon as Amy walked in, he echoed, 'Surprise, surprise!' as Cilla Black used to say on her TV show back in the seventies. Amy gasped as she stared at her dad who opened his arms wide, scooping her into a hug and a few kisses.

'Oh Daddy, you're back!' she uttered with pure delight, grinning from ear to ear.

'Yes, I am. I came last night whilst you were asleep and thought you'd like the surprise this morning. I've got something to show you once you've had some cereal, which is some Cheerios on Saturdays,' he added.

Amy didn't take long eating her breakfast and drinking a small glass of orange juice. Ralph and Amy soon dashed into his bedroom, where he took out a wrapped box from his bag and gave it to Amy. Amy couldn't wait to see what it was and unwrapped the pink foil paper to reveal another jigsaw, this time with more pieces to amuse her for the next hour or two, and a book of *Little Red Riding Hood* to aid her reading skills.

'Thanks, Dad, this is great. I love a new jigsaw and a new book. I could show the book at school next week if Mum lets me,' she said enthusiastically.

Breakfast out of the way, it was time to enjoy the rest of the day while Ralph was still here. Jodie seized the moment quickly, put all the dishes in the dishwasher and got ready for whatever was on the day's agenda –a pleasant stroll around the arboretum as it was such a sunny day and bulbs popping up in every flower bed. Spring had definitely sprung, filling the air with a perfumed scent as if at the Chelsea Flower Show, lifting the mood for everyone.

They soon came to the large play area, with swings and wooden logs to climb over, for children to generally let off some steam, much to parents' and grandparents' delight, as they could sit and natter on wooden benches within the area, which she and Ralph did; having little time alone together, each moment was indeed precious. They sat down on a bench to themselves which was more intimate, with no one overhearing their private conversation and which they naturally preferred. They sat close together, almost rubbing their legs together, which always seemed to send a shiver down her back; enjoying the closeness to Ralph, smelling his natural aroma.

'It is peaceful sitting here,' she spoke out loud. Everyone was going about their day. She loved to sit and people-watch, thinking of everything she used to enjoy whilst growing up. She turned her head towards Ralph and in that split second wanted to kiss him on the lips as a sign of her love for him and to show how proud she was of him, how far he had come on his mental health journey, turning his life around, trying to grab life in both hands and move forward to the next level. Ralph looked at her appealingly, not holding back; leaning towards her they touched lips together for a lingering second then pulled away gently as they grasped one another's hand, gently squeezing fingers, then squeezing hands, acknowledging to one another this was good and OK.

Suddenly they felt relaxed, as if it was their first date again. A new start was about to begin in their lives together, she hoped, as this seemed safe, at last rekindling their relationship as new excited parents, ready to embark on their journey together. Heads looking towards the play area, they saw Amy walking towards them, all steam let out, ready to walk on around the lake, to see the swans and ducks swimming around enjoying their freedom. The sun glistened on the still calm water, giving a mirror effect to the lake. They stood up, holding hands as they turned to walk around the idyllic park. She glanced back at Amy, who was one step behind them, probably noticing they were holding hands, which seemed fine with her as she skipped along to keep up. They soon got to the lake, where one swan was steadily floating along the lake with ease, her cygnets in tow, which was a beautiful sight to see. Amy turned and gasped, 'Wow!' as they slowly swam by, Mum in front leading the way with her five cygnets.

Lunchtime was fast approaching, and they needed to get back to the flat to jump into the car and head to the Toby carvery for a pre-booked table at 12.30pm. A quick bathroom stop and off they went again. On arrival they were shown to their table which was a window seat one, with views onto a small patio area with picnic benches. A young lady took their drinks order; adding a bottle of water to their orange juices she asked if they were having the carvery, ushering them to the counter when they were ready. Perfect, as they could spend the rest of their day reminiscing before Ralph's return home. Ralph took Amy to the desired lunch counter to choose what she fancied: turkey, a Yorkshire pudding with a few vegetables and a ball of stuffing, which she had always loved, ever since her mum had served some up on her dinner plate at home. It was clear to see that Amy loved having her dad around, being a family again. It was Jodie's turn next, coming back with her piled-up plate leaving enough room for a pudding.

They tucked in in silence as they devoured their individual plates, Amy seeming particularly hungry after her workout in the playground. Soon all food was demolished and they were ready for dessert; all had an ice cream sundae topped with raspberry sauce. The waitress brought over the bill, which Ralph kindly paid for, before they went back to the flat to have some much-needed chill-out time before Ralph was taken back to the station; another direct train home to start another busy week ahead at work.

Jodie flicked the kettle switch to boil and took out two mugs for a quick brew before they had to drive off to the station. Amy went into her room to play and do the jigsaw her dad had bought for her, whilst she and Ralph had some last-minute adult time together, which they were thankful for. She thought about a night away, perhaps, next time, just the two of them; otherwise any intimacy would prove awkward to rekindle their relationship, as they were ready to take things to the next level. Valentine's day was on the horizon. She thought a surprise could be waiting; *you never know what*, she thought.

She thought it was a good opportunity to inform him of the solicitor's letter she had received, which had no real bearing on their relationship thus far, but it was wise that Ralph heard about it, nonetheless, so that he understood her end of the week's events.

'Sounds interesting,' Ralph interjected. 'I'm sure everything will soon be cleared up; clear as to the contents of the letter, don't worry about it,' he lovingly tried to reassure her. 'Receiving a sum of money can only be much welcomed and indeed helpful to you both,' Ralph added, with a smile on his face which gave her positive reassurance. Ralph checked the time on his phone again, knowing the final hour was ticking by too quickly. His bags had already been packed that morning, leaving them a few precious moments together. They were sitting on the sofa drinking their last tea when Ralph turned to her, taking her hands, and said, 'I just wanted to thank you again for having me back and giving me such a lovely welcome, even if it has been brief.' He leant in towards her, kissing her on the lips, sending shivers and flutters around her insides. She soon reciprocated, bringing him into a hug, arms around each other were followed by a lingering kiss lasting a few seconds. It felt like a moment in heaven until they finally drew away, both feeling entirely satisfied. They wanted to delve more, but couldn't as time was no longer on their side. A romantic night away was much desired to enable them to go forward and catch up on missed time.

'Amy, time to take Dad to the station for his train home. Use the bathroom quickly and put your shoes and coat on. We need to leave in ten minutes.'

'OK, Mum, I'm coming!' Amy shouted back. Ralph dashed into his room and grabbed his bag, having a final check around, not wanting to leave behind anything he might need in the week. He put his coat on, ready for the off.

'Well, this is it, I guess, till next time.' Ralph looked at her with a hint of sadness as he drew her into a final hug and a kiss on the lips. They locked the front door, heading to her car for the short drive to the station. Amy was very quiet, sitting in the back seat, feeling a bit sad to say goodbye to her dad, yet knowing she'd see him again shortly.

On arrival at the station, Jodie parked up at the front to let Ralph out, as his train was due soon on platform 1, directly on the other side to the rear of the station. A quick hug, followed by one to Amy, and he got out of the car, shutting the door behind him, with his bag in tow. He walked to the station entrance and turned around to wave his final goodbyes to them before disappearing into the small crowd of people mingling around gathering their tickets to put through the slot, to push the silver bar and walk onto the platform, to await the next train, due in the next few minutes. Ralph out of immediate sight, she started up her trusty car and swiftly drove off, taking five minutes to get back home again.

Once home it was time to prepare for the week ahead. Homework first with Amy, to read the book she had brought home from school, another *Biff and Chip* book, with a few sentences this time. Amy loved her reading, which was a huge bonus in that age group, as many couldn't read as well or hadn't had the opportunity to read aloud at home for many different reasons, such as being in a one-parent family, pure lack of interest, too busy or not making the time and effort. Ten minutes was all it took every day to enhance a child's reading, yet for some it never happened. She made a point of spending quality time with Amy, which clearly reaped the rewards. Amy was grateful in her own way, as some of her classmates lagged behind in their reading skills. Jodie noticed these things as she was a teaching assistant and had her quota of children to read every day.

Sunday soon came to an end. They put their PJs on and just lounged about in the living room, playing a game of snap, which they both enjoyed, a bit of down time before bedtime. Amy soon went to brush her teeth, whilst her mum put a small plastic cup of water by her bed for the night.

They hugged each other goodnight, leaving Amy resting on her pillow, soon out for the count as Jodie quietly shut her bedroom door.

Chapter Nine

Jodie woke up with a smile and a warm glowing feeling inside, remembering yesterday's close encounters with Ralph as they kissed and embraced into tight hugs, something that she had looked forward to for a while if she was being honest. Ralph had come on in leaps and bounds since their temporary split years ago; his mental health picked up as he started a new journey, he was more sure of himself, ready to put past misfortunes behind him. He clearly wanted to renew his relationship with her, with whom he had fallen in love many years before. Ralph had changed his career and was doing a job he had always wanted to do, turning what was once a hobby into a living. Ralph had a future with her and their daughter Amy. Hopefully they could be a happy family again and move in together, which would feel more normal for others to see their commitment to each other and a deep satisfaction for themselves. Just one thing needed to be sorted, which was the sum of money she had inherited, to be revealed when she paid the solicitors a visit on Friday. She stretched out as she sat on the edge of the bed as part of her yoga routine. Taking her phone up, overnight it had pinged into action with a few messages. She clicked on her messages to see one from the solicitors reminding her of her appointment on Friday and confirming her visit. Another from Lisa, wanting to catch up soon with the latest news regarding Ralph, no doubt. Noticing a WhatsApp message from Ralph sent goose pimples all over her again.

Good morning lovely. Thank you for a fab weekend albeit short. It was lovely to see Amy again, she's growing up fast. Have a good week and hope to see you soon xx

Jodie melted every time she read messages from him. Desiring to see him asap, it must be love, she muttered. She pinched herself metaphorically to get back to the present, reminding herself it was Monday morning, she needed to get Amy sorted with a quick breakfast and head off to school. Coats, bags ready, they were ready to lock up and jump into the car to drop Amy off at her school.

On arrival she was greeted by Sam and Lottie,, who seemed eager to ask her if Amy was still coming over on Friday.

'Good morning, you two lovelies, did you have a good weekend?' she asked, smiling from ear to ear.

'Yes thanks, and now here we go again!' Sam replied with a grin and a sigh.

'Thank you, Sam for helping me out on Friday. I confirmed to the solicitors before we left this morning.'

Sam gave a thumbs up, knowing she had to dash off to her school or she'd be in their bad books! Jodie parked up to the sound of the early morning bell, alerting all to the school day starting minutes away. Everyone lined up formally in the playground, like soldiers ready to face their enemy; they walked to their individual classes in single file. The day progressed as normal with no real dramas, thankfully, for a Monday, till the end of the day. She was already looking forward to her day off as she needed to prepare for Friday and just generally catch up at home; the usual housework, which most people dreaded after a weekend but, *that's life*, she thought, or else live in a tip, everything littered all over the place, which she could never put up with. She also needed to go and do a food shop. This time she would order online as she didn't have the time to go to the supermarket with Friday fast approaching. She picked up Amy that afternoon again to head home where they had a quick drink before starting homework which was the usual reading and a few spellings Amy had been given in her new blue spelling book. As Amy progressed in her reading she naturally picked up the various spellings which she excelled in, getting ten out of ten most weeks, pleasing Mrs Newbury, her class teacher, who gave her gold stars on a wall chart she had drawn up for them; putting big smiles on Jodie's face at the end of term when she read Amy's progress report. She often took a screenshot of a page, forwarding it to Ralph, as he obviously liked to be involved in her schoolwork.

Tonight's tea was one of her and Amy's favourites, and quick and easy to make; macci cheese with cauliflower and homemade chicken nuggets, which involved crushing cornflakes and dipping chicken into beaten egg then placing on a dish in the oven to cook for twenty-five minutes. Yummy every time and healthier than McDonald's! Jodie fancied investing in a simple air fryer which seemed the latest craze these days, as electricity prices were currently spiralling out of control in the light of a downward economy. She was sure her inherited gift would cover it, she chuckled. Obviously, she could afford one, now things weren't that tight. She also had to make sure that Daisy the guinea pig had her food, consisting of lettuce and carrots and water topped up. As Amy was growing up her daily homework and chores around the house had changed; so far so good, until the teenage years started, which was an entirely different life, fortunately many years ahead of them. She was well aware of starting early with discipline, teaching right from wrong, what was acceptable and what was not in life. She could only do her best, as all parents faced the same problems. She wasn't alone.

The evening was slowly drawing to a close, with homework done. Amy went into her room, put her PJs on, brushed her teeth and was ready to go to bed. School often tired her out as she was only six. Jodie went in to kiss her goodnight before closing the door. She needed some down time before she, too, went to bed. Monday had slipped by in no time.

Spring was definitely here as the morning light started to break through the corners of her bedroom blind; pulling the cord to reveal blue skies gave her a warm feeling inside. Checking her phone there was a text from Ralph.

Good morning hope you slept well and enjoy your day off xx
You too Xx

She promptly showered then knocked on Amy's door to find her already up and dressed. They had breakfast and collected their things to head out to the car. Parking outside the school gate she gave Amy a kiss and a tight squeeze before she stepped out of the car to walk to the school gates. Amy now wanted to just be dropped off rather than have her mum walking her into the courtyard, clearly showing her independence. Tuesday was always welcome as it was her day off; time for herself. This morning was no exception. She decided to head into town for a while and have a quick coffee and a toasted tea cake to start her day off at the café, and to mull over Friday, which was fast approaching. She wasn't particularly fazed by it now; just looking forward to the surprise, especially if it was a good one.

'Good morning, what can I get you?' the lady behind the counter said, as Jodie walked over with a happy smile.

'Good morning,' she said, feeling happy. 'A latte macchiato, please, with a toasted tea cake, if you have one.'

'Yes, freshly baked this morning.' Jodie passed her the loyalty card which got stamped; she would be entitled to a free drink after five stamps. 'I'll bring it over to you. Thank you,' the kind lady replied.

Jodie chose a window seat again to watch the world go by, making her feel more relaxed as time passed. Whilst waiting she pulled out her iPhone, which she had recently bought. It was her first and she loved how everything fell into place; it was so easy to use.

She clicked on her to-do list with her reminders. The top of the list was to get all documents ready for Friday; neatly placing them in one of those transparent sleeves she had lying around somewhere or which she could acquire from school tomorrow. Next, sort out the all-important clothes to wear. Smart casual was the in thing these days; just a smart pair of trousers would suffice. She was relieved she had done an online shop so that there was no need to worry about that. On the arrival of her latte and tea cake she could just sit and watch people, her favourite pastime.

She did think she might just look at a new shoulder bag, as hers was looking rather old and tatty. It clearly wasn't fit to be seen out in; her excuse was she'd just been paid and Valentine's Day was on the horizon. It would be a treat to herself if nothing else, which was very important. Thinking of her new reacquainted relationship with Ralph lifted her spirits even further. Surely a bag wouldn't break the bank! *Mustard colour*, she thought this time, away from her usual reds. *Little things in life make a big difference*, she reminded herself.

She started meandering along the high street, noticing a big stall a few metres away she could never resist a glance. The lady sitting on a chair in front, noticing her interest, asked if she needed any assistance, an offer she took advantage of. The lady showed her a few mustard bags of different sizes; she thought she should better try them out for the size, slipping her phone and glasses inside, as they all seemed different these days. Finally making her choice, she paid the lady and went home. The rest of the day was slipping by and soon it would be time to pick up her princess Amy from school. Jodie started to collate the documents for Friday, checking everything she possibly needed: as a form of identification, she needed to photocopy her passport page and take in an original utility bill. Another tick off the reminder list. Glancing at the kitchen clock it was time to pick up her girl from school. The usual after school routine began once home again.

Unlocking the front door, she was greeted by what she assumed was junk mail, including an electricity bill which she whipped open, seeing how it had gone up in price. Fortunately, she could pay it off directly, for which she could only be grateful, knowing that some weren't in that position. Placing their coats on the coat stand and putting her car keys in the usual place on the table in the hall within swift reach, she flicked the kettle switch on for her usual green herbal tea. Opening Amy's school bag she took out her day diary, which Mrs Newbury updated weekly with her progress and homework for the week ahead. She noticed a note tucked inside with her name written on the envelope. She opened it carefully to read a birthday party invite for Amy from a new girl Amy hadn't yet mentioned: Lucy. Her first party invite and no doubt one of many, as this was the age group of invites and sleepovers. Remembering her own childhood days she was sure her mum had got fed up with them after a while. They always prompted much discussion from parents about what present to buy them as only a small present was really necessary.

'Amy, look what I've just opened, your first birthday invitation, how cool is that!' she called out to Amy, who had quickly changed into her PJs as she usually did once home from school, to feel relaxed.

'Wow!' Amy exclaimed, looking at the colourful balloons printed on the white background of the invitation which read:

To: Amy
Birthday party: February 22nd
Venue: Lucy Thomas' house
Address: 21 Portland Street, Winchester
Time: 5 pm
Looking forward to having you, Lucy xx

Amy reacted with a skip and a dance when her mum read it out. Jodie hadn't yet met Lucy; potentially a new friend for Amy.

'Can you tell me about Lucy, do you like her?' she asked, using words she could understand. Amy continued by saying she was small, had blonde hair, they liked one another and that they played together in the playground. Her mum's name was Karen.

Portland Street was the next street from where the school was, which was easy to remember. She thought it would be best if they replied asap so she grabbed a piece of paper from her desk and wrote a reply to Lucy's mum, placing it in an envelope into Amy's school bag for the morning. Another job sorted, she thought, though nearer the time they would need to buy something small for Amy to take along to her party.

Next on the agenda was to prepare tea for them both so she

asked Amy to check on Daisy the guinea pig who seemed very content in her hutch, occasionally making an appearance in her run. Amy enjoyed watching her dart from one end to the other, giving her adequate daily exercise.

'Pizza tonight, Amy?' she called out to her from the back door. Amy soon came in and took her place at the table, seeing slices of vegetable pizza with chicken ready to eat before it went cold. Within minutes all was eaten and Amy went back into her room to play. Jodie's phone suddenly sprung into life. This time it was from an unknown number which she was always wary about. Recognising a mobile number these days was very difficult as they all had so many digits. She decided to answer it, saying, 'Who is this, please?' not sure whether a please was entirely necessary but polite, nonetheless. A young voice at the other end said, 'Don't you recognise my number, Mrs Smith?' at which she had to stop and think twice before bursting into laughter.

'Oh, it's you, Lisa,' she giggled, feeling somewhat relieved it was Lisa and not Virgin Media trying to get their customer to upgrade their mobile package. She hated those calls and tried to block their number but failed sometimes. 'Oh, hi there, chum, I didn't recognise your number. Normally your name shows up on the screen!'

'Sorry, that's because I'm using a temporary number, soon to be restored to my proper one. I had an upgrade on this one which will take twenty-four hours. How's life with you and your new romance with Ralph?'

'Now you're talking,' Jodie continued. 'All is going to plan. We touched base again at the weekend and hugged and kissed so all is looking swimmingly good. I think you could safely say we have moved on to the next level.'

'Yippee!'

Jodie pulled the phone inches away from her ear as she heard screams from the other end, Lisa was clearly elated. 'OK, let's make a date in our diaries for a catch up as I need to put Amy to bed soon. I'll check my schedule and text you back as soon as possible,' she quickly replied, aware of the evening hour.

They hung up and she called out to Amy. It was time for bed, and she'd see her in her room in five minutes. As she approached her room, she opened the door to see that Amy was one step ahead, lying on her bed with her teddy, ready to be kissed goodnight. Within minutes Amy was fast asleep; another day over.

Walking quickly back downstairs she tidied everything up in the kitchen. Locking the house up she soon followed suit by putting her PJs on ready for bed.

Chapter Ten

Another bright sunny day lightened up the whole room. Jodie folded back the duvet, stretching out as part of her yoga routine, dangling her legs by the side of the bed. She reached out for her bottle of water on her bedside cabinet to hydrate herself after the night's sleep and unplugged her phone, alerting her to a message from Ralph.

Good morning, Jodie, happy Valentine's Day.

How sweet, she thought, as she sprang into action with the usual morning routines before school. She jumped into the shower and dressed before waking Amy, although she was already up, ready for the day ahead. They went downstairs into the kitchen. Jodie filled the kettle from the water filter, flicking the switch to make herself a herbal tea to kick start her day, while Amy had her usual orange juice and Cheerios. Jodie preferred her bran flakes with a few blueberries and a single raspberry, giving her some antioxidants to face anything coming her way. She was alerted by the doorbell so she dashed to the door, as time wasn't on her side; unlocking it she opened, it leaving a narrow gap to poke her head around the door, and noticed a young man holding a bunch of flowers wrapped in cellophane with a pink ribbon around the middle and a little brown envelope sticking its head out from the middle.

'Good morning, she smiled. 'Gosh, are those for me?' she continued, with surprise in her voice.

'Indeed they are,' he smiled back at her.

'Have a nice day, and thank you,' she replied, looking at the display of flowers. She swiftly took them into the kitchen, placing them on the worktop by the sink, and picked out the envelope, opening it to read:

Dear Jodie
Hope you have a lovely day, see you soon
Love Ralph xxx

Nearly choking up with a fine tear of emotion leaving her eye as she read his sweet message with a heart on each corner of the card, she quickly took out a vase from the cupboard. She gently removed the cellophane and, snipping the liquid sachet, she poured it into the vase filled with cold water, then placed the mixed colours of carnations inside with a few green leafy sprays adding to its display. She would prune the stalks later, as time was ticking, and they needed to head out to the car for school. Amy noticed the flowers, saying how beautiful they looked, and Jodie explained they were from her dad.

Amy had a show and tell today, which she always looked forward to, and was bringing her new teddy which had been given to her by her Aunty Sue, Ralph's sister. They all sat down in a spread-out circle in the classroom, taking turns to show their friends what they had brought in that day. Mrs Newbury, the class teacher, passed a baton around to each child, indicating their turn to speak and explain what they had brought in, which prompted discussions about their object, sending laughter around the class. All went to plan. Reading was next on the agenda which everyone enjoyed, reading aloud to their class teacher. The day progressed with lunch time and playtime outside as the weather had picked up and was sunny and dry, which was always a bonus.

The end of the day was drawing ever nearer, the days just flying by. Soon it would be Friday, that being the big event day, and she would be off to the solicitor, finally to find out what was in the letter, and how much money she had inherited. She was looking forward to it yet feeling somewhat nervous as to what might be dug up as she was going down memory lane. There was only one thing for it and that was a big breath in and release and just go with the flow with confidence; after all what deep secret could be unearthed? Just on cue Jodie's phone pinged in her coat pocket, as she was leaving her school day behind to pick up Amy from hers. She quickly glanced at another text from Ralph which immediately put a huge smile on her face.

Good afternoon, Jodie, just checking all is well and wondered if you've got plans next weekend. Xxx

She quickly replied, *No, so far nothing in the calendar, what are you thinking?*

Could you get cover for Amy for a sleepover over perhaps, as I'm planning something. That's all I'm saying for now! Ralph fired a prompt reply with a winking emoji.

Ooh, sounds intriguing, I'll have a chat with one of the mums. Remember I've got to return countless favours as I have not really played my part lately.

OK watch this space. Let me know. Bye for now, Ralph concluded.

Checking the time, she dashed to her car, zooming off to collect Amy, who had been taken back into school as her mum turned up late, putting everything else out of sync. She rocked up just in time, leaving a handful of children waiting to be picked up. Teachers had a life, too, after their long day, no doubt starting all over again with chores at home, etc. which she was very aware of.

Once home and all outdoor gear hung up, she flicked the kettle on to boil for a cuppa and a hot chocolate from a packet she'd picked up from her last shop for Amy. She opened her school bag, noticing an envelope addressed to her. She slit it open to find another invite, this time a sleepover over next weekend; *perfect timing*, she thought, after reading Ralph's text earlier. Lottie was Amy's best friend so how could she refuse, and Sam, being her best buddy, she could entirely trust.

'Amy, can you come here, please, an invite awaits you.'

Amy had just nipped to the loo and came running back in a jiffy. 'Lottie wants you next weekend. Do you fancy that, darling?' hoping Amy would say yes.

Amy did a quick dance, indicating three yesses from her and swiftly went into her room to have a play before her mum called her for tea, as she knew by now what the after-school routine was. Jodie thought she'd better send a text back to Ralph, informing him of the sleepover invite Amy had just received, which would fit perfectly with his plans that weekend, whatever he had in store. She messaged him back that Amy had an invite for next weekend which was perfect timing. She also thought it best to RSVP Sam, saying Amy would gladly accept, and replaced the invite in Amy's bag for the next day, when Sam had kindly agreed to pick up Amy after school, as agreed the previous week, ready for the solicitor's trip tomorrow.

Chapter Eleven

The day of the solicitor's visit had finally arrived. She woke up to another blue-sky morning in Winchester, which always put a smile on one's face and turned the most boring of days into a better one. With the sun shining, sending happy vibes, she had now finished for the weekend. She had read many times about replacing negative thoughts with three positive ones to start the day: being a great mindfulness believer she shared that thought with others who needed extra inspiration. She stretched her legs over the side of the bed before getting out and jumping in the shower. She dressed before knocking on Amy's door; she clearly didn't need waking, as when she opened it, peering around the door, she saw that Amy was already dressed for school. It was Groundhog Day as she flicked the kettle switch on for her usual herbal tea and a juice for Amy. Granola with a few berries mixed in sufficed them for the next few hours. A quick bathroom visit, brushing their teeth, and they were ready to grab their coats, bags and car keys ready to drive off to Amy's school. Amy, now independent and loving the transition, leant in to her mum for a kiss before opening the car door, and walking through the school gates, where she was greeted by Mrs Newbury with, 'Good morning Amy.' She beckoned her in to meet the rest of the children waiting for the bell to be rung, summoning them into school.

After dropping Amy off she was now ready for the day ahead and the drive to Alton, a small market town, where the solicitors were located. She thought she'd start her journey early, in time for a quick coffee somewhere, before making her way to the solicitors in the afternoon; a good combo, to give her that extra boost she might need for any unwelcoming surprise in store. She always loved a good nosey around a new town or place she'd never been before. A quiet little stroll along the high street, window shopping, then finding the next coffee shop for a cappuccino and a bite to eat, which were indeed the simple things in life that broadened her smile, ready to face any situation feeling chilled and relaxed, which was the ultimate purpose. She hated that feeling of anxiety which suddenly arose during the menopause at its worst, hot and cold flushes circling around her head.

The doorbell chimed as she entered the café, informing staff of a new customer in the coffee shop which was already filled with chatter from all corners.

'Good morning,' a bright voice uttered from the counter ahead.

'A cappuccino and a brownie, please, to eat in,' she replied, looking at the pretty face.

'Take a seat and I'll bring it over,' the lady quickly interjected.

'Thank you,' she smiled back. As usual she took a window seat as she liked to watch people meandering by. The café was beginning to fill up quickly. Glancing at her phone to check the time she noticed a message, making a mental note to ignore them today in order to focus on the day's events until the appointment had finished. This one, however, she couldn't ignore, as it came from Sam, who was taking Amy after school.

Hi Jodie, all is fine, just wishing you the best of luck this afternoon. No need to worry about Amy, Lotti is looking forward to having her for tea. Take your time, ring me afterwards if you want to.

She was very grateful to read her kind words of encouragement as she needed to hear them today; how lucky she was to have such caring friends. As she walked down the high street, she noticed the sign above, reading 'Cooper and Sons', the solicitors she was due to see later. She had parked up in the high street car park, which was free all day, much to her relief as she wasn't sure how long the appointment was going to take. She arrived a few minutes early; she thought this was common courtesy as Mr Brown might be running late or on schedule.

———

81

'Good afternoon, may I help you?' the young lady at the front desk asked as she approached.

'My name is Jodie Smith, to see Mr Brown, please,' she politely told her.

'Oh yes, Mrs Smith,' looking in her diary. 'Please take a seat, he'll be free shortly.'

'Thank you,' she replied, as the nerves started to kick in. Within a few minutes a brown door opened, revealing a stylish young man, thanking his previous client. She assumed it to be Mr Brown. The receptionist left her place, walking into his office with a folder. Jodie assumed it was her turn next. She took a deep breath before she was called in by the young lady acting in a professional manner. An older-looking gentleman appeared at the door. He walked towards her, with his right hand stretched out in greeting. She stood up to reciprocate.

'Mrs Smith, I'm Mr Brown. Please come in and take a seat.' She followed him into the office directly in front of them. 'Beautiful day today,' he remarked, as he stepped aside, letting her pass. 'Please take a seat,' he added with a smile of politeness in his voice.

Mr Brown's office was the usual with a large bookcase holding many folders, presumable for reference, and a dark mahogany desk in front of a good-sized window to the rear of the building. A filing cabinet with two drawers housed clients files, neatly arranged in dividers in alphabetical order. He had one of those leather-bound writing mats in bottle green with black corners to finish the look. Mr Brown took his seat behind his desk with a folder in front of him, which she assumed was hers. She promptly retrieved her folder from her bag and placed it in front of her, looking official. After introductions were out the way, he thanked her for coming, then he opened the file in front of him, pulling out the letter he had sent her and the Will which he was about to discuss with her.

He started by saying that he'd received an updated Will from her father's stepson from a past relationship, which she knew nothing about. She just listened, feeling surprised, and gasping at the news of her dad's ex-girlfriend and a son – a stepbrother – initially thinking that she had not known about this and wondering why her mum had not said anything before. *Never mind*, she thought, *what happened had happened*.

Mr Brown continued by saying that the sum in question was £20,000, to be divided between her and her stepbrother, James, who was now forty. James clearly thought that it was only fair to divide it between them, despite their never having met. She was awestruck as she swallowed, confused by this new take on her dad's Will, knowing something had gone adrift since his death and wondering why this hadn't been unearthed before. *Still, here we are*, she thought, as she continued listening to his speech and trying to keep up. He concluded by saying 'If you agree, by signing on the line which I've marked with an *X*, then the money will be transferred into your account, saving you any further visits. We are keen to close the file once and for all, Mrs Smith. It is entirely up to you whether you pursue the relationship with James as, regarding this matter, no further contact is needed; you both clearly have separate lives.'

'Thank you,' she said, with a surprised look of shock and delight. He handed her a pen and she took another breath in and signed for the money to be moved into her account.

'I'm sure that will help you with any immediate plans you have. Use it wisely, which I have no doubt you will, Mrs Smith,' he concluded, closing the file and indicating that the meeting was clearly over. They stood up and shook hands before Mr Brown opened his office door, bidding her goodbye and sending her on her merry way.

'Thank you.' She turned around, smiling at him gently. The deed had been done in ten minutes, yet a huge gap in her life was left for her to understand. Jodie needed a cup of tea to digest what she had just been told, so she went back to the coffee shop and ordered a mint tea, to calm her edgy nerves before she slowly made the journey home. She sat down with her tea and a tea cake and pulled out her phone to see any missed messages. There was one from Sam asking how it had gone, she was happy having Amy to stay, saying Lottie was looking forward to having her and that she'd got spare PJs so no need for her to race back.

She quickly replied telling her all had gone well, not entirely telling her the truth, as she just needed time to digest what had been explained to her. She would text her once home to reveal all. Her thoughts were all over the place; in particular, why her own mum had kept this stepbrother a secret for all these years. She felt slightly angry but didn't want this to spoil her moment, having her much-needed cuppa and tea cake, which was yummy as she spread the butter all around it. She loved her mum, yet this had come as a complete shock. potentially turning every plan upside down. She did not know how to approach this. She had mixed feelings; as lovely as a lost brother sounded, she also felt rather nervous about finding the whole truth about him. Now she had Amy and was just starting to enjoy her re-found relationship with Ralph; he came first and was the most important person in her life right now, together with her princess Amy. She mustn't let anything spoil her future happiness; she mulled it over in her active yet unsettled brain. Strike while the iron is hot, the saying came into her mind. Don't overthink things, Jodie, she repeatedly told herself, which did help to calm the current situation. On that note she replaced her now empty mug and crumb-free plate on the tray by her feet to return to the serving counter; the kind lady thanked her and wished her a good day as she walked out of the café with a smile on her face, feeling more relaxed.

Finally home, after travelling an hour through traffic, from the somewhat of an ordeal at the solicitors and with lots to mull over, she walked into the kitchen, taking a mug out of the cupboard for a soothing camomile tea. Taking out her phone she thought it best to text Sam to say she was safely home now.

Hi Sam I've just got back and am having a cuppa. Thank you for having Amy, hope she's behaving. I'll see you in the morning. Xx.

Her next call was to her mum; she wasn't looking forward to it.

She wasn't feeling very confident, knowing her mum could no longer recall much due to ageing, although she guessed it had its bonuses at times; though never talking about this matter flummoxed her altogether. *Where to start*, she wondered, as she clicked on her recent call to her mum, pressing go to start the call and hoping for the best. She thought, *what's the worst that could happen?* At first her mum didn't answer, then after three rings she picked up, not recognising the number despite her daughter's name being visible on her phone.

'Jodie, is that you, love?' came a faint voice at the other end.

'Yes, Mum, it's me. Are you OK? You sound faint or maybe it's the phone.'

'Oh well, I'm a bit tired today. I'm getting old and weary, no fun this ageing business, dear,' sounding like a sigh in her voice.

'I've been to the solicitor's today and they found an outstanding account of Dad's, and a sum of money owed to me, which was very surprising although welcome. However, that's not all, Mum, as I've just learnt about a son with his ex-girlfriend or wife, making him my stepbrother. Did you know about this and if so, why wasn't I told about it?' There, she'd said it; she drew in a deep breath.

'Oh, well er,' her mum stumbled along, knowing full well this would cause some controversy one day. 'You'd best come over and I'll tell you everything, dear, over a nice cup of tea or something stronger if you fancy, depending on the time of day.'

'Yes, that sounds like a good idea, Mum, as it's too involved to be discussing it on the phone now. Just to say I've agreed for my share of the money to be moved into my account, so no worries there. That will definitely help me in whatever plans I have in the future, and as it happens, I do have ideas.'

'Well, that's the main thing, dear, every little helps as the saying goes!' Her mum added, 'Let's sort a date out for you to come over,' before ending the call.

Jodie felt satisfied with that and agreed it was for the best to meet up soon to discover more about the situation.

She wondered how soon she could see her mum, perhaps on her next day off work. Her mum lived on the other side of Winchester, making it an easy trip. For now, though, she had enough on her plate, so she'd look at her calendar later to fit in a visit to her mum. She was looking forward to seeing a healthier bank balance but the rest was history; she couldn't turn the clock back. After all, what she didn't know she didn't miss, was her thinking so she put the day's shenanigans to the back of her mind, where they belonged for now.

Jodie felt at peace after that day and for now just wanted to get on with her life, with Amy and Ralph being the most important people she loved and cared for aside from her friends. Life was running smoothly, without any really big dramas, which she always tried to avoid. She wanted to pursue her newfound relationship with Ralph, not only for herself but ultimately for Amy; just being an ordinary family again was all she had ever wanted. She knew deep down that Ralph was a steady, loving character who had had a bit of a wobble and was now putting that all behind him, moving on in his life; she couldn't ask for more. She was quickly brought back to the present, hearing her phone vibrate on the kitchen table. She picked it up, seeing that Sam was ringing her.

'Hi Sam, how's life with you?' hoping Sam wasn't fed up looking after her daughter.

'All good here, no need to panic. Just wondering if you'd like to meet us at the café tomorrow for brunch, as they make a yummy one. The kids can chat and have a hot chocolate probably, but I need to shop anyway. What do you think, lovely?'

'Yes, that sounds good to me, a nice Saturday morning treat. What time's best for you, Sam?'

'Say ten, if that's OK?'

'Perfect, see you there, thanks, Sam.' she concluded. She plugged her phone into the USB socket to recharge her phone overnight. She'd better call it a night and get to bed. She placed her mug in the dishwasher and turned off the lights, checking that everything was locked up, then headed to bed. She looked forward to tomorrow, feeling blessed to have a lovely friend, Sam.

Saturday came and she was glad to have a well-needed lie-in, taking things at an easy pace instead of the usual rushing around before driving off to school. A quick shower, and after putting some casual clothes on she was ready to face the day ahead. A quick drink of water and she was ready to walk out the door, looking forward to a catch up.

'Good morning, Jodie,' came a voice after she'd walked through the café door, alerting everyone by the bell above the door. Sam was clearly happy to have adult company after a long day yesterday. Amy turned her head around, noticing her mum, running to her and enveloping her in a tight hug, nearly taking her breath away. Jodie hugged her back, kissing her on the cheek, saying she had missed her. On release, they took to their chosen table before placing their orders. Mini brunches for the girls and two adult portions for the mums, who by now were famished. Two hot chocolates and two lattes sorted. The young lady serving them soon brought over their drinks orders, followed by the brunches consisting of hash browns, fried egg, baked beans and a slice of black pudding for the adults. Lots of giggling and laughter from the girls, who were stuffing their faces and enjoying one another's company. They seemed happy, leaving Sam and Jodie to catch up on interesting gossip happenings at school.

'Any news on this romantic weekend?' Sam asked her, with a chuckle in her voice.

'No, not yet, I'm not pushing him. I'll just wait and see what happens; surprises are always the best,' she replied, feeling hopeful.

'Fair enough, just let me know if you need me to have Amy for a sleepover,' Sam concluded, after which they asked for their individual bills and marched out of the café with the girls tagging on behind. Each needed to go shopping, picking up essentials for the weekend, so they went their separate ways, heading back home first to pick up the car before going to their desired supermarkets. Jodie hadn't had time to make an essential shopping list; having shopped over the years, she always had a rough idea of what she needed. One look in the fridge told her when stock was running low, it wasn't rocket science; the rest she'd get online. Once home she unpacked and put it all away. She then had time to concentrate on any homework Amy had been given for the weekend: usually it consisted of reading, spellings and times tables of late, boring as that was, but it had to be done before anything else. She usually set Amy a task and in between would put the washing on or make a drink to keep them both alert and focused. Weekends were for catching up on housework, especially if you were working during the week, trying to juggle everything. Her aim was to start early, leaving time for Amy. The more homework Amy was able to do herself without her help, the better, a sign of good parenting skills. Work hard, play hard, was her motto, which had worked well so far; until those difficult teenage years kicked in which was every parent's dread as their children always seemed to know best. Her phone suddenly pinged. Noticing it was a message from Ralph put a smile on her face, as always. She instantly opened it to read it, feeling loved up.

Good morning, Jodie, how are you, fancy a chat?

She quickly replied, *I'm just doing homework with Amy and catching up with chores. I'll ring you later, in an hour, if that's OK.*

OK great, chat later xx was his instant response. She looked forward to chatting with him later.

Homework done and dusted, they each gave a big sigh of relief as they were clearly worn out and needed a well-earned drink. Jodie flicked the kettle on to boil, taking two mugs out of the cupboard and making them a creamy hot chocolate from sachets they had bought earlier. She poured each sachet into a small amount of hot water, stirring it to dissolve the thin grains, then adding more water to the drink. The result was a lovely creamy-textured drink with a subtle sweetness to the flavour. Amy packed her books back into her school bag, ready for

Monday, sipping her hot chocolate as she packed her bag. She wanted some down time for herself, going into her room, where she could have a rest or do one of her jigsaws with her teddies sitting on the carpet watching over her. She was in her little world where she could be anyone. That was the best bit of being a child and a stage every child should go through.

It was now Jodie's turn, so she pulled out her phone, clicked on the last number, which was Ralph's, and rang him back as she'd promised. After what seemed a long wait, he picked up.

'Jodie, thanks for phoning back.' She heard his voice with a touch of excitement as if he was just as eager to hear from her. 'Clearly Amy's homework is out of the way,' he swiftly added.

'Yes, she's now in her room, amusing herself,' feeling quite relieved.

'Good,' he added, let's talk about our weekend, shall we?'

She naturally felt excited hearing him mention it. She wanted to move on with Ralph and, if possible, try and start over to become three again; she couldn't deny she needed him to be part of her life again as well as a permanent father to Amy. She was now in a better financial position if they needed to move. She missed him on a daily basis. Despite having her school friends and going out in the evenings, something was missing from her life and that was Ralph. It was becoming apparent that he felt the same towards her.

'So,' he continued, 'are you free next weekend? Did you get cover for Amy?'

'Yes, my friend Sam has already said she would have Amy as I told her you might be planning a surprise. I do feel a bit awkward, as she's just had Amy overnight when I went on Friday to the solicitors, which went to plan, by the way.'

'I've booked a night at a hotel near you so that will help next Friday, if that's OK with you and for Sam?'

'Sounds great,' Jodie replied, 'I'll have to ask Sam if that's OK and ring you back, Ralph.'

'No problem, Jodie, just let me know as soon as possible.' He ended the call in haste, as she heard voices in the background, calling him.

Jodie thought it best to ring Sam and ask if that would be OK whilst it was fresh in her mind. After three rings Sam picked up. Choosing her words carefully, she fired her request at her friend, feeling slightly nervous as she delicately explained the situation.

'Ooh, how exciting and romantic!' Sam interjected with a hint of a joyful flutter. 'Three yesses from me, Jodie! I'll make your dreams come true by taking Amy, as Lottie loves her coming over. She's no trouble at all, Jodie, so don't think twice about it, OK? This is potentially your future in the making, getting back together with Ralph. He's so perfect for you, Jodie, you can have Lottie another time, as I know you're thinking that, my lovely. Ring him back and tell him all is well. Just have the best time, OK?' Sam was getting all emotional and mouthing a kiss down the phone.

'Thank you, Sam, I promise I'll repay you very soon and I love you for doing this grand favour for me, much appreciated!' She couldn't thank her enough. On ending the call, she texted Ralph back; as he sounded busy, she got straight to the point, saying Sam would have Amy and had told her not to worry as it was more important to sort out their future together.

Sam pinged back an instant reply, with a thumbs up emoji. A big sigh of relief came from Jodie as she took a deep breath. She now couldn't wait for the weekend. She jumped up and punched the air with excitement.

Friday couldn't come soon enough as she felt ready to rekindle her relationship with Ralph, knowing he felt the same. They both agreed something was missing, they didn't want to live apart anymore as Amy was growing up so fast. Those days were over; in her opinion, it was time to start afresh and wipe the slate clean. She was finding it increasingly hard to have a social life of her own outside the daily school routines and, seeing Amy growing up fast, she too needed a sense of freedom, away from her mum. She had heard of Rainbows, the group for girls between five and seven before they joined Brownies, learning different life skills and earning badges along their journey. She wanted to enrol Amy; Rainbows was held one night in the local community hut across the high street, which she was keen to sign up for. As everything was online these days, making life somewhat easier, she checked her local area social media page and found her local Rainbows group, where she could register Amy, hoping there wouldn't be a long waiting list. Within a few minutes she received notification of registration and told she would be informed later of a vacancy for Amy to join. *Happy days*, she thought.

Friday was approaching fast, and she was excited about her weekend away with Ralph, something they hadn't done since Amy was born. Life just took over, with a newborn to look after, twenty-four hours a day nonstop; she didn't know what had hit her when she became a mum. She enjoyed it all, despite feeling drained of energy in the first few months: feeding, changing, sleeping, and repeating for the foreseeable future became her daily routine with no end in sight. Fortunately, all first-time mums felt the same, so she wasn't alone. Fathers took on the easier role, she concluded, as they walked out the door going to work, assuming they had a job. That said, working was equally tiring, just different.

She needed to organise packing a bag for Amy, ready to hand her over to Sam at school that morning. Amy was equally excited to see Lottie again and spend time with her. Breakfast out of the way, they set off in the car to school, Jodie having sent a quick text before she left saying she was on her way. She parked by the school and jumped out with Amy in tow, with her school bag as well as her rucksack packed with all she wanted for her stay, to be greeted by Sam and Lottie as they walked towards them, clear excitement beaming from Amy's and Lottie's faces. Hopefully Sam felt not too overwhelmed.

'Good morning, girls, ready for some weekend fun?' Sam

asked, smiling at them. Jodie drew Amy into a hug, kissing her goodbye and saying, 'Have a great time and be good for Sam. I know you will be,' as Sam took the girls, walking hand in hand, through the school gates. Jodie quickly walked back to her car as if it was just the usual drop off, as she was eager to move swiftly on before any emotions set in, as they usually did.

Parking up back at the house she had an hour to kill before she set off on her romantic weekend in Bibury, in the Cotswolds, a very pretty village with a stream flowing through it, with beautiful walks surrounding the area. She started packing for all kinds of weather and a dress for the evening, placing her phone by her bed. Seeing a text message from Ralph, giving her the hotel address, and postcode which she needed for the satnav, sent a chill but good feeling down her spine, adding to her excitement. She sent a quick text back.

Thanks, Ralph, just packing to leave soon, can't wait to get this weekend started xx

Swiping back to her checklist, she ticked off things she had packed, making sure she wouldn't forget essentials such as her phone charger, purse, coat and hat, just in case it turned chilly, a spare pair of shoes and, not least, a favourite book to read if the opportunity arose to sit on a park bench to read. She, being an avid reader, could never go away without a good paperback. Ralph also liked a good read, an escape, murder mystery being his current favourite genre. She felt happy that they both enjoyed a good book. Already packed, she did a quick bathroom stop and looked into the mirror, checking her appearance; she was good to go. Taking her small suitcase downstairs she grabbed her coat, bag and keys to lock up and headed out to her car. She thought it best to set the satnav up, ready to start her journey first, stopping to fuel up. She turned her radio on to Radio 2 for the afternoon show, in particular Sarah Cox at 4 pm. She loved to join in with the fast-track songs for a laugh; the very slow ones sounding as if the singer was drunk, very hard to guess. She loved her music, and it kept her happy and stress free. Life couldn't be better at the moment, knowing she would soon be rekindling her relationship with Ralph, with whom she had fallen in love nearly six years before. Could this be the start of something new? She sincerely hoped it would.

Chapter Twelve

After a nearly two-hour drive through the countryside lanes, passing through many beautiful towns and villages, she finally heard her satnav's ossi voice, 'You have reached your destination. Windows up, grab those sunnies and don't let the seagulls steal your chips!' She knew at last her hotel was almost in view. She breathed a huge sigh of relief, feeling in need of an espresso once in the hotel. She parked the car in the hotel car park to the rear, dismantled the satnav, placing it in its case in the glove box, glanced in the mirror checking her hair, adding some lip gloss to her lips as they had become dry, and opened the car door, to be immediately greeted by fresh air. She retrieved her case from the rear seat and clicked her car fob to lock up. She was excited yet a bit nervous, wondering whether Ralph had arrived yet, as she didn't fancy walking into the hotel alone, considering he had booked it presumably in his name. All became clear as she walked up to the entrance. Her phone pinged with a message, which she was rather relieved to read, saying:

I'm in the foyer, waiting.

The mystery had begun, she chuckled to herself with a beam across her face. She approached the entrance, with its double automatic doors, and walked up to the check-in desk in front of her. Placing her case on its wheels by her side she glanced around to see if she could see Ralph. Suddenly she felt a tap on her right shoulder. She turned around to see a medium-height, smart-looking fella in light brown chinos, wearing a casual red knitted jumper over a chequered red and white shirt to add to the look; immediately recognising it was Ralph, albeit smartly dressed to impress his date.

'Well, hello Mr Smart Guy! Do I know you from somewhere?' Jodie leant in to kiss him on both cheeks as the French do.

'Bonjour, Madame Jodie,' as Smith didn't quite have that ring to it, being a common English surname. She smiled back at him affectionately. He proceeded to ring the bell on the desk, alerting a member of staff that someone was waiting to check in.

A smart lady dressed in a black blazer soon appeared behind the desk, saying, 'Welcome to the Bull Hotel.'

Thanking her, Ralph said he had a double room booked under the name Mr Stevens for two nights including dinner.

'Perfect,' she checked her screen for the booking. 'Oh yes, Mr Stevens, room 108 on the first floor. The lift is over there,' as she pointed to the right. She placed a printout of the booking form for his signature, handing him their room key card. 'I hope you enjoy your stay with us. Please ask if you need anything during your stay,' she concluded, with a smile towards the loved-up pair. 'If you would like coffee and cake, we are currently serving it in our lounge to the left.'

'Thank you,' they replied in unison. They both desperately wanted a drink and a yummy piece of cake after their long individual trips, so they quickly took the lift to the first floor, finding their room off the corridor to the right. Ralph took out the card to insert into the slot above the door lock, showing green to open, pulling the door handle down. A quick 'Wow,' uttered at the smartly decorated room with ensuite to the side, then they placed their bags onto the bed and hung their coats up on the hooks by the door. Closing the door, remembering to take the card out of its slot, they made their way back downstairs to the lounge, where the lady directed them to a lovely area serving coffee and cake. On walking through to the lounge, they were greeted by a waitress, who directed them to a table in the restaurant; a table for two, with a table lamp with a light pink lamp shade adding to the ambiance.

Ralph pulled out the chair for her to take her place at one end of the table, Ralph sitting down opposite. The lady came back, taking their order for two lattes. Ralph asked about the cakes, and she went through the list, each choosing a slice of carrot cake, which was always a favourite of theirs. The waitress went back to tap out the order on the screen by the till. They were suddenly engulfed by an aromatic smell of coffee as they ground the beans in the coffee machine. Within minutes she was back, carrying a round tray with their coffees in a glass on a saucer with two long spoons to stir sugar, or scoop up the frothy milk they could no longer reach to drink. The cakes followed, sitting on a plate with a fork, and a white serviette on the side.

How romantic, Jodie thought as she started to relax and forget about everything else happening at home. It was their time to share and enjoy the moment and indeed the two days they had to rekindle their relationship and find a way forward for themselves. They raised their lattes, clinking glasses and saying, 'To us. May we enjoy this time together.' They smiled at each other. They soon broke into their cakes and sipped their coffees, feeling refuelled, ready to return to their room, unpack and take a wander outside, pretending to be a tourist and exploring the vicinity around the Cotswolds. They asked for the bill and headed back to their room. They unpacked the essentials, leaving the rest for later when they came back to dress for dinner.

The weather was pleasantly warm with the odd breeze, so a light coat sufficed. They walked alongside each other, soon linking fingers, then hands, firmly grasping each other's, sending a warm glowing sensation through one another as if they had been longing for this moment; if the truth be known, they were making up for the lost time spent apart. She realised Ralph had found his way again in life after his meltdown, with the farm becoming too much to cope with as well as having a newborn girl to entertain. She was certain that he had put that past life behind him and was feeling relieved that he had moved away from his dad's farm to start a new life of his own, trying to find himself again. He felt thankful to her for showing signs of immense patience and kindness towards him, as she had tried to steer him through this dark time, offering help and guidance; suggesting talking therapy, which Ralph knew he needed.

They continued their sightseeing tour on foot, walking along the riverside as it meandered along a path lined with trees either side, with views of delightful cottages in Cotswold stone, a picturesque sight to see whatever the weather. They linked hands as they enjoyed their peaceful walk along the promenade with all stresses slowly leaving their thoughts, just enjoying the moment, which always felt good. Few people were about, which made it extra special, enabling them to stop and take in the scenery before them. At the end of the walk they turned to face each other, looking deeply into one another's eyes, at which point only one thing could happen; they drew each other closer, their mouths touched as they kissed, feeling the electricity between them, arms starting to rise, engulfing one another in a hug, arms around their bodies. They stayed there a few moments, enjoying once again their clear fondness for each other, both feeling safe in each other's love and affection; a moment of stillness blocking out everything and anyone. Moments after, they stood back, still facing one another.

'That felt good,' she said appreciatively, squeezing Ralph's hand. She added, with a chuckle and a hint of embarrassment, as they stood surveying the scenery, 'Thank you for bringing me here to this beautiful part of the world, and indeed, the lovely hotel. It's all gorgeous.' She kissed him, this time on the right cheek, inhaling the natural scent on his smooth-shaven face. Jodie was lapping up their getaway break with pure delight and excitement. She wanted this to continue forever. She suddenly missed Amy, knowing she would love the idea of Mummy and Daddy reuniting in their affection for one another and hoping they would become one again, which they both deserved.

After a quick glance at his watch, Ralph thought they should slowly meander back, as time was ticking away. They needed to get back to the hotel to change for dinner, which they had booked for 6.30, giving them ample time to shower and spruce up. They both needed a meal after their long journeys.

'I wonder what's for dinner?' she asked Ralph, turning her head towards him.

'We'll just have to wait and see,' he replied, smiling back.

Back at the hotel they made their way to their room. She slotted the card in the door to open immediately, noticing a single red rose wrapped in cellophane with a few twigs of green fern to add to the initial decoration and a red ribbon tied around it. Next to it were two foil-wrapped chocolates with a picture of a thatched cottage on the front. 'So sweet,' she said out loud to Ralph, who was unpacking his suitcase and placing the items neatly in the drawers provided. 'Ah, how romantic is this! Did you have anything to do with it, Ralphy baby, must be love,' she muttered.

No sooner had she uttered those words she felt two arms around her middle. Little kisses were placed on one side of her neck, then the other. The arms brought her into a tight embrace. 'Steady on, Mr S, we need to get ready for dinner.' She turned round.

He let his arms drop and twirled her around to give her a quick kiss in appreciation of her thanks. 'I love you, Jodie, always have, since the day we met. First one in the shower is a winner,' he concluded, flirting his way with her again, knowing full well she loved every minute of it.

This was hitting on dangerous territory so she thought it best to undress in the bathroom before any further advances got out of control, as it was soon their dinner time. She went first, as girls usually took a bit longer, fixing their hair and makeup, though in her case all she needed to do was brush her hair, so she could be ready in minutes. She took out the block-coloured dress she had bought herself at Christmas; it was orange, black and grey. She slipped on a pair of wine-red tights to keep her warm and matching ankle boots to finish the desired look. She took a look in the full-length mirror in the bedroom, and she was good to go.

Ralph spruced up with smart tan trousers, a chequered shirt and a khaki green jumper. Each looking lovely, they made their way downstairs to the dining area, where they were shown to their table by a waitress. A tea light in a red foil case, bedded in white crystal chips, sat on the far edge of the table which she lit, giving an extra lovely touch to the occasion. They took out the menus which were stacked in a holder, and browsed through them before placing their drinks order, each having a bottle of still water. Looking at the mains, they choose dauphinoise potatoes with fine greens beans in garlic, with venison slices in a red wine jus, which tickled their taste buds. Although they didn't need to choose their dessert at this stage, after perusing the choice they were both tempted with the crème brûlée, as it had become one of their favourites from past times eating out. The lady soon came back to take their order, drinks arriving first.

'Well, this is very pleasant,' Jodie remarked. They clinked their wine glasses together, both looking very relaxed and enjoying one another's company. She had noticed a leaflet in the room, with the usual blurb about the hotel and things to do around the area; the hotel spa in the basement with a pool, sauna and various treatments on offer at a special price during their stay. 'We should take a peek tomorrow morning perhaps, Ralph, if you fancy, or later in the afternoon.' They agreed that would be fun. They just had to book a time with reception, which they would do after their meal. Their meals arrived shortly, looking delicious and inviting, so they tucked in with enthusiasm, leaving no crumb on their plates. Desserts followed, which also looked very tasty, with a lightly crunchy topping on the crème brûlée, followed by two cappuccinos. They had ordered these to be taken to the nearby lounge and were delivered on a round tray with a white doily in the middle by a young gentleman in a smart suit. He obviously enjoyed his job as waiter, making polite conversation with customers, asking them how far they'd travelled and wishing them a pleasant stay at the hotel. It was lovely to have that extra special touch to the evening. All done and finished they retired to their room. A TV was on the wall and they browsed through the channels. An episode of the much-loved *Repair Shop* was just about to start, so they plumped up the cushions by the headboard, taking off their shoes, and sat back to watch it, feeling very cosy and in tune with each other. On Facebook she had come across Jay Blades' thoughts for the day, which she loved to read whilst having breakfast and sipping her coffee. He was a master craftsman.

On Saturday morning they slowly came to feel the love as they slept side by side, after such long time, never wanting to be apart again. Their minds were made up: to move back in together, knowing this was the right thing to do, especially where Amy was concerned. The details would be discussed over time; now it was time for a fresh start. They gave each other a high five which sealed it all, making them the happiest couple, affectionately kissing each other, wrapping each other around in hugs: perfect. A tray was on the table with a small kettle and a selection of teas, including Pukka, which were Jodie's favourite flavoured teas to suit the mood and soul. Ralph went to fill the kettle, asking her which tea she'd prefer. 'Let me guess,' he added, 'Morning Fresh, which gives uplifting energy for the day.'

She replied with a big grin. Ralph had an Earl Grey tea and placed their mugs on each side of the bed, before they showered and dressed before breakfast, chatting about their plans for the day. It was another sunny warm day so they decided to stroll around the town before enjoying an afternoon in the spa, where she had already pre-booked a body massage with essential oils, which she was really looking forward to. Ralph would take to the pool. with its jets and bubbles in one area. melting all stresses within minutes as he soon relaxed into the weekend ahead.

Breakfast consisted of croissants and pains au chocolat, different types of bread, yoghurt, fruit or scrambled eggs with smoked salmon and a cheese platter; all looking mouthwatering and healthy with a selection of fruit. *A healthy diet is preferable for a long life, feeling fitter in yourself,* she thought. Juices and tea and coffee added to the feelgood factor and they were fully charged to face the day ahead. The went back to their room to collect coats and off they went to see what was out there. They went for another stroll along the riverbank, stopping off occasionally to sit on a bench, taking in the surrounding scenery, followed by a coffee stop, sitting outside a coffee shop which had tables outside as the weather dictated it was warm enough. They discussed the way forward for their moving back in together. Ralph would put in for a transfer to a local company, as his contract was ending soon. The inheritance would certainly come in useful if they thought of buying a bigger house; Jodie's flat was rather on the small side. They might add to their family later on, which both wanted, as Amy was growing up so quickly.

The afternoon was spent at the spa, lapping up the luxury. First was Jodie's massage followed by resting on a lounger as suggested for at least half an hour. It was not wise to return to the pool due to the oils used, so she did rest, taking out her latest book, *The Olive Branch* by Jo Thomas, which she found addictive, being a very keen reader lately. She felt so relaxed and chilled, falling asleep at odd moments. Ralph decided to join her on the adjacent lounger after being in the pool and sauna. He too needed a rest before it was dinner time again, their final evening. They showered at the pool before returning to their room to dress for dinner. This time she wore a deep pink blouse with black trousers and wine-red shoes: a more casual look. Ralph wore mid-brown cords with a chequered shirt and a red jumper. Each ready, they took the lift to the ground floor, heading to the dining room, which was filling up by the hour.

'As it's our last night, I thought we'd have a glass of bubbly if you fancy?'

'Perfect, thank you, two glasses of prosecco it is, then,' she added. The waitress soon obliged with their bubbles and took their meal orders. Each wanted the sea bass with dauphinoise potatoes and fine green beans. The dessert had to be another crème brûlée, with two cappuccinos in the lounge afterwards, finishing the evening off on a high.

After dinner they returned to their room to prop up cushions and pillows on the bed, ready to select a movie on Netflix, thinking *La La Land*. They'd seen it numerous times but still loved it as if they were seeing it for the first time. There was something about the film that brought a comfy and cosy feeling yet with a joyous musical talent flowing throughout the musical. So, it was PJs on and get comfy as they sat alongside each other waiting for the grand entrance where they descend from their cars into a jumping jack onslaught. Having the latest tech knowhow they paused the film for a drinks interval, which was a herbal camomile tea for Jodie and a hot chocolate for Ralph, with another chocolate, adding to the romantic night in. Life was at its best for now, having made the decision to move back in together and share the load, as couples do with children. Ralph having decided to put in for a transfer to a new post they could immediately move back in together, giving them plenty of time to look for a new house later. That was settled, putting any unwanted stress and anxiety behind them. After the movie had finished, they were so tired from the day's events that they just visited the bathroom before kissing each other goodnight and turning the lights out.

Chapter Thirteen

Sunday morning was their last morning, before checking out at midday to return to their everyday lives and they reunited forever under one roof. All good things came to an end, so they made the most of their precious time together. First, they had a lovely cuppa to energise them before breakfast: this time it was Jodie's turn to roll out of bed to fill the kettle and decide from the array of teas on offer which they'd prefer. She noticed her all-time favourite, A Fresh Start, a Pukka tea she usually drank at home, so opted for that one and Ralph an ordinary Tetley tea bag. Returning to bed, pillows propped up with an extra cushion for added sitting up comfort, they drew one another close for a kiss and cuddle before sipping their early morning brews and firing up their phones to peruse any urgent messages. Fortunately there was nothing urgent as they wanted to savour their last hours together before they parted to make their separate ways back to their normal daily routines. On the plus side they both had lots to look forward to as they rearranged their lives to become a family again, which excited them both.

Ralph had to ask for a transfer to a local company near Jodie and give notice to his landlord at the flat he was currently renting. He had always intended to rent the flat on a temporary basis, knowing that one day he would probably move on in his life, even if things didn't work out with Jodie. Now he was naturally over the moon as he wanted a permanent contract with his daughter, so he strived hard to aim for that. From today onwards life was on the up for them both, no more secrets, all out in the open was their best way forward. They soon showered and dressed, ready for breakfast one last time before they packed their bags, Jodie to drive back to Winchester and Ralph catching the train to

Wolverhampton, where he had a return ticket and a direct connection early afternoon. They had a hearty breakfast with two cappuccinos and then felt ready to face their long journeys home. Returning to the room, they packed, checked they hadn't left anything behind and went back to reception, where Ralph picked up the invoice for their stay. All that remained was to load up the car and take Ralph to the station for his connecting train to Wolverhampton.

Jodie set the satnav in motion to return home and off they went to the station. She pulled up at the drop off stop outside the front entrance, leant in for a final kiss, and Ralph grabbed his suitcase from the rear seat, opened the door, and soon disappeared into the crowd heading into the station, swiping his ticket through the machine to open the barrier leading to the platforms. He looked up at the TV above to see that his train time showed no delays so far and find the platform number. Jodie quickly picked up her phone which she had placed on Ralph's seat after he left, thinking to send a text to Sam as she was on her way home and telling her the good news that she and Ralph had decided to move back together as soon as possible.

Within minutes came her reply.

Oh Jodie, that's brilliant news. I'm so happy for you. Let's catch up once you're home. All is well here so no need to worry, safe travels Sam xx

Thanks, I must go as I'm at the drop off part by the station.

She was soon on her way to the motorway which, thankfully, was pretty fast-flowing, which would reduce her travel time, she hoped. She turned her radio on to listen to *Elaine Page on Sunday*, with those hilarious laughs that were interjected if something funny occurred. She loved her music on the go at home too, having her mini-Google in the kitchen playing her favourite tunes at breakfast time, or when she was home alone needing a pick me up. *Sounds of the Seventies* followed, which she loved equally, usually singing along.

Three hours later she parked up outside her flat and left her car to run, which was always a good idea before turning it off after a long journey. With a big sigh of relief to be back home again she packed up the satnav placing it in the glove box, removed her suitcases from the rear seat and walked up to her front door. She suddenly felt tired, needing a coffee once inside. Opening the door, the floor was covered with scattered mail, so she collected it and took it into the kitchen, placing it on the table to be sorted after the important coffee she desperately needed. Everything could wait but her energy levels needed refuelling. She filled her trusty new coffee machine with filtered water, turning it on to heat up, then poured some milk into a plastic IKEA cup she had in the cupboard and placed the milk pipe, letting it flow through the machine. The cappuccino button was pressed to grind the beans, making the cappuccino, adding the frothed milk, finishing with a few chocolate sprinkles from a shaker with little holes at the top; she enjoyed this with a Hobnob, starting to feel recharged with each gulp. 'Amazing what a coffee does to you as an instant pick me up,' she said out loud to herself. She picked up her phone to text Ralph that she was home and ask him how his journey was going.

He pinged back:

That's good, well done. We're just chugging into the station now chat later xx

Brilliant, she thought, *next text to Sam.*

Hi Sam just home and refuelling with a coffee, what time should I pick Amy up? Hope you're both OK xx

Sam texted back:

I'll bring her over after tea at McDonald's; been to the cinema. Having a great time, catch up next week with all the goss.

No need to worry, she told herself and started flicking through the post, of which most were the usual ads, until she noticed a letter from an unknown sender. She whipped it open with her thumb underneath the seal and pulled out to read a letter from the stepbrother she'd just learned about. He wanted to meet up; *putting a spanner in the works*, she thought, *just as everything was coming together with Ralph and me.* She immediately went on the defensive, thinking what did he want, which she then guessed was a bit cruel, as he might not want anything, only wanting to connect in her view after all these years. Did she really want her life to be suddenly thrown upside down, unravelling the layers of the past and present events, which really Amy didn't need to hear about for now. She reread the neatly written letter, analysing it as she read each sentence, making her mind up if she wanted to finally meet James. It would be interesting but really this wasn't the right time. She replaced the letter to reply another day. She swiftly unpacked her suitcase, placing dirty washing into the empty washing machine, to add Amy's later before setting it into motion tomorrow. Fortunately, she had cleaned everything before she left, making her Monday morning start as easy as possible as they embarked on a new school week. She decided to check on Daisy, hoping she hadn't died of starvation or loneliness whilst they were away. Seeing a face appear through the hutch she breathed a sigh of relief and delight.

At a ring of the doorbell, she sprang back into life, thinking that it must be Sam and Amy. She opened the door to see her neighbour, Jenny, who she'd not seen in ages. She looked slightly flustered, as if something had just happened.

'Oh, hello Jenny, long time no see. Are you OK?' she asked with slight concern in her voice.

'Oh, it's nothing, I just saw your recycling bins out over the weekend which weren't taken in again, leaving me wondering if you were OK.'

She replied with a smile on her face, 'No problem, I was away for the weekend. I've only just got back now and I'm waiting for my friend to bring Amy back.' She said reassuringly, 'It's very kind of you to enquire about me,' bidding her goodbye and closing the door. Moments later there was another knock at the door and this time it was Sam and Amy. Amy flung her arms around her mum's waist, pleased to see her.

'Yay,' her mum embarrassed her by inviting Sam in.

'Welcome home, lovely,' Sam leant in, giving a French kiss to Jodie.

'Thank you so much for having Amy. I really did appreciate it,' she replied, looking very happy. Sam, recognising the happy signs, handed Amy's bag over before saying goodbye and that she'd see her in the morning, as both needed to get on.

Jodie soon heard everything about Amy's weekend which seemed to be all wonderful. Unpacking her bag, she filled the washing machine with her underwear and suchlike before Amy dashed into her bedroom and changed into her PJs, as she was accustomed to doing. Jodie enquired about any homework that had to be done before Monday, which to her delight Sam had already covered. All she needed was a quick drink of hot chocolate and Amy was ready for bed. Fortunately, she didn't ask about her dad as it was getting late, and that would need more explaining that he was going to move back in with them. *That was for another day*, she thought.

Chapter Fourteen

Monday arrived with a reality check. The weekend over, a fresh week awaited, the run of the mill school run with possible hidden surprises to brighten up the day. One thing was certain; Ralph was moving back in, which was something to celebrate each waking morning. She did her morning stretch before taking her morning shower and getting ready for school. She loved this time of morning with quality time for herself before Amy appeared downstairs for breakfast. She soon got back into the morning routine as they grabbed their bags, keys and coats, walking out of the flat. They were soon in the car on their way to Amy's school, where she now just dropped her off, having mum walk her inside the school gates now a thing of the past; independence kicking in. Life was getting a little easier for her. Indicating as she moved out of the drop off lay-by onto the main road, she continued the journey to her school with a deep happy feeling within, after her rekindled weekend with Ralph. It felt like the first day they had set eyes on each other; a love never really lost. She was so excited to tell her friends she felt young and full of the joys of spring. After she'd parked up and made her way to the staff room she was startled to see a yellow sticker on her locker, saying 'Welcome back'. *How sweet*, she thought, unlocking the door to hang up her coat and taking her phone out before leaving her bag on the shelf above. She turned around to see Sam standing by her side.

'Meet me later for a catch up.'

'I'll text you later. Must go before I'm in their bad books,' she quickly added, walking out of the room to her class.

She was greeted by 'Good morning Mrs Smith' as she entered the class.

Feeling a little overwhelmed yet clearly happy, she replied, 'Thank you. Good morning to you all.' Mrs Newbury started calling out their names from the register. All present and correct, she asked Jodie to take her readers out into the corridor so as not to disturb the class, leaving them to continue their learning in peace, maths being the first subject of the day.

Lunchtime soon was upon them, and it was her turn on playground duty which she didn't particularly enjoy, but today was at least bright and cheerful. From time to time, new pupils would join the school within the term, due to a family move or similar, and today happened to be one of them. Another teacher walked up to her, holding a shy little girl's hand, who clearly needed one-on-one attention.

'Mrs Smith, this is Kitty, who's just joined us today. She's our latest Reception pupil. I wonder if you could help her mix with the others out here today.'

'Absolutely I can,' she replied, thinking of another string to add to her CV. She enjoyed the one-on-one personal touch, which every child so deserved. This added extra enjoyment to her day. She soon took young Kitty's hand, giving a gentle squeeze, hopefully indicating to her that she was in safe hands, noting the pun. Jodie thought she'd sit with her on the bench provided outside, which was named the Friendship Bench. She thought this was a great idea as those who felt lost could sit on the bench, knowing others might sit beside them and befriend them. One of the dinner ladies supervised this. She had always wanted to be a one-on-one teaching assistant, possibly to a special needs child, as she had experience of this, having had a second cousin from her mother's side who had only walked at the age of ten years; now married and happy. It took courage and dedication to overcome any disability in life and not all truly understood the journey they encountered. As they sat and chatted it was apparent that Kitty only had a mum, which she could currently relate to, knowing how hard it was for her, no doubt. Kitty was also five, the same age as

Amy, so perhaps they could befriend one another, possibly inviting Kitty for tea.

'What's your mum's name, Kitty?' she asked, her bending towards her ear and seeing that she was shy, possibly softly spoken.

'My mum's called Debbie, my dad lives far away. I don't see him much.' She started to open up more, which she thought was good progress.

'OK, is she collecting you today after school?'

'Yes,' Kitty smiled back, as if she couldn't wait to see her.

'Great, I'm sure I'll see her later today.'

Home time was fast approaching, and she was feeling a bit worn out after the weekend. There was lots to process amid the excitement of her and Ralph moving back in together. Her class started to gather up their books, preparing for home time when they'd soon form a straight line by the back door, ready to walk into the playground to meet their respective parents waiting behind the school gates. Kitty was clearly very clingy, grabbing her hand, feeling secure after their conversations on the Friendship Bench, having opened up to her with confidence. The end of day bell rang, all getting excited for home time and, for some, the after-school club for those who had working mums who couldn't pick up their children. She took Kitty by the hand into the playground, where another member of staff opened the school gates, letting parents and grandparents alike flood in to collect their children. All needing to let off steam after a long day, the children ran towards them, some with open arms, some who couldn't get off the premises quick enough. Plenty of shouting and screaming, as was the custom after a school day. Kitty led Jodie to her mum as they walked towards one another.

'Hi, I'm Mrs Smith. I've been looking after your daughter today. We had a great chat at lunchtime as she told me about you and that she's just moved into the area.'

'Oh, thank you. I've been worried she'd feel a bit overwhelmed by her first afternoon.'

'My pleasure. I've enjoyed our chats,' she added, letting go of Kitty's hand and handing her over to her mum. She waved them goodbye, moving swiftly back to the classroom to gather up her things and back to her locker to retrieve her coat and bag to leave, walking to her car to dash off to Amy's school.

On arrival at Amy's school Jodie parked in the lay-by, seeing Amy walking towards the car. She jumped in and off they drove home, to chill and start again as families do. Flicking on the kettle switch, Jodie made herself a green tea, and a hot chocolate for Amy. They sat down, chatting about their individual school days before Amy opened her school bag, taking out her book to read and her spellings for the week to practise with her mum. This took half an hour which was enough, as neither was really in the mood, it just had to be done. Amy checked on Daisy, who poked her head out from her hutch on hearing her name, proving to Amy that animals are very clever and blessed with intelligence. She couldn't live without a pet. She was an animal lover, hoping that one day she would have a dog. All chores out of the way, Amy went back to her room to amuse herself till her mum called her for tea.

Jodie picked up her phone, checking any messages and noticing one from Sam, wanting to meet up on her day off on Wednesday, an excuse to go to the café for a catch up after dropping the girls off.

Hi Sam, yes let's meet at the café after morning drop off on Wednesday, 9.30 OK.

Great, look forward to it hun xx Sam replied instantly.

Moments later another ping. Jodie saw an email offering a Rainbows place for Amy, due to a cancellation, to start on Monday from 5pm to 7pm, which was lovely as Amy needed something other than school. Jodie instantly wondered if Lottie was going or anyone else. Amy might know others as she was an easy mixer. Jodie replied instantly, accepting the offer. She also thought she would help out, if they needed extra adults, furthering her skills such as crafting or baking, which she enjoyed adding to her ever-growing CV.

Within a few minutes she got confirmation of Amy's registration, followed by an attachment listing the uniform required, of which they would have stock at affordable prices at her first meeting. Suddenly Amy came dashing out, obviously getting hungry, asking what was for tea. Jodie thought she'd tell her the news about her Rainbows place, knowing she would be excited about getting a new uniform, too. She jumped for joy.

'Macaroni cheese tonight,' Jodie added, knowing it was one of her favourites.

'Can Lottie come over soon, Mum? She needs to come to ours as I've been several times to hers now,' Amy asked.

'Absolutely. I just had to do a few things. How about this Friday? She could sleep over, to go to the cinema or something?'

'Yeah, thanks Mum.' Amy walked over, hugging Jodie and planting kisses on her face, clearly elated.

Jodie promptly clicked on Sam's number. She answered after two rings.

'Hi there, lovely, you OK?'

'All good. Amy was just wondering if Lottie wants to come over on Friday for a sleepover as Amy's been to yours so often. Is that OK?'

'Just checking the calendar, nothing planned, so it's a yes from me, hun!'

'Great, sorted, details later this week. Bye for now.' She hung up, beaming at Amy, confirming the event. Both were happy as Jodie owed Sam a few favours. Lots of new things were happening in Amy's life now, which brought great pleasure to them, including Ralph, whom she thought she must update re Rainbows. She felt at peace with everything as her life was taking a new direction. Amy went back into her room and put her PJs on as she felt more chilled in them and would be ready for bed later Jodie took the opportunity to message Ralph, telling him about the Rainbows place and Lottie's sleepover on Friday. He immediately replied with a thumbs up emoji with two kisses.

She decided to catch up on an episode of *The Repair Shop*

before bed which got her into a deep sleep. 'Another day over,' she mumbled to herself. She checked in on Amy who had taken to her bed, kissed her good night, shutting the door gently behind her, switching all lights off, put her PJs on and jumped into bed, lights off, hitting the pillow.

The week was slowly ticking by and soon it was midweek and Jodie's day off and meetup with Sam at the café. She was looking forward to it, knowing full well Sam would want to hear all the latest news about her and Ralph, and the next steps towards living back together, all three under one roof again, which filled Jodie with delight and much to look forward to. Groundhog Day again as the morning light seeped through the side of the windows before the blinds revealed all, once they were pulled up by the cord. Jodie slid her way out of bed with a stretch, showered and dressed before setting the kitchen table for breakfast. Amy soon appeared, ready to launch herself into the day. Within the hour they went to the car. Making their way to school she dropped Amy, continuing to her school. Entering the classroom, she was greeted by her new little friend, Kitty, who walked towards her.

'Good morning, Kitty, lovely to see you again.'

Kitty smiled back at her, feeling the love bond between them. Jodie had now been assigned to look after her on a one-on-one basis, giving her any extra support she needed in her first days after joining, an idea which she loved. She was pretty much her own boss, so she thought she would take her to one side to assess her reading ability. The usual Biff and Chip books came out, which were graded according to ability, starting off with words then gradually progressing to more words and sentences. Kitty clearly enjoyed the pictures. Jodie asked her to explain what she saw in the pictures, tapping into her imagination, which would lead her to writing short stories later. She wrote her progress in the new exercise book, with Kitty's name in bold letters on the front cover, placing it back into her school bag to take home to show her mum along with any further homework she needed to do. Kitty soon joined the rest of the class after their group activities.

The morning continued smoothly till the sound of the bell for lunch. All the children lined up by the classroom door to walk quietly into the dining room, where they sat at their assigned class table. Staff would walk alongside the tables, indicating when their table should walk up to the serving counter to choose their meal. A vegetarian dish was always an alternative to the usual meat dish along with a variety of desserts from ice cream to brownies or apple crumble, all homemade, which would please Jamie Oliver no end with his wacky methods these days! *There was always method in his madness*, she thought, chuckling to herself. It was Kitty's turn in the queue but when asked what she wanted she became a bit shy, even after the dinner lady leant towards the counter, trying to listen with all her strength. Jodie had to take over, explaining what was on offer and asking what Kitty wanted. All sorted, the children carried their red or blue trays with dividing slots back to their table. Lunch lasted forty-five minutes before the next sitting, which was for the upper end of the classes.

Tuesday afternoon meant PE, so everyone in the class had to pick up their gym bag from their coat peg and bring it into the class to change into their kit. There were always moments of chaos, as some had forgotten to bring back their washed kit from home or had lots of items or didn't have various items in the first place, bringing everything into confusion. It often involved spending more time sorting it out than the class itself and others needed help dressing, too.

Kitty was one of those who didn't have the right attire, being so new to the class. Fortunately, there was always a stock in a cupboard in class. Kitty wasn't a keen gym fan as a few others weren't either, but physical fitness was a vital part of the curriculum, leaving little excuse for not taking part. It was only half an hour once a week, which most children could surely endure. Tuesday afternoons were always a bit of a palaver, to say the least, with changing and putting all kit back in their bags ready for washing at home. After the usual bell rang for playtime, the final part of the afternoon was spent sitting in a circle on the carpet in class, telling each other about something special that might have happened over the weekend, which she and her colleagues always found interesting and amusing. A baton was passed from one to another, much like passing the parcel, where the child holding the baton had to say a couple of words about the weekend's event or anything that would interest the others, usually resulting in heaps of laughter and bringing joy as they recalled their stories. Finally, the school bell rang out loud, alerting everyone to the close of day, all feeling agitated and raring to go and meet their waiting parents outside the school gates. A sigh of relief usually emanated from all the class teachers as they started to tidy their classrooms before the evening cleaners descended, ready for the day ahead. Sadly, not all teachers had the pleasure of going home, as staff meetings occurred from time to time, especially once monthly for all to catch up with the latest events in the school calendar year. Regular staff meetings were held on different days to meet everyone's home life needs as often staff had extra children to cater for.

Wednesday finally arrived, which was her favourite day of the school week as it was her day off. Café meetup with Sam and a good natter, putting the world to rights as they say. Suddenly her phone sprang into action. Jodie looked at the screen, noticing it was from Ralph.

'Good morning, young man, all OK your end?' she quickly replied, hoping everything was, as she was just about to leave for the café date with Sam.'

'All good, my sweet, just checking in, as you do.'

It sent shivers down Jodie's spine every time she picked up his call. She gave him a quick synopsis of the day ahead, as she was running late for her date at the café down the road.

'Chat later tonight, if you want,' Ralph added, before hanging up.

Jodie grabbed her keys from the table in the hall and zoomed over to the café in her car. Sam had only just arrived when she walked in, hearing the bell ping above the shop door, and walking over to the table Sam had chosen in the corner of the room.

'I've ordered,' Sam said, feeling excited to see her.

'Perfect, thanks,' Jodie added.

The lady soon brought over a cappuccino for Sam and a latte for Jodie, asking, 'Any cakes today, ladies? We have carrot cake, a walnut Victoria sponge or a light lemon cheesecake today.'

'Oh, yummy choices. Er, a Victoria sponge for me,' Sam indicated, 'and a cheesecake for my friend here, thank you,' she swiftly replied.

'Coming up,' she added, leaving them to chat. They each took a sip of their drink before waiting for their cakes.

'Well, I'm all ears,' Sam smiled up at her, 'about what's happening between you both and when,' Sam continued with further enthusiasm, eager to know the details.

'OK, OK, Miss Nosey.' She started from the beginning, when they met up at the Cotswold Hotel.

'I see, sounds very promising and exciting,' Sam replied, patting her hand and giving her a gentle squeeze of delight. 'Lots to work out, then. I'm sure it will all come together in the end,' she continued, winking at her in acceptance. 'I'm so happy for you both, perfect for Amy too before number two child appears.'

'Sam, shh, let's not jump to conclusions, please, though I know my biological clock is ticking. I don't fancy a baby at forty,' she quickly replied, laughing and cringing at the thought. The cakes arrived, the girls drooling in anticipation of the delicious taste. 'Oh, they look so yummy, enjoy,' she added.

'They taste good, too,' they said to each other, both taking a bite with their fork. Sipping their coffee in between bites, Jodie went on to say she'd received an email from the Rainbows co-ordinator, Mrs Drew, offering a place for Amy, starting Monday at the hub up the road, which Amy was looking forward to. 'Is Lottie thinking of joining?' Jodie asked, feeling hopeful.

'I'm waiting to hear anytime soon; it would be lovely if the girls could go together. We live in hope,' Sam concluded.

Sam changed the subject to the romantic weekend away with Ralph, eager to know how it went and what was next in their new world. 'So, tell me about your weekend with Ralph, with any dishy details. I mean did you kiss and walk hand in hand and, more to the point, did you sleep together?' she asked with a wink, laughing as she carried on, feeling more and more inquisitive.

'OK, OK,' she held her hands up in defeat. 'The short answer being yes, yes and yes, the long answer is that we rekindled our love for one another in beautiful surroundings, lovely walks around the village and staying in an old but beautiful hotel with food to die for and waiters to love but not touch, satisfied!' she continued with enthusiasm.

'Wow, that sounds very promising, and I'm so happy for you that finally life has taken a new direction for you all. Amy must be delighted, assuming you've told her, obviously leaving the intimate bits out – she'd only say, "Yuck, Mum".'

'Yes, I've told her in simple terms that he's moving back in with us at some point. He first has to ask for a transfer to a local building company here and then it's full steam ahead. It's now or never, Sam, as we're both getting older and plan to give Amy a brother or sister as I'm on a ticking time clock,' she explained with excitement, regarding Sam as she reached out, placing her hands on top of hers with affection and almost shedding a tear as it sounded like a soppy love story.

'I think we should drink to that. Another coffee, Jodie? Shopping can wait.'

'Oh, go on then, why not?' she quickly imparted, before she could say she had things to do.

Sam got up and made her way to the counter and asked for two more cappuccinos and returned to her seat. Jodie continued to thank Sam for being such a great supportive friend; she was so grateful to have met her. 'Long may our friendship last,' she continued. They quickly checked the time on their phones and for any messages, but for now they put their phones back face down on the table to take away the temptation to check every so often, which always proved difficult in this age of technology.

'Moving on, what's the rest of your day looking like, Jodie?'

'The usual weekly shop, return home to do house chores. It's all very exciting!'

Sam added, 'Mine's much the same, lovely life, isn't it, Jodie? It could be worse,' she concluded, stacking the plates and mugs on the tray by the table. They parted company after they had paid the bill.

Jodie soon arrived home again with the shopping, putting it all away. She didn't really enjoy it other than that she could tick that off her to-do list and concentrate on more important things. As it was her day off, she didn't feel like doing much so she thought she'd make herself a herbal tea, sit down on her sofa and read a chapter or two before driving off to school to pick up Amy, which she always looked forward to. She made a quick call to her mum to ask how she was, feeling it was more of a duty than a pleasure but nevertheless important. She reminded herself not to moan as she only had one mum. She was aware things could turn around in a flash without warning and even the worst could happen.

'Hi, Mum, it's me, Jodie. How's life your end?' she added, once her mum had picked up after five rings. Mum wasn't too quick on her feet at seventy, as most were yet to experience in the distant future.

'Oh, I'm fine, love. I'm ticking along nicely, as you do at my age. No great excitement or drama; not much has happened this week so far, I'm afraid, perhaps things will brighten up. We'll see,' she added, with a sense of sadness yet upbeat.

'Oh, never mind, you sound perky, so that's the main thing, Mum, no worries,' she added to comfort her, pleased to hear all was well. 'Well, I had better go and pick up Amy or she'll wonder where I am, if I don't get to school on time. Let's chat again and arrange a meetup somewhere soon.'

'Oh, that'll be lovely, you could bring Amy to see me. I haven't seen her for so long, dear. Bye for now.' Her mum hung up.

'Another tick off my list,' Jodie muttered to herself. She picked up her phone and keys to go and collect Amy from school, as she didn't want to be late.

Amy was pleased to see her mum after walking towards the car as she pulled into the lay-by, before indicating off again into the main street. The usual chit chat about the day continued till they parked outside their house. The usual after school regime continued after a little snack break with a cuppa for both. Reading and spellings was tonight's homework. Looking at Amy's progress in her exercise book updated by her class teacher she had got all last week's spellings right. *She is heading in the right direction, my clever girl*, she thought. She was a proud mum with Amy reading another new book this week. This all reduced homework time which they both liked, making more playtime for Amy. Jodie could also catch up on her chores, something that had to be done. It was washing day today and putting clothes away or stacking in a pile for another convenient time. Every mum found it difficult to juggle work and home life and did the best they could under the circumstances. It was only when visitors were due that Jodie made an extra effort to make the house look presentable, perhaps she tried too hard, overthinking it all. Next, she thought they would have pasta with meatballs in a tomato sauce, which was easy enough. Amy was already in her bedroom doing one of her jigsaws, one that her dad had bought her on his last visit. While she was boiling the pasta, she thought she'd quickly send him a message.

Hi gorgeous, how are you doing? Miss you lots xx

Within a few minutes he replied: *Hi lovely, good to hear from you. All well here, miss you too. Just waiting to hear about my transfer which should be imminent meaning I can move in sooner than I thought. I'll ring once I have more news. Stay strong and love to our cherub xx.*

She gave a thumbs up in response, showing her excitement. Finally, they were getting nearer to becoming a family again

---

which she knew in her heart was right; not turning back this time.

'Amy, tea is ready,' she called out, hoping she'd hear from her room as the door was ajar. Within a few moments Amy was standing in the kitchen, looking at her portion of spaghetti with three meatballs and Parmesan cheese grated on top.

'This looks yummy. I love spaghetti,' Amy said as she peered down, sniffing the aroma coming from the plate.

'I'll give you a fork and spoon, as it's easier to eat the spaghetti by swirling it around in the spoon before lifting it to your mouth, if you get my gist. Just watch me as I attempt to show you how my dad showed me years ago. It takes a bit of practice, but it works well and is far easier to eat, especially if you are out with friends.' She demonstrated, enjoying every mouthful. Amy admittedly found it a struggle on her first attempt but soon got the hang of twirling her fork around some spaghetti, then placing it onto the spoon before lifting it to her mouth, managing it in delicate style. This soon became an added favourite to their weekly menu. Jodie's aim was to introduce a diversity of foods to her palate, trying to eliminate any fussiness when out and about. So far, she was succeeding very well. With everything eaten up she stacked their plates in the dishwasher whilst Amy went back into her room to put her PJs on, ready for bed later. Jodie thought she'd pour herself a glass of the wine she had left in the fridge. Half an hour later she was also ready to hit the pillow, checking on Amy first, who was sound asleep. She shut her bedroom door, tiptoeing back downstairs to lock up then back to her room and got into bed, turning her bedside light off. *Another successful day over*, she thought. *Roll on the weekend.*

Chapter Fifteen

Jodie woke up from a deep sleep that morning, realising Friday had finally arrived. She pulled the side cord of the window blind up, noticing a ray of red and yellow sky. It was 7am, time to face the day, reminding herself that Lottie was coming for a sleepover after school, with a meal out or cinema, whatever the girls fancied. She was ready for some down time. There followed the usual routine of breakfast, gathering all coats and bags, ready to drive off to both schools, to face what seemed a long day ahead.

Kitty was waiting patiently in the classroom, eager for Jodie to walk through at any moment, wanting to fling her arms around her waist, but school rules didn't allow this as it was a public place. Nevertheless, Kitty was allowed to take Jodie's hand if she needed some comfort. Friday was show and tell, in a circle on the carpet, passing the class baton between them to share what they had learnt in the week, how they could improve and what they were looking forward to at the weekend. When it was Kitty's turn to share she spoke honestly. 'I'm going out with my mum.'

'That's interesting,' Mrs Newbury reacted with a smile towards Kitty.

'We're going to see *Frozen* at the cinema,' she added, before the baton was passed on to the next girl, which was Molly, who was a little timid. Jodie enjoyed these sharing times together as she, like all teachers, could get to know their pupils and their home backgrounds too. Molly was a newbie, who'd only just joined the class the previous week. She was a blonde girl with pigtails, who seemed eager and ready to integrate with the class, making friends.

'I'm Molly and I'm seven years old. I live with my mum and dad and my dog Lily,' she continued telling the class.

'Thank you, Molly,' Mrs Newbury concluded the show and tell time. 'It was lovely to hear all your news, thank you.'

Lunchtime was soon upon them, with the opportunity for a play outside to let off steam and re-energise for the afternoon before home time. Jodie wasn't on home-time duty so she was able to pack up and drive off to Amy's school, where she was greeted by Sam and Lottie, with Lottie's backpack holding her essentials for her sleepover, which the girls were really looking forward to.

'You sure you're OK with having the girls? Lottie loves your Amy, so I'm sure they'll have fun. Ring me if you want to. I'm taking the weight off my feet, chilling, doing absolutely nothing!' Sam told her trusted friend, patting her on the shoulder and pecking Jodie on the right cheek.

'Sounds good to me,' she replied. Sam levelled with Lottie, bringing her into a final hug before Amy and Lottie walked together with Jodie to her car. On reaching the car, which was parked in the school car park this time, for Sam to hand over Lottie, Jodie raised her voice to the girls, looking in her rearview mirror.

'It's time to get this weekend started!'

'Yeah,' they roared back with excitement. Jodie parked up outside her cottage, the girls jumping out of the car and heading to the front door, eager to get in and start the weekend together. Jodie clicked the car fob to lock it and she soon joined them inside. Amy showed Lottie where to hang her coat up, which Jodie thought was very grown up, as most children would just leave them on the floor, bags scattered around. Jodie took them into the kitchen, asking them what

they'd like to drink before they went off into Amy's bedroom, which she'd tidied the night before. Each opted for orange juice. Jodie offered them a couple of flapjacks to keep hunger at bay before tea later. Jodie asked them if they fancied a McDonald's later as a celebration at the end of the week.

'Yes please,' they answered in unison.

'Great, well we'll head off out in an hour,' Jodie confirmed.

Amy took Lottie by the hand, leading her into her tidy bedroom. Jodie thought she'd sneak up behind the door in a few moments, after they'd settled in, listening to the giggling and knowing they were happy playing together, no doubt doing a jigsaw or playing a board game.

'Come on, girls, it's time to go!' Jodie shouted towards Amy's room.

'Coming, Mum,' she heard Amy respond, with a shrill tone in her voice. The door soon opened with the girls racing downstairs to collect their coats. Jodie soon joined them wearing her red puffa jacket. She looked at the house and unlocked the car, the girls jumping in the back. Jodie had a short drive to McDonald's. They parked up to eat in, rather than do a drive through.

'So, what are you having, girls?' Jodie asked them. They looked at each other. They each opted for a chicken burger meal with orange juice. Jodie had the same but with a cappuccino instead. The girls found a table for four while the order was being prepared. Jodie brought it out on a red tray and within minutes they were all tucking in, enjoying their treat.

'Thanks, Mum,' Amy replied, 'looks yummy.'

'Tuck in, girls, and enjoy,' Jodie added, smiling at them. They all tucked into their burgers and chips, sipping their drinks at regular intervals, chatting about anything and everything. The sun shone through the windows, making it cosy and warm.

'So, here's the deal,' Jodie said, putting a scenario to them. 'We can either go to the cinema after and watch whatever's on or go back to ours. I'm sure you'd prefer the cinema option, what do you think?'

Each looked at the another then they said, 'Cinema,' in unison.

'Great, cos I feel in the mood, too.'

Jodie looked up the local Vue cinema to check what was on and the times.

'It looks like *Frozen* is on soon, so we had better get a move on and get down there to select our seats, on the screen they show us before buying the tickets.'

They tidied their rubbish, putting it on the tray which they took to the recycling bins, before a mass exit to the car, to park near the cinema. Tickets bought, they were allowed to go into the screen, located within the long corridor, all feeling excited to watch the movie lasting just an hour and a half, which was long enough. As they had just eaten, no popcorn was needed, saving a bit of money.

Everyone feeling tired, once home Jodie offered them hot chocolate with marshmallows, which was a lovely end to a great evening. Amy's room was big enough to put a blow-up mattress down for Lottie. They changed into their PJ's, feeling very excited as they jumped under their individual light duvets. They each had a book to read with plenty of pictures which always inspired story imagination. Amy had loved her books from when she was first introduced to them at school. They were beginning to invent their own stories from a set of pictures placed before them, adding captions to the story. Lottie wasn't as keen to begin with, yet soon followed her closest friend, not wanting to be left out. As with many sleepovers, they had their little torches, initially to read under the duvet, though both found it too dark in the end, so they were used for bathroom stops in the night to guide them, saving them from bumping into anything along the way. Around ten o'clock, Jodie peered round their door and all seemed very quiet. She whispered, 'Good night, girls,' hoping they'd heard, before quietly closing the door behind her. Phew, she muttered to herself, a good day was certainly had by all.

The next morning, they both decided to sleep in a bit as it was the weekend, much to Jodie's delight as she needed the lie-in too after a school week. Breakfast was in the form of brunch. Jodie asked the girls what they would like, once they had both appeared, slightly blurry-eyed, in the kitchen, while she was putting the kettle on.

'Good morning, girls, good night, was it?' Jodie asked Lottie, who'd sneaked in first before Amy followed behind.

'Yes, thanks,' Lottie giggled back, yawning.

'Fried egg, hash browns, baked beans or peas this morning, was my idea for both of you, is that OK?'

'Ooh, yummy,' they answered together.

'Coming up in a few moments,' Jodie smiled back at them. She gathered all the ingredients, taking the hash browns from the freezer, turning the oven on as she passed. Jodie then took out her trusted frying pan, placing it on the stove and adding a little olive oil before cracking in the eggs after the hash browns were cooked. Timing was essential throughout, though not always easy to achieve. So long as it all tasted yummy, that was the main thing. Jodie remembered her dad basting the eggs, making sure the egg yolk was cooked, not leaving it runny, which wasn't really edible. Within moments Jodie served up the brunch onto three warmed plates, with nothing left after it had all been eaten with relish. The girls stacked their plates together, taking them to the counter where the dishwasher was.

'Thanks, Mum,' Amy walked over to her mum, giving her a hug.

'You're very welcome, and thanks for clearing the plates, girls, my little helpers,' she added with a smile. Both girls soon walked back to their room to do whatever girls do after a sleepover. Jodie couldn't be happier as everything had gone very smoothly since yesterday afternoon. Jodie decided to message Sam, taking her phone from the table beside her.

We survived, just had brunch. Girls behaved very well and were very impressed. Xx

What time shall I pop over as I need to go shopping later? Sam texted quickly back.

Come after you've been shopping, they'll be fine Jodie replied.

Ok I'll text you once I'm done, Sam promptly replied.

Two hours later Sam was standing at Jodie's door, shopping all done, needing a cuppa. Jodie leant in, giving her a hug and a kiss,

---

and welcoming her inside. They headed to the kitchen where Jodie flicked the kettle on for that all-important cuppa. Jodie had her usual lemon green tea and Sam had an ordinary one. Jodie took the flapjacks out of the cupboard, placing some on a plate, ready to be demolished in minutes.

'Well, I only have good reports as the girls behaved so well, very polite too,' Jodie smiled enthusiastically at Sam, who beamed back with gratitude.

'That's good to hear, Jodie, thank you for having my Lottie.' Sam placed a hand on Jodie's as a sign of affection.

'You're such a lovely friend, Sam, you mean a lot to me.'

'Aww, stop it, you'll make me cry! Onwards and upwards, I'll take my little cherub back home. We need to get sorted for tomorrow.'

Sam reached out her hand to Jodie before getting up and seeing where the girls were hiding. She noticed they were both looking after Daisy, who was in her run enjoying her freedom, munching a carrot and holding it in her little furry hands; a lovely sight to see as one could watch for hours with not a care in the world.

'Lottie, we need to go now. You'll see Amy tomorrow.'

Lottie didn't need to be told twice so she got up, skipping towards her mum, grabbing her hand on arrival. The girls hugged one another, and Lottie picked up her overnight bag and coat as they walked to the front door, which was now open. Jodie waved them off as they made a beeline to Sam's car. Jodie closed the door behind them, her mind racing with a million things to do before a new week landed tomorrow.

Amy went back into her room, beavering away and feeling happy. Jodie followed her to strip Lottie's bed and deflate the mattress; rather than leave it till tomorrow she'd wash the bedding, and that would be one less thing to worry about. All homework was done, leaving just the usual reading before Amy went to bed later. Suddenly Jodie's phone rang. Noticing it was Ralph, she clicked the green light.

'Good day, stranger, how are you doing?' she asked with a big smile across her face, which Ralph could sense down the line.

'Oh, I'm good, missing you lots. I'll have to come over soon, maybe on Friday unless your diary is filling up!'

'I think I can squeeze you in, my love. I'll just dismiss the others, you're more important.'

'Ha ha, good to know, Jodie,' he replied, feeling the love. 'Shall I put Friday in my calendar? We could go out to eat with a cosy cinema trip for two, if Sam can babysit, though Amy's no longer a baby.'

'I'll see what I can do and get back to you. Bed awaits me, must go, sweet dreams Ralph,' ending the call.

Monday morning came around too soon, as Jodie's alarm buzzed into life at seven o'clock. She was tempted to set it to snooze but, knowing everything would be a rush, she decided to bite the bullet, stretch her tired legs dangling by the side of the bed before attempting to get up and face the day. *Another new week, fresh start,* she thought, *how hard could this be.* She heard movement outside her door; Amy had definitely stirred. Jodie headed to the bathroom, showered, came back and dressed and knocked on Amy's door, saying, 'Rise and shine, see you downstairs.'

'OK, Mum, coming,' Amy replied, sounding upbeat. Jodie rushed downstairs, switched the kettle on then set the table as per usual. She thought about her conversation with Ralph last night, and his wanting to come over on Friday. She surely couldn't ask Sam again, so she wondered if her friend Jo would oblige this time. Amy did have other friends she liked to mix with outside school, Molly being one, who she hadn't had seen in a while. Jodie remembered that this week was the start of Rainbows, which was tonight in the local community hub, starting at 5pm. Jodie could pick up her uniform tonight as they would have a table laid out for newcomers. A quick easy meal later would have to suffice. Jodie's phone pinged with an email and saw that it was a reminder about Rainbows later. Amy could go in her own clothes until her uniform was sorted, putting Jodie's mind at rest. Breakfast all sorted, they gathered their coats, bags and car keys, locking the door behind them as they walked to the car ready to go to school.

Turning the key, her trusty Polo soon sprang into life although she noticed the petrol gauge was nearing to empty, which wasn't so cool. However, having enough juice to get to both schools she'd fill up at lunch time as she wasn't on lunch duty today. Not the best of starts to a Monday morning, as Jodie usually preferred to be organised. *Never mind*, she thought, as she drove on to Amy's school, dropping her off at the pull in.

After a quick peck on the cheek Jodie was soon on her way to her school. Jodie walked into her class to be greeted by all the children, Kitty coming up to take her hand. They all sat on the carpet, ready for register call. Molly was the only one marked as missing; *perhaps she was ill,* Jodie thought. She might have to revert to plan B for Friday. The morning flew by and on hearing the school bell lunchtime was upon them. All the pupils lined up by the classroom door to walk slowly into the dining room then afterwards went outside to play. Jodie seized the moment and took her car to the nearest garage to fill up, ready for after school followed by Rainbows. She picked up some tuna mayonnaise sandwiches from the shop and drove back to school, eating them along the way as hunger soon kicked in. Jodie went into the staffroom, placing her coat and bag in her locker, and made a quick herbal tea. While sipping it in the staffroom, sitting on the green sofa a parent had kindly donated some while ago, her phone suddenly rang. Picking it up from the coffee table in front of her she saw that it was Sam. She'd better accept the call before class started in ten minutes.

'Hi, Sam, are you OK?' Jodie duly answered, feeling slightly nervous and thinking that something had happened.

'All well, I'm just checking that you realise it's Rainbows tonight, as you left in a hurry this morning.'

'Oh yes, I was running a bit late, which was why I shot off. I've just been to refuel as I noticed I was very low. I'll see you at school in an hour, must go back to class, hun, bye for now.'

Jodie ended the call. She placed her cup on the draining board by the sink and made her way back into class for the last part of the afternoon. Everyone sat in a large circle on the carpet, ready to tell everyone about their weekend. Jodie always loved this time, hearing interesting things from the children, giving an insight into their family life. The final school bell rang ready for home time and the children went to their individual named drawers, putting all their books neatly away for tomorrow and taking their school bag out with homework packed inside. They lined up to walk into the playground and wait for the gates to be opened by the duty teacher, ready for the onslaught of parents, grandparents and the like to collect their little cherubs. Jodie noted Kitty was more confident; she made a beeline for her mum as she walked through the gates, placing a smile on Jodie's face. It was the little steps which made her job more worthwhile, which she loved, helping others being her main aim. Kitty's mum waving back impressed her one step further, acknowledging her agreement that Kitty was making great strides. They were all growing up so fast; seeing their daily progress was always a delight.

Monday night was the start of Rainbows, which meant that Jodie had to make a quick dash to Amy's school, go home, have a drink, then get Amy changed into some leggings and a sweatshirt, as today she would be able to purchase her new uniform which would be displayed on one of the tables in the room. Amy was getting excited as Jodie was explaining it all in the car on their way home.

'Will Lottie be there, or Molly, Mum?' she asked, as they drove along.

'I'm not sure, you'll have to wait and see,' Jodie answered her, looking in the rear mirror. Jodie soon parked in front of their cottage, both springing into action as she unlocked the cottage door, placing their coats and bags in the hall. Amy went straight to her room and changed out of her school clothes, taking out a pair of black leggings and a jumper. She went back into the kitchen, where Jodie had already poured orange juice into a glass and placed it on the table where Amy usually sat. Jodie made herself a lemon green tea in her favourite mug with roses printed all around. Forty-five minutes later they were back on the road heading to the community hub for Rainbows. Even Jodie was excited by it all, it was something new and different to do after school. Those baby days were most definitely over, Jodie sighed with relief to herself. As much as she loved it, as all mums did, it was time to move on and explore something different.

'Welcome, everyone, to Rainbows. Tonight is our first meeting this term,' the lady heading up Rainbows declared with her opening sentence. 'Please take a seat on a chair in the semicircle and we will go round introducing ourselves to each other,' she continued with a beam across her face.

Eight red chairs formed a semicircle in the middle of the room, the Rainbow leader facing them; she was named after a flower. 'My name is Rose and I'm your Rainbow leader for this unit. We have a promise motto which is in the book which you can pick up from the table behind you at the end of today's session. You need to learn this as we will be practising it together next week in our circle at the start of every session,' Rose continued with enthusiasm, hoping that they were all enjoying this time. Now it was time for them to introduce themselves to each other.

'Let's go around the circle, introducing yourself to the next on your right. I'll give you a book to pass around to prompt you to tell us all about yourselves.' Rose passed the book to the first girl on her right.

'Hi, my name is ...' as each took it in turns to introduce themselves. Amy found it all interesting, but nerves kicked in when her turn approached.

'Hi, I'm Amy. I'm new today. I'm seven years old and I have a guinea pig called Daisy, who is light brown and white. I go to the local primary school,' she bravely told her fellow Rainbows. The book continued, like passing the parcel, around the group to the end when Rose got up and took it back. Rose continued by explaining various activities and today they all had to draw a picture of their family, including any pets, after they had stacked the chairs, placing them at the back wall of the room out of harm's way. They all took a seat behind the table, on which were drawing paper, pencils and coloured pens to start their drawings. They wrote their names at the top right of the paper to be left in a pile for Rose to see after the session. Everyone enjoyed this activity despite some only being able to draw stick men.

Home time was fast approaching and they had all had a brilliant time. Their parents waited patiently outside the door to collect them and choose any uniform, which was displayed on a table especially for any newbies; all at affordable prices. Another volunteer stood behind the table taking orders and cash or card payments, the latter being the most common in this day of technology. Jodie perused the items, picking out the right size for Amy, swallowing hard at the final payment which always hurt at the best of times!

Julie, the volunteer, placed the items in Rainbow environmentally friendly bags, handing them out to each buyer. Jodie and Amy thanked Rose for the meeting before Amy skipped out into the corridor to exit the hub. They got into the car and drove home to start all over again; *homework, a meal before bedtime, another end to a fruitful Monday*, Jodie thought to herself. Reading was tonight's homework, which was a blessing, as they were both getting tired. Jodie heated up a macaroni cheese dish with a few broccoli florets, making it an easy yet tasty meal.

Chapter Sixteen

Tuesday morning arrived with a reality check; it was back to Groundhog Day, the morning ritual once again. Just one more day before her day off, then on Friday Ralph was due to stay with them and she couldn't wait. She hadn't yet spoken to Amy about her dad's visit, knowing that she would be so excited and she didn't want to give her any distraction from her school work.

'Morning darling,' she smiled at her, as she came into the kitchen, all dressed for the day ahead.

'Morning, Mum,' she replied enthusiastically. They sat at the table eating their breakfast, sipping their morning drinks in between bites. She decided to keep her dad's visit as a surprise till the end of the week. Breakfast out of the way, they gathered up their gear and headed towards the front door to make the daily trip to school.

Jodie dropped Amy off as usual with a quick peck on the cheek before she jumped out of the car, noticing Lottie walking in the school grounds and soon they were both chatting away without a care in the world, as it should be at their age. Jodie shot off shortly after until she joined a stop-start traffic jam ahead, resulting in her being a little late arriving, one of those things you couldn't do anything about. She parked in her usual place and made a quick dash to the staffroom, putting her coat in her locker, then headed to her class.

'Good morning, Mrs Smith,' they spoke out in unison as she walked through the door, putting her at ease after being ten minutes late.

'Good morning, everyone,' she replied with a smile. Jodie walked up to Mrs Newbury, whispering in her ear and apologising for being late, explaining that she was held up in traffic saving the long version for later; for now, the short version would suffice.

'No problem, Jodie, the main thing is that you arrived safely,' Mrs Newbury whispered back politely. All settled, the class carried on as normal. First off, reading with individuals, which was Jodie's favourite task. She was always impressed how much progress pupils had made, especially when extra effort was made at home with reading aloud either to parents or older siblings; the key being practice, practice, practice, making reading easier and more interesting each time. She noticed that Kitty was absent today; hoping all was well at home she'd enquire at break time. Lunchtime fast approached and at midday all lined up neatly by the class door, to walk quietly into the dining room, sitting and waiting to be ushered up to the serving counter by one of the lunch break supervisors to get their lunch. They walked up, waiting their turn to be served by the five dinner ladies. Their meals were soon finished and they all headed outside into the playground, where they could let off steam playing with their pals. Jodie was on duty today, keeping a lookout in particular for anyone making their way to the Friendship Bench, for those who felt a bit lonely or not mixing well with their peers. Jodie enjoyed chatting to them, trying to resolve their minor problems, giving non-judgemental advice when needed. She suddenly looked up, noticing Kitty from a distance, which immediately sent relieved vibes throughout her body, thinking she might have had a medical appointment or similar. Kitty was happily playing with others so she would catch up with her later in class.

The end of lunchtime bell rang, and all quickly walked back to their classes for the final afternoon session before home time. Painting was the afternoon activity in Mrs Newbury's class, which they all enjoyed, despite it being a bit messy, especially when paint was flicked onto the paper forming pretty pictures. Tidying up was always the worst, so newspapers were used to form a tablecloth, gathering up the spillages. A white deep old-fashioned sink was nearby to rinse out water pots and paint pallets and rinse the various-sized paint brushes under the tap. Always a messy job at the best of times and not one which Jodie ever enjoyed, as art was her least favourite subject at school. All paint pots and pallets tidied away, and pictures laid out to dry, the day finally drew to a close. *Home time at last*, Jodie thought, as she'd had enough for the day. Tomorrow couldn't come quickly enough, it being her day off. She thought of her regular café meetings with Sam, catching up on all the gossip. She was eager to chat about her Rainbows experience last night, wondering when Lottie was due to join. She bid her farewells to the class before they all gathered in the playground, waiting for those gates to open releasing them to their parents and guardians. Jodie made a point of going to Kitty and saying that she had noticed that she was missing this morning and hoped all was well; she would see her soon, as tomorrow was her day off. Jodie made her way to the staffroom, collecting her bag from her locker, and swiftly made her way to the car park to drive off to Amy's school. On arrival Amy was waiting at the drop off bay, ready to jump in the car to go home. They were both clearly tired, needing a bit of peace and quiet. No sooner had Jodie turned the key in the front door than she heard her phone buzzing in her bag. It was a message from Sam, asking her if she fancied the usual meetup at the café after school drop-off in the morning. Jodie immediately responded with:

Oh yes please, it's been a hectic week so far, so looking forward to it Xx

Amy took off her coat as usual and went into the kitchen for a hot chocolate which Jodie made for her; she had her usual lemon green tea. They sat down feeling rather blah. *Just a few hours until bed*, Jodie thought, so she pushed through as best as she could. Reading homework for Amy, which they did immediately, so that it was done and dusted and Amy could then have some "me" time in her bedroom.

'A veggie risotto tonight, OK my love?' she asked Amy, hoping she would be happy with that choice. Amy signed her reply with a thumbs up. 'Perfect,' Jodie said, smiling back at her affectionately.

Amy skipped back into her room, closing her door behind her. Jodie started to prepare everything for the risotto, which she loved making and which was so easy and tasty. She gathered up all the ingredients, looking in the fridge for suitable food that needed using up. She could then "whack it in" which was Jamie Oliver's favourite phrase when demonstrating his new recipes on TV. She liked to gather up all the ingredients onto the kitchen surface so that everything was at hand before starting her signature dish. Chopping an onion and courgette into a medium hot pan with olive oil, she set it all to cook before adding a cup of risotto rice and seasoning, not forgetting vegetable stock, before putting a lid on top, letting all the flavours mingle till all the liquid was absorbed. In half an hour the risotto was ready to be served onto warm plates.

'Dinner is served, Amy,' Jodie raised her voice, hoping she would hear. Amy soon came running into the kitchen, PJs already on, tucking into the colourful plate of risotto in front of her.

'Yummy in my tummy,' came the instant reply, as she forked some into her mouth. Both feeling full, Jodie placed the empty plates into the dishwasher. They each had a glass of water to aid digestion. Amy went straight back into her room, clearly in the middle of something, whilst Jodie took herself into the lounge, making herself comfortable on the sofa, feet up on her red squishy poof, picking up a book she was currently reading. What more could she want after a day's work, she muttered to herself. After a few hours she was feeling rather tired so decided to call it a day and checked in on Amy, who was already in bed, virtually asleep. She quietly shut the bedroom door and walked back to her room to settle for the night. Within moments she hit the pillow and was in dream land!

Chapter Seventeen

The alarm went off as usual this time but she had already been woken by the dawn chorus outside her bedroom window, birds chirping away to one another in the trees, no doubt wishing their mates good morning! *Midweek at last*, she thought, as she swung her legs over the side of the bed, stretching out before she headed for her wake-up shower, turning the temperature down a notch to kickstart her body into action. She loved these solo mornings before Amy woke up; she practised her yoga poses to calm her mind, body and soul, ready to face the day, which was vital in her opinion. She remembered that she was meeting Sam later at the café so she put on her favourite bright joggers, that she recently bought online as a treat. Passing Amy's room, she knocked on the door, saying, 'Rise and shine,' as she headed towards the kitchen. She flipped the kettle on to boil for a Fresh Start Pukka herbal tea; orange juice for Amy and a bowl of cereal and they were good to go. They were soon on their way to Amy's school, and Jodie dropped her off in the usual place, Amy blowing a kiss to her mum as she indicated out and moved swiftly towards the high street, where she parked in the car park. She sent a message to Sam: *Just parked up see you in the café.*

Sam messaged back within seconds: *Just sat down by the window.*

Jodie grabbed her coat and bag, zapped her key fob once for the car and walked to the café a few yards away. Noticing Sam through the window, she waved at her with a big smile. The bell chimed above the door as she walked in, and Sam rose from her chair, embracing her.

'I haven't ordered yet. What do you fancy? My treat,' Sam continued, as they both marched up to the counter, eyeing all the lush cakes and cookies.

'Morning ladies, what can I get you?' remarked the girl behind the counter, who recognised them from last week.

They looked at one another like excited schoolgirls. 'Carrot cake for me,' Jodie said, 'and coffee and walnut sponge for my friend.' Jodie finished with, 'Two cappuccinos, thank you, Julia,' reading the name tag on her blouse.

'On their way,' Julia replied, tapping the order into the screen beside her. Sam swiped her card on the card machine before they both returned to their table.

Julia soon brought the order on a large tray, putting their orders on the table and placing the tray on the floor beside Jodie's chair. They sipped their coffees and demolished their cakes within minutes, catching up on everything. Sam asked about Rainbows on Monday night and said Lottie was looking forward to starting next week.

'That's great news!' she exclaimed, 'Amy will love that,' as she took another sip of her cappuccino. She continued by telling Sam that Ralph was due on Friday, which she was very much looking forward to. Sam said she would have Amy if they fancied a night out to themselves.

'Oh Sam, that's so sweet of you. We were thinking about a cinema trip, possibly Saturday, or just a meal out. I'll see what's on,' Jodie replied.

'Good, just let me know. We've got nothing planned this weekend,' Sam smiled back. They finished their cakes and coffee and left the café. They both needed to do a weekly shop at the supermarket as time was ticking and before they knew it, it would be time to pick up the girls from school. They made their separate ways to collect their cars. Jodie went to Tesco up the road and Sam went to Lidl, armed with their shopping lists. Boring as it was, it had to be done.

After an hour's mooching around Tesco, she drove back to the cottage and started to unload the shopping, placing it onto the kitchen work tops and quickly putting the contents in their correct place, aware of the time before she jumped back in the car again to pick up Amy. She quickly gulped down a small glass of water to quench her thirst, grabbed her keys to lock up and drove off to school. She arrived just in time as they were all about to walk out of the school gates ready to jump into their waiting parents' cars. Amy soon spotted her mum's Polo parked up in the waiting bay.

'Hi, Mum, did you have a good day?'

'Yes thanks, Amy. I had a lovely catch up with Sam at the café,' she added, smiling into the rear mirror. 'How was your day, darling?' she continued the conversation.

'Good thanks, I made friends with Molly. Can she come over sometime?'

'Of course she can, we just need to fix a date. Dad's coming on Friday, by the way.' She thought she'd throw that into the conversation while the mood was upbeat.

'Yippee,' Amy reacted with excitement in the air. 'Can we go out somewhere?'

'I'm sure Dad is up for that, Ams,' as was Amy's nickname for special people only. 'We can Facetime him later if you want, we'll see how time goes,' Jodie added, feeling excited.

She turned into their drive to park up. They were both feeling upbeat as they walked to the front door. On opening it they were greeted by some post scattered over the floor which she immediately picked up, placing it on the hall table before hanging up her coat. Amy did the same. She took the post into the kitchen and flicked the kettle on to have the tea she hadn't had before the school run, taking a mug from the cupboard, and putting the tea bag in it. Amy had a hot chocolate as usual, without the marshmallow this time. Amy came into the kitchen after she had changed into her comfy PJs as was her done thing these days, taking her place at the table to drink her hot chocolate. Jodie sipped her tea and started to look through the post; it was mainly advertising. She noticed an envelope addressed to Amy and she wondered who it might be from. She handed it to Amy, who was delighted to see her name, Miss A

Smith, in the middle of the white envelope. She opened it, pulling out the letter and noticed it was from her dad, which placed a big smile all over her face. She unfolded it, placing a kiss in the middle. Jodie soon realised how close she was to her dad. Amy attempted to read it.

Dear Amy,
Hope you are well as you read my letter. Mum told me you have just started Rainbows, which I hope you are enjoying. I will see you on Friday so you can tell me all about it then. We can go out to eat too.
Bye for now
Dad xxx

Amy showed her mum the letter, which Jodie thought was so touching that she began to well up, hoping Amy wouldn't notice. She was particularly pleased with how well Amy's reading was progressing. Amy finished her drink and zoomed off to her room, her happy place to amuse herself before the all-important dinner.

Jodie picked up her phone from the table and went into her favourites, clicking on Ralph's number to send him a message.

Amy was chuffed to receive your letter, reading it with no problem, a proud mum moment. She's looking forward to seeing you this weekend of course. I am too xxx.

A few minutes later Ralph replied: *See you soon xx*

Jodie pulled out a vegetable lasagna from the fridge which she had bought the other day; it served two, sufficient for tea tonight, with a portion of peas. That was tea sorted.

Finally, Thursday arrived, leaving one more sleep before Ralph arrived for the weekend. She was getting very excited for the day when he finally moved in. Perhaps he had more news about his job move which he could enlighten her with. The day moved swiftly by, with the usual school day. She started planning the weekend in her head, thinking a family meal out would be preferable, where they could all chill out together. Amy had her dad around which she so needed now, as she was growing up fast.

They would have so much to talk about, having just joined Rainbows, which she clearly loved, as an extra activity outside school. Jodie, being house proud, gave everything the once-over, vac and polish, adding a few homely touches, such as carnation flowers in a vase on the lounge coffee table. She changed the beds, too, adding to the freshness of the place. She was now happy they shared a bed, as their relationship had moved up a notch to almost how it used to be when they had first met, only a more improved version. She couldn't be happier with Ralph back on the horizon and seeing his beloved daughter growing up to become a caring young lady, a version of her mum, she hoped, feeling smug. *Girls and their mums were always the best*, she thought. After tea and settling Amy in for the night she made herself a camomile tea and settled on the sofa in the lounge with a book. A buzz from her phone made her jump, thinking it was probably from Ralph.

Just checking everything is OK for tomorrow, can't wait to see you both Xxx, she read, smiling, feeling goose bumps all over her body with excitement.

She fired one back: *Yes, all good, just text me when you get to the station. We'll pick you up pronto.*

Chapter Eighteen

Jodie woke up with a jolt, realising it was finally Friday and that she would see her Ralph in a few hours. 'The weekend is in sight,' she spoke out loud with a gust of enthusiasm, a thumbs up, and punching the sky above. She brought her tired legs over to the side of the bed, giving them that all-important morning stretch before she went to the bathroom for her shower. Feeling refreshed afterwards, she dressed before she walked downstairs into the kitchen, flicking the kettle on to boil for her usual morning cuppa.

'Morning, Mum.'

She turned around, seeing Amy walking through the door. 'Morning, lovely,' she smiled back, 'Sleep well?'

'Yes thanks,' Amy answered, taking a glass out of the cupboard for her orange juice and placing it on the table. Jodie took out the carton from the fridge, topping up her glass. She made some porridge for them, which would keep hunger at bay for longer, she hoped. She reminded Amy that her dad was arriving later and that they'd pick him up from the station. This put a big smile on her daughter's face.

'Looking forward to that, Mum,' she said, beaming with excitement.

'I think the plan is that we'll go out for a meal somewhere, possibly Frankie and Benny's; we'll see,' she explained, whilst clearing the breakfast dishes and placing them in the sink. As time was of the essence, they needed to get a move on to school. After a quick bathroom stop they were out the front door, heading towards her car. A short drive later she dropped Amy off at her school before dodging the morning traffic to hers.

'Let's do this,' she said to herself, locking the car before going to the front entrance of the school and into the staffroom, hanging her coat in her locker. No school assembly today, just sharing time in individual classes, telling everyone what their weekend plans were, which she enjoyed; *nothing too taxing for a Friday*, she thought. They sat in a semicircle on the carpet, Mrs Newbury at the circle's entrance with her baton, wrapped in red foil paper, ready to be passed around like passing the parcel to everyone.

'Let's get started,' she announced to the group, first stop being Kitty. She was clearly excited, judging by the beaming smile across her face. Jodie sat next to her in case she lost her nerve midway.

'So, are you doing anything exciting this weekend, Kitty?' she whispered in her ear. 'It's your turn to share with your friends,' she added, squeezing her hand gently for encouragement.

'My older sister is coming to stay,' Kitty uttered, which was a surprise to her as she had not known that she had a sister. She guessed her sister was from a previous relationship. She looked at Mrs Newbury, who looked equally surprised, as if to say we need to follow this one up, making sure Kitty was loved and cared for. That was the mantra of the school, which was very important to all the staff. After her turn, Kitty passed the baton to her neighbour to the left on the carpet, a new girl who had only just started after her family recently moved house to just down the road. Mrs Newbury introduced her to the class before they continued.

'This is Sophie, our newest member, who has just moved to her new house near this school. Please bring your hands together in clapping, welcoming Sophie to the class,' she continued before the class started to clap, looking at Sophie, which was a little embarrassing for her, as it would be for anyone.

'Please introduce yourself, Sophie, to all of us,' Mrs Newbury continued, encouraging her.

'My name is Sophie. I'm seven years old and live with my mum and dad and my brother Jake, who is ten.'

'Perfect,' Mrs Newbury added, 'and thank you, Sophie.'

The baton passed around till the end when the mid-morning gong sounded for playtime outside in the lovely sunshine. Everyone got up and lined up by the classroom door to put their coats on, if needed, which were hanging on their named pegs in the corridor.

The day continued with Jodie taking her reading group at the back of the class one by one. The day ended with a short assembly in the main hall with a few songs and prayers led by the head teacher, before dismissal at 3pm, with everyone going back into class to collect their homework, placed in their blue school bags for home time. Everyone cheered at the sound of the end of day bell, lining up by the back door of the class to walk out into the playground where the gates were nearly ready to be opened, letting parents and guardians in to take their children home for the weekend. A moment of joy for all the teachers as they gathered inside to tidy up before going to the staff room to gather their belongings from their lockers and leave the building for the weekend ahead.

Jodie rushed off to her car, dashing towards Amy's school to collect her before it was time to pick Ralph up from the station later. She parked outside her cottage and they both got out of the car, eager to get inside, change into more comfortable clothes, have a drink and a snack before heading off to the station. Picking up the post scattered over the door mat Jodie took it into the kitchen to examine the damage, if any. Flicking the kettle into life she made herself a lemon green tea as usual and poured a glass of water for Amy as requested. They had an hour to kill before the weekend exploded into action. She swiftly looked through the post, most of which were promotional adverts which she suitably put in the recycling bin.

Five o'clock soon arrived as she called out to Amy, 'Time to go and get Dad.'

Amy didn't need calling again as she ran into the kitchen, coat on, ready to go, surprising Jodie since she hadn't got that far yet.

She soon grabbed her keys, locking the cottage up as they stepped outside to get into the car, ready to zoom off to the station. She parked in the drop-off bay, turned off the engine and listened to the radio, waiting to see Ralph appear outside the station, which he did after ten minutes.

'There he is!' She soon spotted him as he came towards them with his overnight bag in tow. She looked into the mirror, noticing that Amy had dropped asleep on her booster seat. She made no attempt to wake her, as she wanted to kiss Ralph once he had stepped into the passenger seat. She leaned her body into his for a quick kiss on the lips before starting the engine to drive swiftly off. Ralph turned his head round, placing a hand on Amy's knee and causing her to wake from her slumber.

'Oh, Dad, you're here!' she yelped at him with enthusiasm. They started to chat to one another before deciding on their evening meal venue, which they all agreed would be Frankie and Benny's, not far from the high street where they lived. It wasn't worth going home first then going out again, which had been the initial plan anyway. She continued driving, chatting as they went along, finally pulling into the car park and promptly finding a space. They got out feeling hungry, ready to tuck into a hearty meal, locking the car and walking and talking to the restaurant. A lady was waiting by the entrance, ready to book them in, then showed them to their table for the next two hours, which everyone was allocated.

'This is lovely,' she exclaimed, as they made themselves comfortable, manoeuvring their chairs into position. Their assigned table waitress soon came over with her mini tablet in hand to take the drinks order. Ralph and Jodie opted for a glass of Liebfraumilch white wine to kick off the weekend and a bottle of water, Amy having her usual orange juice. She reached out for the menus in the wooden stack, had a quick glance at the mains and possible side orders. They had all made up their minds when the lady came back with their drinks, placing them on the table.

'Are you ready to order?' looking at Jodie with a smile. She started the order followed by the others. 'Any sides?' the waitress added. Jodie asked for four garlic breads to go with their lasagna and Amy's child portion. 'Perfect, thank you,' as she finished tapping into her screen which processed it to the kitchen.

Jodie picked up her glass of wine, toasting with Ralph and Amy, 'To us and good health,' as they clinked their glasses together, holding them in the middle.

'Yay!' they all agreed. Ralph took this opportunity to update them on his impending move back to the cottage, saying he had been offered a transfer to the sister company ten miles away, where he was due to start in the next few weeks, giving him time to start moving his belongings in. This wasn't a big deal as he had only his clothes and personal items; the flat he rented was part furnished and most of his time was spent either at work or in the pub with his mates, making the move much easier. Jodie was naturally thrilled with his news, looking forward to them being a family once again, starting all over, wiping the slate clean, a fresh start to their relationship.

Amy seemed to pick up the gist of what was said. People watching around her noticed a cute little girl sitting in her high chair with her tray, which had a colouring sheet and a pack of coloured pencils to amuse her while the adults chatted to their hearts' content. Shortly afterwards their main meals were brought by the waitress, who placed them down in front of the correct person with a plate of garlic bread in the middle for all to share.

'Tuck in, all,' Ralph told Jodie and Amy. They all started attacking the garlic bread, taking bites of lasagna in between mouthfuls. Each mouthful of lasagna was delicious with the garlic bread demolished after ten minutes and washed down with wine for Jodie and Ralph.

'That was delicious,' they said to each other, 'now for dessert,' as Jodie flipped the menu over to see the list of desserts on offer.

'Crème brûlée for us, I reckon,' looking at Ralph with beady eyes as he nodded in agreement.

'Chocolate brownie with ice cream for me, Mum,' Amy added, licking her lips. The waitress came over, clearing the plates and taking them back to the kitchen, then popped back to take their dessert orders, saying, 'Thank you,' as she walked away to place the order. Within moments she brought their individual desserts.

'We'll have two cappuccinos, too, please,' Ralph sneaked that in before she left the table.

'Thank you for coming up,' she replied, smiling back at Ralph.

'OK, what do you fancy doing tomorrow, Amy?' Ralph asked, looking directly at her. 'We could go for a cinema trip, perhaps, or a walk in the park. When we get home we can check what's on. Homework first though,' he insisted.

'OK,' Amy said, giving her dad a thumbs up.

They were soon home from their night out, feeling relaxed and ready to sit and do nothing. Amy disappeared into her room, changing into her PJs for the more relaxed look. It was a golden opportunity for the adults to sit back on the sofa, resting in one another's arms, cuddling each other and enjoying the moment of bliss, peace and happiness, feeling happy that their lives were finally coming together once again, with Ralph's imminent move back home where he belonged.

Amy seemed delighted that she was getting her dad back on board; they could play board games as a proper family unit just like her mum used to do back in her day.

'Fancy a game or something?' Jodie asked, after having a cuddle, feeling enthusiastic.

'Sounds good to me; Lexicon?'

'Yes, I bought it the other week from a game shop on the high street. We used to play it at home. Seven cards which have a letter are dealt out to the number of players, and each player takes it in turns to make a word, placing it face down on the table in front of them. It's great fun and helps your spelling ability, keeping you on your toes,' she went on to explain at length. 'Fancy a cuppa before we start?' looking at Ralph.

'An ordinary tea for me,' he said.

She promptly went back into the kitchen and flicked on the kettle to boil, taking two mugs from the cupboard above, a tea bag from the tea caddy and a camomile tea bag from the box in the herbal tea stash. Once made, she brought them back into the lounge, placing them on coasters, then taking the box of Lexicon from the table underneath. She gave the cards a good shuffle then dealt them out one by one.

'This is brain taxing!' Ralph commented.

'That's the whole idea,' she added, smiling back at him. 'Pick up a card from the pile in the middle where the first letter in the alphabet starts.'

'OK, here we go,' Ralph continued, picking up a card.

'My turn,' she added, feeling pleased with herself. 'Now you've got your card we'll see who goes first.' Jodie started off by placing the card she had picked up from underneath the pack of cards on the table, as that was how the game worked. She started to place her cards in alphabetical order in her hand, making it easier to make a word, which she did within minutes, placing it fanned out on the table. 'Your turn now, and so on, till you have no more cards to put down. Simple and fun,' she concluded with a smile.

They continued playing their first game then Ralph walked back into the kitchen, grabbing a few Hobnobs on a plate for stamina for their final game of the evening before they turned in for bed. All seemed very quiet where Amy was concerned as she played happily in her room. Ralph thought he'd better check up on her, knocking before he entered, only to find her asleep on top of her bed in her pink PJs. He found a blanket at the end of her bed which he covered her up with, unwilling to disturb her as she looked so comfy and peaceful. He kissed her goodnight, whispering, 'Sleep tight, my angel,' closing the door softly behind him on his way back to Jodie.

'I just checked on Amy. She's fast asleep on top of her bed so I pulled the blanket over her and kissed her goodnight. We could have an early night,' he winked at her, 'to make the most of our time alone,' he suggested, feeling tired himself. She agreed as Ralph gathered up the playing cards, placing them back in their box.

'I'll put the biscuits back in the tin and follow you in shortly,' she added, brushing past Ralph, patting him on the shoulder then checking everything was locked up. She went upstairs into the bathroom and cleaned her teeth before going into her room, or rather, their room now.

She opened the door to see Ralph already in his PJs; she thought, *they'll be off soon*. Having the romantic thought brush past her sent a shiver down her spine, wondering if he felt the same. *The night was still young, as the saying goes; an opportunity missed is often regretted,* she thought lustfully. Jodie decided to put her PJs on to slip under the cosy duvet she'd only just freshened up the day before Ralph's arrival. Within minutes he opened the door, closing it softly behind him. Noticing Jodie already in bed he jumped in next to her, cuddling up to her as she lay on her side, his arm cradling around her torso, kissing her head of hair, showing his affection, hoping she would turn around to face him and look into his eyes like the big softy that she was lurking behind her facade. Jodie was fully awake and aware of his feelings and intentions if she gave him permission. She was in the mood for a bit of fun; they explored one another as she gently found his lips with her index finger, feeling his silky-smooth lips as their foreheads touched and their lips touching, their tongues in and out, growing ever more intense.

Jodie rolled back over in excitement, pulling off her top and revealing her nakedness. This intensified their desire for intimacy to the next level, as he too pulled his top off, revealing a few black chest hairs. She started to glide her finger over his bare chest. Ralph was clearly enjoying the moment as murmuring sounds came out of his mouth, which excited them both more. Jodie's hand slipped gently down towards his crotch, pulling at his underwear and clasping her hand around the bulge inside, slowly pulling over the top of his Y-fronts. His hand reached down towards her bottom, squeezing her cheeks as he moved his hand round in-between her crotch, placing his finger inside her as he tried to add to the electricity between them. She lay on her back and opened her legs, inviting him inside her. He slid gently inside, pumping gently then with more intensity, enjoying every second. He pulled out after a while to lower himself into position, licking her vulva till she burst out with excitement as everything began to let go.

Exhausted after their moments of sheer passion they lay back on the mattress. Pulling back the duvet they soon drifted off into deep sleep. A few hours later Jodie awoke, needing the bathroom with a sense of urgency. She wanted to avoid Ralph, who was still deep in sleep, so she pushed the duvet over her side, grabbing her PJs to avoid any embarrassment if she met Amy in the corridor, making a beeline to the bathroom. After washing her hands, she was back in the room, quietly getting back into bed. Ralph was still out for the count, *thank goodness*, she thought. She was far too tired to make the smallest conversation at that hour.

The early hours soon appeared as the sun started to beam through their bedroom with blackbirds chirping in the distance with their morning choruses. Ralph was beginning to stir as he rolled from side to side, eventually facing Jodie head on, looking into her soft hazel eyes. His eyes were still in a squint while he gradually came to.

'Good morning, darling.' He kissed her right cheek, tapping her leg underneath the covers.

'Good morning, sleepy head Mr Ralph,' she replied, feeling the love. 'Fancy a tea?' she continued, grinning at him.

'Oh, er, yes please. That's a treat I miss, living on my tod,' he added, with a sense of anticipation.

'Coming right up,' Jodie confirmed, as she sprang out of bed, slipping her feet into her pumps.

'Oh, you've got your PJ's on,' Ralph noted with a wink.

'I had to go to the loo so put them back on. We don't want Amy catching us in the nuddy, do we, and besides, I feel too undressed without them, if you get my drift,' she concluded, lightly smacking him on his arm. Jodie opened the door quietly and tiptoed down towards the kitchen, where she filled the kettle from the water filter, letting it drain through before filling the kettle enough for two mugs of tea. Jodie took an ordinary tea bag from the caddy and the Fresh Start Pukka tea she loved from its box. Placing the two cups on a flowery oblong tray, she carried them into the bedroom, placing them on the bedside tables. They plumped up their pillows to sit up, reaching out for their brew, sipping and blowing in between morning chats, which they enjoyed. It was a special time, bringing back the happy times when they had spent their first nights together. Ralph and Jodie were back where they started, only this time their relationship was more solid; with Amy growing up they were reaping the benefits of a rooted relationship once again.

Their drinks consumed, they each made their way to the bathroom to shower before Jodie wiped it down with her soft scraper. Wrapping their towels around them they quickly walked back into the bedroom to dress, before knocking on Amy's door, saying breakfast was ready at ten. No sooner had she knocked on Amy's door than she appeared round it, which almost made Jodie jump out of her skin, hardly expecting that response. She was obviously excited that her dad was there if she was showing her eagerness to get up in haste on a Saturday morning.

Within ten minutes Amy joined them around the kitchen table, where Jodie had laid everything out, looking very inviting. Jodie had bought a selection of croissants and pains au chocolat at a nearby bakery the other day, as a treat for Saturday, when Ralph would be there. *Two mugs of tea and a jug of orange juice for anyone who desired a remotely healthy boost for the morning*, she thought. Amy wasn't a tea lover at the moment, which no doubt would change as she grew older.

'So, what's the plan for today?' Ralph asked anyone who was listening. Before Jodie or Amy interrupted, Ralph reminded Amy of homework and guinea pig duties before any pleasure activities, smiling at her. She was up for that challenge, Jodie agreed, taking a croissant from the plate in the middle of the table. Amy seemed in a hurry, knowing she had to do all her homework before any fun activities in the day ahead. Fortunately, Amy only had reading and spellings and hoped she could persuade her dad to delay it till later; after all, the sun was shining brightly so they had to take advantage of being outside. Daisy needed releasing into her run for some all-important fresh air. Ralph was feeling generous and, seeing that the weather was so lovely, he let her off the hook. Daisy's needs were more urgent, as she loved being outside enjoying the weekend sun. She was just happy having a carrot and some broccoli leaves or lettuce to amuse herself.

Jodie cleared the breakfast dishes away, stacking them into the dishwasher, knowing if she just left them on the side they'd be there forever. A woman's work was never-ending, she tutted to herself.

'So what's the plan today?' she asked, feeling excited, raring to go and feeling in the mood for outdoor fun. 'We could go to the park; Amy could play as we sit on a bench watching the others pass the time; have an ice cream; go to Burger King after; generally just chill out, soaking up the sun's rays for a change. My thoughts anyway,' she added with a sense of freedom, looking at Ralph for alternative suggestions. They agreed to go to the park so they all got ready to jump in the car to the park.

'What a beautiful day,' Ralph remarked, getting out of the car, followed by Jodie and Amy, before she pressed the fob to lock it. Amy, with a spring in her step, took her dad's hand, skipping occasionally as they all made a beeline for the play area, which at mid-morning was still reasonably empty. Amy wore her trainers for extra bounce and comfort. She started to swing, dangling from the lovely wooden logs suspended overhead supporting the frame. Ralph and Jodie meanwhile sat on the adjacent bench, watching her enjoying herself and having the time of her life. Jodie remarked about the lovely clothes one could buy for children. Amy wore pretty, light pink, flowery joggers with a light pink T-shirt with the logo "Be Kind" on the front, written in rainbow colours. Jodie thought she looked stunning, biased or not. She looked at Amy, knowing she had no care in the world, free as a bird or kite flying high, like Mary Poppins. She was instantly reminded of the classic song "Let's Go Fly a Kite" from the original movie in which Julie Andrews had starred. Ten minutes had elapsed, and the park was gradually filling up, with more people walking along the straight and zigzagging paths, enjoying one another's company as the sun engulfed them, filling them with warmth. More children joined in the fun around the play area as parents and grandparents sat on the benches, watching from a distance seeing their precious ones enjoying every minute.

'OK, I've had enough now, Mum,' Amy's voice came from a distance as she ran towards her mum and Ralph. They both felt the same.

'OK, fancy an ice cream? I heard an ice cream van wander down a few moments ago,' she suggested to Amy and Ralph as they got up from their bench. They were met by a little spaniel which came from nowhere, sniffing at their feet, wagging her tail, enjoying the numerous scents along the path in front of them, no doubt sniffing any crumbs from crisp packets or other snacks accidently dropped by those sitting on the parked benches. Jodie was usually cautious but this time couldn't resist a pat or a stroke along the dog's white and fawn furry back. She loved dogs very much and was hoping they would be able to rescue a lost puppy needing a forever home, as seen on TV with the late Paul O'Grady, who helped at Battersea Dogs Home in London, where he smothered the lost dogs with love and affection. He was one in a million; everyone loved him. He would be sorely missed by droves.

They walked hand in hand, forming a chain towards Mr Whippy after saying goodbye to the spaniel, which continued its adventure then began to follow them as they continued walking. Jodie instantly wondered who it belonged to, seeing no one in sight. They soon arrived at the ice cream van, where there had already formed a queue, mainly of children. As they patiently awaited their turn, they eyed the board on the side of the van with its many different flavours of ice cream and a variety of lollies. The queue filtered down to single numbers until finally they faced the front of the van.

The man looked down at them, waiting to hear their order. 'What can I get you,' he said, looking at Amy with a smile.

'Oh, a 99 please, with a flake,' she replied with enthusiasm. He turned his body towards the ice cream machine; as he held a cone in his right hand he pulled the lever to extract the white smooth ice cream, which stood up like a steeple, then took a Cadbury flake from a box, placing it into the middle of the ice cream, before handing it over to Amy with a serviette to soak up any dribbles. Amy accepted it with beady eyes, twirling the cone around, licking the sides before it melted. Jodie and Ralph had the same. They stepped aside from the ever-growing queue only to notice the friendly spaniel, sitting this time by Amy's feet.

'Oh, hello again,' she looked down at it with a smile. 'Where's your owner, then?' she continued to ask, as the dog tilted its head from side to side as if it understood every word. Jodie tried to distract her as she hoped the dog would soon get bored and would walk away. They continued walking around the arboretum, noticing a sign for the bird sanctuary, so they decided to visit it, seeing the colourful parrots with their red and yellow wings and bodies. They all enjoyed peering into the wire cages, gasping with oohs and aahs as they moved from one cage to another, avoiding bumping into the wheels of pushchairs as parents pushed their little ones along the line. The day was proving very enjoyable as they came to the end of the bird sanctuary. They carried on walking around, watching the odd goose waddle along the grass verges and across the lawns before finally finding a lake to dive into, joining a few white swans as they glided along the lake with little effort, a very pleasant sight. From time to time Amy looked behind her, hoping she might see the dog walking behind them. Sure enough a few yards behind them it was trotting along, clearly enjoying all the open spaces.

'Mum, look there's the dog again. It keeps following us.' Jodie was a bit concerned by this time. Noticing a light brown collar, with a few eye-catching studs in places, she thought she'd look for a name tag, once the little friend came beside them, to see if it was chipped. Jodie thought she might ask a warden if they had seen the dog before. She knew what the next question would be from Amy, which was if she could take the dog home, or at least to a vet to check her out. Jodie was starting to fall in love with the wee dog. It finally sat beside them, so Jodie seized her opportunity to look for a name tag, which had a number engraved on one side of it. Suddenly the spaniel stood up, with her paws begging to be lifted up which Jodie couldn't resist, thinking this dog needed a forever home. She was surprised at how co-operative the young dog was, obviously loving the attention she was being given. Chatting to one another Ralph agreed to take the dog to a nearby vet, as no park wardens seemed to be around; they were probably all busy with different jobs around the arboretum. Ralph did notice one official chap in uniform walking around, so he asked him if he knew of a nearby vet so that he could get the dog checked out, as no one seemed ready to claim it.

'There's a vet across the road, sir, who we often use for our animals. He's very pleasant and comes highly recommended,' the warden replied in haste, remarking he had noticed this young whisper of a dog roaming around over the last few days.

'Thank you,' Ralph and Jodie replied in unison. They continued walking towards the exit until they were on a side street with a level crossing. They crossed to the other side. They noticed a signpost above, saying Veterinary Surgery, which pleased them, and they knew they were one step closer to solving the mystery of the lost dog. As Ralph pushed the glass door to open it, a bell above alerted staff to their entrance, as well as barking dogs of different shapes and sizes. Amy was in her element as she surveyed them all, spotting the odd mini cages housing cats and other small furry friends.

'How can I help you?' a young lady behind the front desk asked Jodie as she approached her. Jodie started to relay the story to the listening lady, who peered down at the dog from time to time, saying hello as the spaniel looked up at her with appealing eyes. She noted the details, tapping them into her computer, and asked them to take a seat and a vet would call her in shortly. Jodie felt relieved and confident that they had done the best thing by bringing the dog to the vet. It was becoming more clingy as they walked around the park, perhaps feeling lost and was in need of some proper attention. Within a few minutes a vet appeared, opening his door, and walking towards her; as the dog had no name he couldn't call it out.

'Hi, I'm Mike, the vet on call today. I understand this dog has been roaming around the arboretum with no owner in sight. Please come in. I'll check if it's been microchipped and take it from there,' he said as he walked back into his room, opening the door for Jodie and crew to pass through. She lifted the small dog onto the raised bench, ready for a full examination by Mike, the trusted vet, who seemed keen to help and solve this poor lost dog's problem. Amy eagerly watched every move as he took out his stethoscope, placing the end under the dog's tummy, listening for a healthy heartbeat, which was all good. He then took out a handheld scanning device, placing it near the dog's neck to detect a chip. Much to his dismay he couldn't see one on his monitor so he promptly decided to chip it, giving the dog her unique identification. A few moments after his examination he gave them his update and thought it was time to give this wee character a name. He looked at Amy, smiling, as she probably wanted to give the dog a name.

'So, think of a name. Any ideas?' he suggested to her as Amy stared into his eyes. 'Rosie' she announced, as she liked the ring to the name. They both looked at Amy in approval.

'Rosie sounds like a lovely name,' the vet confirmed with a

smile. On hearing the name, the little spaniel tilted her head towards Amy, giving the impression that she approved of her new name. The big decision was whether Ralph and Jodie were ready to take Rosie home, knowing the commitment this would be with Jodie's current job; yet how could she resist taking her, knowing that Amy would be delighted. How could she look Amy in the eye and tell her that they couldn't adopt her? They thought they would somehow find a solution to this temporary problem or else Rosie would just be back in the park again, finding her next potential owner.

Chapter Nineteen

Driving home from their day out to the arboretum, they had never thought they would come home with a new dog. The vet estimated she was probably only three years old, judging by her canine teeth to establish her age.

'Welcome to our family and cottage, dear Rosie,' Ralph said, as they parked the car outside. The vets had had a wide selection of small leads to choose from, as well as the essential two bowls, one for her water and the other for food. They had suggested a dry food mix which they donated to Jodie as a big thank you for taking little Rosie, which would keep them going for now till they visited the local Pets at Home later in the week. On opening the front door Rosie was unhooked from the red lead which Amy had chosen; soon nose to the ground, she walked and sniffed her way through the hall which once again was scattered with the day's post. As they were all in need of a drink, they headed to the kitchen, where Jodie filled the kettle from her water filter jug and switched the kettle on to boil whilst taking three mugs from the cupboard and one herbal tea bag and an ordinary one which Ralph and Jodie shared for that all-important cuppa. Placing one of Rosie's bowls on the floor by the back door, they filled it with water, ready to be lapped up whenever she was thirsty. Rosie also found her place on a couple of old but comfy fleece blankets; she circled around to get comfy, rolling up her body in a tight ball as dogs often did. Rosie had finally found her happy place; feeling very snug she soon closed her brown eyes and fell into a deep blissful sleep, knowing she was safe in her new forever home.

After they had all consumed their drinks with a few biscuits, Amy retired to her bedroom, amusing herself as Rosie slept away the next hours and Jodie contemplated how she was going to manage Rosie in her busy daily schedule. Adjustments had to be made, even notifying her school, as she clearly understood the responsibility lay with them. *There must be a way*, Jodie thought, voicing it out loud to Ralph, listening, and seeing how he could give some practical advice. 'Where there's a will there's a way,' Jodie added with a giggle.

So far all had gone very smoothly with little Rosie; no major potty-training hiccups as she was regularly shown out in the back garden ten minutes after drinking and after a meal, sniffing for a favourite spot until bingo, she performed. How lucky, they both felt, bringing Rosie back home, as she seemed to adjust so easily into Smith family life. Amy enjoyed talking about her at shared time in class, bringing in the odd photos her mum printed off at home. Life couldn't be happier in their opinion.

Sunday mornings were looking very different now, since they had acquired dear Rosie, who had settled in nicely, enjoying her new surroundings. It was another sunny morning as Ralph pulled the window blind cord up, letting in beaming sunshine and lightening up the whole room. Ralph went downstairs to make two mugs of tea and let Rosie out the back door before carrying the teas up on a melamine tray and placing them on either side of the bedside units. He was shortly followed by Rosie, who curled up beside their bed. Ralph suggested they should buy a second bed for upstairs, which Jodie could do in the week. They took their time sipping their tea and chatting about yesterday's unexpected events before Jodie headed for a shower. Seeing Jodie walk out of the room Rosie got up and trotted behind her, until Jodie turned around. Looking down at her she said, 'I'll be back in a mo, go back and see Ralph,' thinking she would get the drift. Rosie sat by the closed bathroom door before walking back downstairs where she felt more comfortable, knowing it was her spot.

Half an hour had passed before all three came down for brunch, as Ralph had to return home later. Jodie peered into the fridge and took out eggs, bacon and mushrooms for a quick fry-up, adding baked beans. After making a scrumpy brunch, which everyone enjoyed, Ralph reminded Amy of her homework, which he wanted to get involved in before heading back on the train in the afternoon. Amy agreed and she went into her room to fetch her school bag, placing it on the kitchen table as she pulled out her spellings and reading books, those being the weekend tasks. Jodie cleared the table, stacking the dishwasher, then continued with other chores, making sure she was up to date for the week ahead.

'This won't take long, Amy, if we start now, then we can take Rosie for a walk,' he added, to encourage her to push hard in the next half hour.

'Great, thanks, Dad,' Amy smiled back, as she placed her books in front of her, ready to start her homework. Reading first, then ten spellings which they raced through so that they could spend as much time as possible with each other before they needed to drive back to the station for Ralph's train. All homework done, and packed away, they had a quick drink before taking Rosie out for a much-wanted walk. Jodie grabbed the lead hanging in the hall. Rosie shortly followed her, probably realising what was happening as Jodie rattled the lead deliberately at Rosie who wagged her tail from side to side enthusiastically, a sudden and first "woof" voicing her excitement.

'Come on then, Rosie, time for walkies,' as Jodie bent down to her level, clipping the lead to her collar, laughing as she did so, being amused by her sudden bark. 'Woof woof,' Rosie answered back, adding to Jodie's amusement. Ralph and Amy arrived on hearing the commotion then they all stepped outside the front door, Jodie locking up behind them. Jodie took Rosie's lead as she trotted alongside her, walking remarkably well to heel.

Amy was keen to take the lead later once they started to walk around the block. They all took turns as she knew both Ralph and Amy needed to get used to the dog as quickly as possible. Jodie had thought about how she'd initially cope in the week when she was at school; they would have to change their morning routine, rising earlier to give Rosie a short walk after their breakfast before driving off to school. This was initially a slight culture shock yet they had agreed to give Rosie a forever home and they had no regrets, as it had been love at first sight, seeing the little spaniel wandering aimlessly around the arboretum. It was a mad idea that was very much a spur of the moment decision, but which felt right at the time, Amy being the real reason they took her on board.

The afternoon flew by. As they returned from their walk she turned the key to the front door, bending down to unclip the dog's lead and hanging it back on its hook in the hall. Rosie raced to the kitchen to her bowl of fresh water, quenching her thirst after her adventure, then curled up in her fluffy bed to rest till the next event. Time moved on until Jodie had to take Ralph to the station for his six o'clock direct train to Wolverhampton; soon to be a thing of the past, as he was due to move back with Jodie within the next two weeks, making family life much easier and happier with their new furry addition. She decided to cut her hours to three days a week, as she could work from home catching up with admin work, which was hard to incorporate at school with her reading duties, initially solving the problem of leaving Rosie for many hours in the house which seemed rather unfair. Ralph gathered up his weekend bag and grabbed his coat from the coat stand before they all headed to the car, leaving Rosie asleep in her cosy bed, oblivious to the goings on as she snored slightly with the odd yelp, no doubt dreaming in her doggy land sleep. After a quick drive down the road to the station and pecking Ralph on the cheek as he got out of the car, Jodie turned around to drive back to the cottage, with Amy nearly asleep on her booster seat. When she opened the front door into the kitchen, she was pleasantly surprised and relieved to see Rosie still in her bed, but she suddenly burst into life when she heard voices, getting up from her bed to greet them as she spun around a few times as if they had been gone for hours. Jodie bent down to stroke her with Rosie starting to lick her face, thanking her for the love and attention she gave her, filling both of them with pure delight and satisfaction.

Bedtime was fast approaching as she walked into the kitchen, looking at the clock on the wall. She flicked the kettle switch on for another cuppa whilst Amy changed into her PJs ready for bed, as it had been a long but more than exciting weekend. She made her favourite bedtime drink, which these days was hot chocolate, before Amy retired to her room in desperate need of an early night. She would no doubt follow her, as she grew wearier. Letting Rosie out for her final toilet stop, she hoped, before locking all the doors, she made her way upstairs and this time Rosie was happy to stay snuggled up in her bed in the kitchen. She bent down to kiss her goodnight, stroking her back, reassuring her all was well, at which she raised her head before curling up in a ball.

Chapter Twenty

A new chapter was about to start in the Smith family; with Ralph due to move home and now Rosie being the latest addition to the family everything was beginning to fall into place. Amy was delighted by her new dog, as it meant they would get out more on regular walks after school. Their lives had just been turned upside down for the better. *Bring it on*, Jodie thought, as she got herself dressed for the new week ahead. She walked past Amy's door, knocking as she announced, 'Time to rise and shine, Rosie needs you,' as she headed quickly downstairs, hoping she wouldn't be greeted with puddles and piles, which fortunately she wasn't. Rosie had been able to last the night.

'Clever girl!' She went over to pat her side, kissing her head as Rosie turned onto her back in her bed in submission, tail wagging from side to side, feeling chuffed with herself.

'Come on, let's open the door as you must be desperate to go out,' Jodie continued talking to her, soon noticing that Amy had sneaked in and was standing alongside Rosie. Whilst she was exploring the garden, sniffing as she trotted along, Jodie focused on getting breakfast, prepared cereal being the easiest as winter was now behind them. No sooner had they cleared the breakfast dishes, placing them in the sink for quickness, than they locked the back door so that they could walk Rosie before going to school. A quick walk up the road would hopefully suffice before she returned in her lunch break; she could then gauge the situation as to how Rosie was coping with being left alone. She would chat to Mrs Newbury about their new furry addition, knowing that she would be more than willing to adapt her hours for now until things had settled at home.

Once both Jodie and Amy were at their schools, she felt more settled, as normal practice had resumed for now. Mrs Newbury was keen to hear more about the weekend's events, so she asked Jodie to share with the class, as it was sharing time, which she was naturally happy to do. They all formed a semicircle on the carpet, Jodie leading the class this time, as they shared the duty.

'Good morning, everyone,' she opened the initial chat, before telling them all about the exciting adventure at the weekend of acquiring Rosie; she left out all the details as it might bring some confusion to the class. Simple terms were always the best, in plain language, until they progressed to the upper classes.

'Wow,' and, 'Ooh,' they gasped in reaction to the news. Kitty showed particular interest as she asked, 'What sort of dog is Rosie?' putting her hand up before Jodie had invited anyone to ask questions, which always led to further information. After half an hour the sound of the school bell alerted them to morning play, which was much needed, before reading time. Afterwards she took the opportunity to go into the staffroom and make herself a herbal tea. and to catch up with any messages on her phone. One stood out as it was from Ralph; she thought she'd better read it now as he might have an update on his job and home move. She quickly opened it, reading:

I've been accepted for the job transfer to a company near you to start next week. I have just accepted, and they are happy to have me on board, so that's great news. I'm coming home forever, love you, Ralph xxx.

It placed a huge smile on her face as she fired one back:

That's brilliant news. Let our new chapter begin. Must go, was just on my break xxx ps. Wait till Amy hears this Jodie xxx

Playtime over, she had to focus on her reading buddies as she retreated to the back of the class before calling the readers from her list one by one as they brought their current reading books to her, all seeming eager to read for the ten-minute time allocated slot. Monday was the day they all changed to a new book, some moving to the next one in the series, others to more words, as Jodie noted their progress in their individual exercise books for their parents to see and continue their reading homework. She had ten children to read with until lunch break. The day continued until bell rang. Everyone gathered together in team work to tidy the classroom before getting their coats and bags from their individual coat hooks and forming an orderly line to go into the courtyard, soon to meet their parents when the gates were opened. Jodie made her swift exit to the staffroom, unlocking her locker to gather up her things before walking towards her parked car. Opening the car with her key fob she drove off towards Amy's school. Amy soon noticed Jodie's car, walking towards it, and she soon indicated to return home where Rosie was no doubt crossing her legs, wanting to go out into the garden once they opened the front door.

'I'm home,' Jodie called out as she entered the cottage, hoping she might hear a woof coming from the kitchen. She rushed to open the kitchen door, only to find Rosie nice and snug in her bed, seemingly oblivious to Jodie having been away for most of the day.

Amy soon came rushing in to see her beloved Rosie, who immediately jumped out of her bed, twirling herself around a few times, showing her excitement as Amy ran up to Rosie. Bending down to her level, nearly sending her backwards, patting and stroking the smooth body before Rosie rolled over, legs in the air, on her back, inviting Amy to stroke her belly as she wagged her tail from side to side, loving the attention. The love of dogs was endless as they lapped up all the attention their owners gave them. As it was Monday it was Rainbows night so there was time for a quick drink and snack then to change into her uniform. They soon headed out again to the community hub for another night of activities with the other Rainbow girls. Jodie had thought about messaging Sam to meet up to discuss sharing transport, as Lottie had now joined. This would make it easier so that young Rosie wasn't left unattended for too long. It gave Jodie the opportunity to walk her around the hub area which they would both benefit from after long days. Jodie soon parked up in the car park; seeing Sam's car they met near the entrance, where the girls went into their group, whilst both mums chatted, exchanging their thoughts on car sharing, agreeing to the idea of solving the initial problem.

'Perfect!' They high-fived each other, hugging, before they both drove off in opposite directions. Sam would pick them up later whilst Jodie could potter around the house ensuring Rosie didn't feel left out. At least they had come to an amicable solution, *sending happy vibes to all included*, she thought. Life was indeed looking pretty rosy; excuse the pun, she chuckled to herself, with Ralph moving back in for good. What's not to like, she thought to herself as she went about her early evening jobs, one being what she would cook for tea – something simple – the other taking Rosie for a walk around the block, giving them both some much needed fresh air. Rosie kept following Jodie around the kitchen, as she liked it, the fridge then freezer, looking for something quick and easy for her and Amy before unhooking Rosie's lead from the coat hook in the hall to muster up the energy to go on their walk.

Grabbing her key bunch to lock up, Jodie shut the door behind them on their way up the path, Rosie's nose to the ground, sniffing all the way to the end of the drive, pulling Jodie along, stopping at the particular scents she enjoyed. Jodie was really enjoying her new life chapter, embracing the new changes with Rosie, then Ralph moving back in in less than a week's time. She realised her time was soon becoming a thing of the past, well different, as they became a family of three. Was Jodie ready for this; a sudden moment of doubt hurtled through her inquisitive mind, yet she knew the answer before it popped into her head. She quickly pushed it to the back of her mind; only positive thoughts were welcome. Time was ticking now as they both walked around the block; she needed to get back before Sam appeared on her doorstep with the girls. She thought of fish fingers and peas tonight as being an easy meal, knowing Amy probably would be tired with an early night in store for them both.

Jodie placed the fish fingers in the oven ready for Amy's return, along with the peas, leaving the rest of the evening for her to chill on the sofa with her usual camomile tea before she turned in for bed. 'Another end to an eventful day,' she muttered to herself. Amy would no doubt change into her PJs after her meal, then join her for her last drink before retiring to her bedroom. She picked up Rosie's food bowl and placed it on the kitchen top as she scooped a small level of her dry food, mixing it with a fork and adding a little water, stirring it all together then placing it back on the floor near her water bowl. Rosie watched every move as she started to drool with anticipation. She soon dived in, chewing each mouthful before swallowing and within minutes she had eaten the lot, licking the bowl clean as dogs usually did, showing their owners their satisfaction. A quick lap of water and she was satisfied with her lot as she curled back into her bed before needing to go out for her final toilet stop before Jodie locked the house up before bedtime.

Jodie woke up the next morning with a sense of longing for the week to end, knowing that Ralph was on his way home forever, all three becoming a family unit once again, only this time having Rosie, their latest addition, bringing much joy, laughter and fun along the way. Amy soon got very attached to her as they changed their daily routine to regular walks after play in the garden, inviting her school friends to join in the merry fun. On hearing her phone ring, she picked it up from her bedside table, swiping the screen to open.

'Good morning, my lovely, sleep well?' came the light-hearted voice at the other end of the phone.

'Oh, good morning, Ralph, yes a good night was had by all,' she replied quickly before dangling her legs by the side of her bed to stretch before dashing off to have her shower.

'Not long now until Friday, better let you get on enjoying your day,' he continued, adding kissing noises before he hung up. He was gone before she had bid him goodbye, knowing how her mornings were always a bit rushed; nevertheless it was lovely to hear from him. Showered and dressed, she passed Amy's door, knocking twice to get her up before running downstairs, hoping not to be too late to let Rosie out in the garden. Rosie was already waiting at the back door, nudging her nose against it, willing her to hurry up and open it lest she puddle the floor.

'Good girl,' she praised her as she unlocked the door to her swift exit. She went back into autopilot as she filled the kettle from the water filter to boil, ready for her first brew. Amy soon appeared fully dressed, ready for the day's events at school. The usual breakfast and drink were consumed and after a quick pat with Rosie they gathered up their belongings to walk out to her car ready for the school run. *So far so good*, she thought, encouraging herself as she chatted to Amy, driving along, and reaching the drop-off point within minutes. Amy undid her seat belt to reach over the back seat to give her mum a kiss before a quick exit to the school gates, where Lottie was waiting, having just been dropped off by Sam. Jodie waved to Sam before indicating, continuing her journey to her school. Fortunately the roads were reasonably clear, which helped. She parked up as usual, swiftly walking to the staff room, opening her locker to place her jacket on the coat hanger above, taking out her phone from her bag before placing it on the shelf above. She never liked to be late, knowing Kitty would be waiting for her in anticipation. They had become good friends in such a short time, filling her with smiles all the way.

'Good morning, Mrs Smith,' came a voice from behind the classroom door; it was Kitty's.

'Oh, good morning, Kitty.' She turned round, seeing Kitty standing before her, looking smart and radiant. The weather helped with everyone's mood as the sun shone through the slightly smeared windows in the classroom, showing all the smudges since the cleaners had attacked them. Today was PE day, as they called it in Jodie's day, so everyone could run around outside in the yard, letting off their energy after their morning lessons, which were reading and maths times tables, which Jodie had just about mastered in her day, as maths wasn't her strongest subject. She preferred languages, French and German being her strongest, as her mum had German origins. She took a few children gathered around one of the blue round tables as her latest group for maths, which she wasn't keen on doing, as she felt she was still on the learning curve herself. She had already discussed this with Zoe, the class teacher (known as Mrs Newbury to the others). Each child had to recite the times tables; that morning it was the three times table.

She was always pleased when it was over, as maths was really not her forte. She was saved by the morning bell as she muttered a 'Phew' under her breath. They all left their books neatly piled on the desk before making a quick exit outside, to run around releasing their energy. She headed back to the staffroom, making herself a herbal tea and taking a seat on the green sofa armed with her phone, checking any missed calls and messages. She saw one from Sam, reminding her of their usual catch up at the café on their day off, which they always looked forward to.

Just on my break looking forward to seeing you tomorrow, see you later xx she replied in haste.

No sooner had she sent the text than the school bell rang at the end of play, leaving just enough time for a ladies stop before rejoining the class. She kept focusing on her catch up at the café tomorrow then Ralph's homecoming on Friday to get her through the remaining school week. The afternoon continued after lunch with sharing time where everyone enjoyed catching up on each other's outside school activities or whatever they wanted to share with their classmates. The usual semicircle on the blue carpet was formed; this time Mrs Newbury headed the forty-five-minute session with the baton in her hand, ready to pass around like pass the parcel only this time without the music. Kitty was always delighted when she got the baton as she seemed to prepare herself for what she was going to share with the group, sparking lots of laughter along the way, which pleased both Zoe and Jodie. The final end of day bell rang, and they all cleared up as quickly as possible so that they could escape to the gates to go home. Once all the children had gone home, Zoe and Jodie raised their hands in the air, glad the day had ended and eager to get home.

Chapter Twenty-One

Wednesday had finally arrived, which was when she met up with Sam for their usual morning coffee and cake after drop-off from school at the local café. It was sharing time with her class, a special time they always looked forward to making a point to stick to each week; nothing would interfere with "their" time.

'Good morning lovely,' she said, embarrassing Sam, seeing her in the café. She had chosen a table looking out of the window so that they could occasionally watch in between sipping their cappuccinos and eating cake. It was Sam's turn to go to the colourful cake counter, placing their order.

'Good morning, ladies! Your usual or something different today?' the girl asked, smiling at those who were on duty today.

'The usual two slices of coffee and walnut sponge,' Sam replied, smiling back.

'Coming right up,' she added.

'Well, here we are again; the week has flown by.' Jodie remarked, seeing their order being carried over on a tray with a pretty white doily. She removed their coffees and cake from the tray, placing the tray on the floor beside her. They soon tucked into their cakes, leaving no crumb in sight as they put the world to rights, looking out, watching people passing by going about their day. Suddenly she had a thought, noticing a water bowl in the corner. She could have brought young Rosie as they welcomed well-behaved dogs. Just on cue the doorbell pinged as an elderly lady led her dachshund into the café, sparking much attention. Heads turned, all taking a good look at the fawn-coloured dachshund which walked obediently alongside the lady as she walked up to the counter and asked for a coffee and a lemon slice. She then turned round to seek out a table where the dog could lie beside her. The waitress was obviously taken by the cute dog, asking the lady if her dog was allowed a doggy treat in the form of a little beef bone; it was always best to ask, as some owners didn't like their dogs being fed for many different reasons. She brought her order over to the table, placing the bone by the lady to give to her furry friend; it gently took the bone from her fingers whilst the waitress watched, smiling at the lady. She went back behind the serving counter feeling chuffed, clearly a dog lover herself.

After an hour, Jodie and Sam left the café. Jodie needed to get back home quickly to Rosie who had been left alone and was probably desperate for her walk. Hugging one another they waved their farewells until they collected the girls after school. On opening the front door Jodie placed her keys on the hall table before heading straight to the kitchen to see if she was going to be greeted by a big puddle, as Rosie had been left for several hours since school drop-off. She sneaked around the door to find Rosie where she had left her in her bed, no puddle in sight, which took Jodie by surprise considering the time. Noticing her, Rosie came towards her, circling around a few times indicating she was excited to see her and finally being allowed out to relieve herself! Jodie turned the key to open the back door. Rosie shot outside, wagging her tail as if she'd been released from prison! She found her freedom, racing around the garden, nose to the ground, sniffing the scents till she went racing back indoors, straight back into her bed; tongue hanging out by the side of her mouth, panting.

Jodie decided to take her out once Amy returned, as Rosie seemed happy enough being just out in the garden. Jodie spent her time wisely, doing a few essential jobs around the house and deciding what to have for tea later, to give her more quality time with her daughter. Amy was always her priority, as was helping her with her homework, which was starting to increase as she improved, learning new things, demanding more concentration and effort both in class and at home. These years were the most important ones in any child's life. A few hours later she was back on the road, collecting Amy to start all over again, after a well-deserved cuppa and a snack. Once back home she did the honours, making two drinks and placing a plate of flapjacks in the middle of the kitchen table as they caught up with the day's events. Amy opened her school bag, taking out her reading book and spellings, to start before taking Rosie out for her obligatory walk before dinner. An hour later Jodie helped Amy put Rosie's lead on, ready to head out for their walk.

Rosie always knew when it was time for walkies as she spun several times around Jodie's feet, waiting impatiently to go out of the front door. With a skip and some pulling on the lead they were soon enjoying their spring walk, Rosie nose to the ground, sniffing as she went along.

'This time next week Dad will be able to join us,' she explained to Amy, giving them both something to look forward to.

'Yeah!' she jumped in excitement, thinking of all activities she'd like to undertake with her dad, walking with Rosie being high on her to-do list. On returning home Jodie found an old towel to wipe Rosie's paws and her undercarriage to avoid mud being trodden around the house; *a good habit to adopt*, she thought, as she refilled Rosie's water bowl. She could start dinner, which would be pasta and meatballs, a yummy and easy midweek meal. She started to prepare the dinner whilst Amy amused herself in her room, her happy place. Hearing her phone ring, she swiped to see who it was. Noticing it was her mum, despite knowing it wasn't the most convenient time, she thought she'd better answer it anyway even if she only said she would ring her back after they'd eaten.

'Hi, Mum, how are you doing? I'm sorry I haven't been in touch lately. It's been full on here, with school and now Ralph moving back on Friday,' she continued, hoping her mum didn't feel like a lost sheep and left out.

'Oh, don't worry yourself, darling, life gets so busy in this modern world. I understand, just don't forget your mum!' which made her feel worse, although at least she understood.

'Just doing our tea. I'll chat to you later, I promise. Bye for now, Mum,' Jodie concluded.

Half an hour passed by and they finished their tea. Amy retreated into her room and changed into her PJs ready for bed later, feeling all comfy and cosy, whilst Jodie stacked the dishwasher, flicking the kettle switch on for a herbal tea before going to the lounge to phone her mum back as promised.

'Hi, Mum, I'm back now, just finished our tea. I've just made myself a cuppa, thinking I'd ring you back so you now have my undivided attention,' she explained to her mum, smiling as if she could see her.

'Oh, thank you, love, I appreciate that,' her mum added, feeling less intrusive. She continued chatting away, recalling the last week's, events giving her the full rundown. Fortunately, her mum sounded upbeat; it was all going like clockwork at home, with no major drama to report, which she was relieved to hear. Dot, her mum, had neighbours either side to call on when she needed or wanted company; she was living on her own now, since her husband had died last year. They had had a great relationship, having their disputes, as most long-standing relationships did, but generally they were there for each other. being soul mates. Dot did like her girly company, as all women do; it was essential to have other friends, especially if you became widowed, something which anyone might have to face one day in their lifetime. She sipped her tea in between her lengthy conversations, checking the time on her phone, being aware of Amy's bedtime and hers; however, she didn't want to give her mum the impression that she didn't have time for her. Her life was very different now, she'd been there, done that, got the T-shirt, as the old expression went. After nearly an hour she had to draw the conversation to a close as time was ticking.

'OK, Mum, lovely talking to you. It's past Amy's bedtime so I'd better see her before she wonders where I am. Chat soon.'

Jodie mouthed kisses down the phone before hanging up. She drew a breath in exhalation as she sighed with relief, thinking she'd done her duty even if it didn't sound good. She quickly knocked on Amy's door, much relieved to see she had already taken to her bed without any fuss, *not that she is usually fussy*, she thought; after letting that thought enter her head, she pushed it to the back of her mind. She felt worn out after today's events, thinking she would lock up and send Rosie out for her final wee before settling her in her bed in the kitchen and taking to her own bed, where she was soon cosy in her PJs, easing herself into bed and switching the bedside light off.

Friday had finally arrived as Jodie came to, feeling slightly panic-stricken yet very excited that her Ralph was finally moving back home so that they could start a new chapter, all four of them as one happy family. She had thought she would never see this day after their break up all those years ago but how wrong she had been. She was feeling very grateful for this second chance in their relationship and for not having given up at the first hurdle. She pulled herself into a table-top yoga pose, before rolling on her side to place her outstretched legs to the floor and getting out of bed to have a tepid shower. She really enjoyed her me time in the early morning before the day started; it was a time for body, mind and soul to become one. Once dressed, she went into auto pilot, knocking on Amy's door before racing downstairs to let Rosie out in the garden. She was clearly desperate to go out as she pawed at the bottom of the door.

She had arranged to work a half-day, finishing at midday so that she could get ready for Ralph's homecoming, doing last-minute grocery shopping and generally tidying up the cottage, showing him that she wanted to make the extra effort to welcome him home. They would celebrate by having a meal out at their local Italian restaurant. They loved an Italian, whether it was pizza or pasta, every time; it was special, finishing off with a mouth-watering dessert. She decided to drop Amy off at school then head off for a quick coffee stop at the café before going to

Tesco to shop, to help kickstart their first weekend together for many years. She parked in the car park before her first fuel stop at the high street café. She pushed the door open, triggering the doorbell above, and was immediately welcomed by, 'Good morning, what can I get you?' the young lady announced behind the counter.

'A cappuccino, please, with a sneaky chocolate brownie for energy to do the weekend shop, thank you.'

'Take a seat and I'll bring it over,' she replied, smiling at her. Jodie sat in a corner so that she could have some me time before starting her day properly. She swiped her phone, looking at her shopping list, adding a few things she had forgotten about or fancied. As she looked up, others were starting to walk in, no doubt having the same idea of a refuel before their day started. Her phone bleeped with an incoming text, which she swiped open to see it was from Ralph.

Good morning, lovely. Today's the day of the big move home. Well, only me and my suitcase. I come very light. See you later xx

She decided to ring him instead of texting, which probably would surprise him.

'Good morning, Ralph, I'm just having a quick coffee stop before going shopping. I've taken a flexi day as I've got time in lieu. Text me once you start your journey, giving me some idea of your arrival time. Bye for now,' she concluded by pressing red to end the call. She suddenly felt slightly panicked by uncomfortable feelings of doubt about her newfound life changes. Had she made the right decision by letting him move back in? It was a very silly thought which she soon pushed back to the back of her mind, knowing full well that she desperately wanted him home, to be a family again, and now Rosie had joined them everything seemed perfect. So what was she worrying about; it was just tummy butterflies; a mix of excitement and nerves. She was head of heels in love with him and wanted the very best for Amy. She was gradually getting fed up with being a single mum, juggling every move, being lonely too; that was the real reason for adopting Rosie, knowing a loveable hound would turn their lives around for the better and that surely had to be a good enough reason. She wanted to become a family again as life was too short for anything but pure happiness, despite the daily challenges they would soon be facing together. She started to mentally make a list of pros and cons, pros winning every time. She looked forward to waking up to him, his smell and radiant smile, once fully awake, was top of her list as surely it must be in most relationships. There was no doubt in either of their minds; it required daily work, pulling together with one goal to love, support and cherish one another, a solid rock to all happy relationships. Now she had put her mind to rest she finished her coffee and cake, placing the empty crockery on the tray, picked her bag up and marched, head held high, out of the café. The sun shining above warmed the air as she made her way to Tesco to start her shop, pulling out a trolley and placing her phone in the slot, she proceeded up and down the aisles.

On arrival home she turned the key in the door; seeing a scattering of post around the mat she bent down to gather it up, placing it on the hall table to peruse after she'd put the shopping away and made herself a cuppa. Her instant reaction to any post was that most would be junk mail and flyers which would immediately be going for recycling. Occasionally she would get some happy mail which gave her instant excitement, like a child in a sweet shop, or in her case, a coffee and cake shop, as she never was a fan of sweets, being more of a savoury person. She swiped her to-do list, marking off jobs done so far; *a very handy tool*, she thought, *on iPhones these days*. Next was to load up the washing machine, placing the washing afterwards in the dryer which her mum had given them as a wedding present. She went into their bedroom to strip the sheets and remake the bed with the fresh-smelling, lavender-scented ones. She stripped Amy's bed too, adding to the feelgood factor. Checking her phone for the time, it was time for a quick snack, so she made a ham sandwich before her habitual walk with

Rosie, who was now lying outside on the lawn enjoying the sun, occasionally rolling on her back, legs bent at the elbows, stretching in the air, lapping it all up, not a care in the world. Perhaps she would leave the walk till later, seeing as Rosie was so relaxed in the garden, which would give her more time to take the vac out to blitz and dust, as she wanted the house looking lovely on Ralph's return. A woman's touch always went down well; as she liked the house looking shipshape from time to time this was her incentive.

How time flew by; she soon had to call Rosie before locking up and driving off to Amy's school. After a quick bathroom stop she was off again in her car to pick up her daughter. Amy stood waiting as she drove into the lay-by; seeing Sam she blew a kiss and a thumbs up whilst Amy jumped into the car for them to drive back home. As soon as they had parked up on the drive her phone pinged with a WhatsApp message, now set as "family", from Ralph saying he was now on his way, driving his car, sending shivers all over Jodie's body in anticipation of his return; *this is it*, she thought.

'Dad's on his way to us now, how cool is that, Amy?' she told Amy, who was sitting in the back; looking in the rearview mirror to see her reaction, which was a thumbs up, placing a big smile on her face. She had to leave a space next to her car; they were now a family of VW lovers, as he had a light blue metallic Golf which he had owned from new.

'So, the plan is, once he arrives with just his suitcase, we will go out to eat at the Italian restaurant, which I have booked for 6.30, which will be a lovely homecoming. We can take Rosie for a walk when we get home, leaving plenty of time before he gets home.' She chatted away her thoughts to Amy, getting more and more excited by the second, now longing to see him.

'Sounds good to me, Mum,' Amy added, looking out of the window and watching the cars pass by, counting them as she went, feeling bored until they finally parked up by their cottage, leaving a car space for him next to theirs.

They went straight into the kitchen to have a quick drink and let Rosie out the back. Amy went to change into her pink cropped trousers, adding a red T-shirt to her relaxed look as it was Friday and would start her weekend off in style. There was a definite excitement in the air, as this marked a very special day in their marriage reunion; new beginnings to a future where anything could happen, so they were going to celebrate in style. After they had had their drinks, they locked up, putting Rosie on her lead to take her for a walk around the block, which she always loved, sniffing to the ground as she stopped along the way, inhaling a new scent where other dogs had passed by, wagging her tail from side to side as she moved on. Half an hour elapsed and they were nearly home, to be greeted by Ralph's car parked up next to Jodie's She hadn't expected him for another half hour, *clearly a good run, then*, she thought.

'Yeah he's arrived!' She let out a short scream of joy as she parked beside him, turning off the ignition. They each jumped out of the car in haste, ringing the doorbell and knowing that Ralph was lurking around inside. After two rings he opened the door, greeting them both with open arms pulling them into a tight embrace and kissing them both on their foreheads. They were all over the moon to see each other. Amy got out to let Rosie out of the kitchen whilst her mum and dad took the opportunity to have a long-awaited kiss, enjoying the moment before Rosie ran out to greet them.

'Oh, hello you,' she bent down to pat Rosie as she twirled around several times before pushing her bottom up the small step back into the cottage before she found her freedom and escaped down the road. They soon followed her inside, Jodie closing the door behind her. She couldn't quite contain her excitement on seeing Ralph looking healthy and smart in his chinos, with a light brown jumper dropped over his shoulders. He placed it on the side as he faced her, lifting her off the floor and kissing her on the lips a few times before landing her back on her feet; both enjoying the moment, feeling elated. Ralph suddenly brought out a bunch of flowers from behind his back, lighting up her already happy face even more.

'Aww, thank you, Ralph, they are beautiful,' as she saw the different coloured carnations of red, yellow and light pink. She leant forward, giving him another kiss on the lips.

'To us, new beginning, a fresh start,' he replied, taking her hand as they walked into the kitchen. There was a crystal vase waiting on the surface to be filled with fresh cold water; adding the attached sachet she poured it into the water. She took some scissors from the drawer to snip the wrapper and tied elastic bands holding the flowers and foliage together, and cut the stems to make a nice flower arrangement in the vase. She stood back, pulling out her phone to snap a picture to send to her family via WhatsApp, which also included Sam, her bestie.

Amy, meanwhile, was amusing herself with Rosie, leaving Mum and Dad to their embrace before she joined them in the kitchen, admiring the flowers in the vase. Ralph quickly took his case into the bedroom to unpack later, after their meal out at the Italian restaurant, which they were all looking forward to as hunger started to kick in. A quick check on Daisy to make sure she was fed and watered, then they all headed back to the front door to jump into Jodie's car and head to the restaurant, which wasn't far up the high street. They arrived, pulling the door open to be first in line of the queue waiting to be seated. A pretty waitress soon spotted them waiting patiently. Seeing the booking on the screen, she picked three menus up before leading them to their reserved table for the evening. Once seated, the girl gave them time to look at the drinks menu before returning to take their order.

'Two glasses of pinot grigio and a small orange juice, please.' Ralph gave their order as she tapped it onto her handheld screen. Ralph reached out his hands over the table to clasp Jodie's, giving her a light squeeze of affection before the drinks order arrived, which it soon did on a round tray. Placing them in the middle of the table, the waitress left them to peruse the menu for their meal.

Within minutes she was back to take their order, which was pasta for all in a carbonara sauce, with four slices of garlic bread which they could all share.

'Let's drink to us as a family, new beginnings, as we bring our glasses together, saying cheers to us,' Jodie continued, as they raised their glasses in unison.

Amy was feeling slightly overwhelmed, shedding a small tear down her right cheek, not yet fully understanding the idea of why they had just clinked their glasses together; but it was evident that her mum and dad were very happy. After all, she had still been so young when they first went their separate ways. A few moments passed before their mains were brought out by two waitresses, carrying them individually and placing them on the mats in front of them, as well as a plate of garlic bread in the middle to share.

'Enjoy,' she added, before walking back to serve others. They soon devoured the garlic bread as they took a slice each to munch whilst forking a mouthful of spaghetti.

'Yummy,' Ralph remarked, circling some spaghetti onto a spoon to make it easier to eat. Jodie followed suit as Amy struggled with hers, being inexperienced yet eager to learn.

'I'll show you how at home, next time we eat spaghetti. It's a bit tricky at first, but easy once you know how,' Jodie added, looking at Amy as she tried to help her with hers. They polished off their meals with gusto, leaving just about enough room for ice cream, and crème brûlée for Jodie and Ralph, finishing the evening in style. Ralph asked for the bill, before they left to return home. A good evening was had by all.

Arriving home, Jodie flicked the kettle on to make a camomile tea for herself and an ordinary tea for Ralph. Amy had a cuddle with Rosie after she came back from her trip around the garden, before returning to her room to change into her PJs, to read in bed before lights out when her dad came to kiss her goodnight. Jodie and Ralph finished off their drinks before retiring for an early night, leaving the unpacking of Ralph's suitcase until the morning. They just fancied time together before they rolled over for the night. Jodie enjoyed cuddling up to Ralph, putting her head on his chest, feeling in heaven, embracing their fresh start, and they offered one another kisses before they finally lay on their backs, holding hands as they fell into a deep sleep.

Chapter Twenty-Two

On Saturday morning the weekend kicked off with a bang; Ralph had finally come home and they were playing happy families again. Jodie rolled over, kissing Ralph gently on his cheek, caressing her fingers gently over his bare chest, feeling so lucky to have him back. Seeing he was still fast asleep, she jumped out of bed, put her cosy dressing gown on and tiptoed to the door, opening it gently, not wanting to wake him, and went down into the kitchen. Seeing Rosie still curled up, she filled the kettle from the water filter and put it on to boil, taking two mugs from the cupboard and a tea bag from the caddy and placing it in a mug before transferring the tea bag to the other. She turned to look at Rosie, seeing her roll over as she came to. Jodie grabbed the key to the back door, unlocking it and letting Rosie out. She was soon sniffing the air, holding her head high with her nostrils twitching, as they do. Jodie carried both mugs upstairs to their bedroom, placing them either side of their bed.

'Good morning, sleepyhead,' Jodie uttered, bending down to his level and kissing him on the lips.

'Good morning,' he replied with a smile on his face, looking at the mug she had just placed on the bedside table.

'I had better go and check on Rosie,' said Jodie, 'as I let her out and need to feed and water her before she gets restless. Back in a mo.'

Once back, she climbed back into bed, propped up her her pillow and sat up, sipping her mug of tea with her husband beside her as she chatted about the day ahead, noting any urgent tasks to do before allowing themselves some fun time together, while taking the day as it came. First on the to-do list was empty Ralph's case, adding to the existing pile of washing, then create his own space in the wardrobe. Ralph, hearing a tippy toe sound, soon noticed Rosie walking into the bedroom, wagging her tail as if to say "found you". She was such a sweetheart that they couldn't tut tut; knowing she wasn't really allowed in the bedroom she jumped into her upstairs bed, knowing her place. After their morning drinks they showered and dressed to have a Saturday family brunch in the kitchen. Ralph made it this time, giving Jodie a much-needed rest so that she could just sit back and relax. Finding his way around the kitchen cupboards, he pulled out a frying pan to start a somewhat healthy all-in-one fry up which consisted of an omelette with ham, cheese and frozen spinach florets, just as Jamie Oliver demonstrated on his easy meal recipes on TV. They both loved experimenting with new dishes. She heard a ping from her phone which she immediately swiped open. She saw it was from Sam, wondering if they had any plans and asking her if she fancied going to play mini golf with Amy and Lottie in the afternoon in the arboretum. Telling Ralph and thinking it was a great idea, she rang her back, accepting her kind invitation which would give them all a fun activity for today.

'Perfect! Meet up at 2pm, if that's OK,' Sam responded with excitement in her tone.

'Something different,' she voiced to anyone who was listening, thinking they could bring Rosie and attach her lead to a tree so that she could lie on the ground, basking in the sun with a water bowl beside her to keep her hydrated.

All crockery stacked in the dishwasher, Jodie started to pack a rucksack for the afternoon, including Rosie's bowls for treats and a water bottle she could refill her bowl with, adding a few snacks to keep them going. With water bottles they were all ready for their afternoon adventure at the arboretum fun day event. Amy attached Rosie's lead to her collar, and off they went to Ralph's car for the short car trip where they parked by the side of the road at the arboretum. They locked up and followed the signs to the mini golf course near the playground. Amy happily walked

Rosie, as Mum and Dad carried the essential bags, all feeling excited about their day out. Jodie soon spotted Sam and Lottie as they walked towards them, equally loaded with rucksacks filled with their essentials for the day.

'Hi there,' Sam waved, seeing them from a distance, Lottie picking up the pace as she spotted Rosie wagging her tail as they got closer to one another. The weather by this time was heating up to a bearable temperature for all to enjoy. On arrival they placed their bags on a bench around the pitch whilst Ralph, Jodie and Sam went up to the kiosk to pay and pick suitable clubs and balls and tot-up cards to score as they played. They strolled back to their bench where Amy and Lottie were happily chatting away whilst Rosie sniffed out a place to bask in the sun beside them.

'OK, here we go girls,' Ralph announced, lifting the golf clubs up as they walked towards them; two junior ones, the others adult size. Each picked one and a light small ball to putt with as they went round the circuit of twelve mini golf holes. Jodie gave the scoring cards to the girls with a small IKEA pencil, to write down their individual scores as they went along, making the game more enjoyable and competitive. The girls giggled and laughed as they took turns, gliding their balls into the desired holes, taking a well-earned break after half an hour to hydrate, making sure Rosie had her water bowl regularly topped up. The afternoon proved extremely entertaining as they all got into a friendly competitive mood with oohs and aahs along the way. Two hours elapsed and the game was over, everyone feeling a bit drained as the girls returned the clubs and balls to the kiosk.

It had been a "good game" as Bruce Forsyth would say on the classic *Generation Game* back in the seventies, loved by millions.

'Anyone fancy an ice cream, as Mr Whippy is parked over there?' Jodie pointed out by the edge of the playground.

'Yes, please,' they all shouted. Ralph and Sam gathered their things together in the rucksack, united Rosie and off they walked towards Mr Whippy, where they all indulged in a "99" with a flake, sitting on a bench to consume them whilst planning their next move. They all agreed to finish off the day by meeting at the local McDonald's, to save cooking an evening meal, which became a chore after years on end. Ralph and Jodie made their way back to the car, with Rosie leading in front, sniffing the numerous scents around the nearby bushes and wagging her tail, enjoying the moment, whilst Sam and Lottie returned to theirs. They all met up at McDonald's inside, the girls loving the idea of spending more time together and regarding each other as sisters, giggling and laughing as they walked.

On arrival they chose a table whilst Jodie and Sam discussed meal options for the girls and Ralph walked up to the large touch screen in the middle, tapping in their main orders then sweets, which were two vanilla McFlurrys for the girls and three mini chocolate brownies with cappucinos. All were satisfied, not wanting any more toys as they only accumulated in a pile at home, waiting to go into the next charity bag such as Great Ormond Street, being her preferred choice of charity. Ralph brought their orders, with Sam providing an extra pair of hands to carry them over. Soon they all tucked into their meals, unwrapping burgers, placing their chips on the same wrapper, relishing every bite with extra sauces.

'Yummy,' the girls commented together as they tucked in, licking their fingers as they went. They all chatted about their mini golf game which they agreed they'd like to play again one day, as they had enjoyed one another's company. Placing their empty wrappers on the red plastic tray, which Sam added to the named recycling bins, they walked out to their respective cars in the car park, with hugs and kisses before they drove off home, all feeling deeply satisfied after their day out.

Sunday was always a chill-out day a day to catch up on everything before a new week started. After their day out they all needed a laidback day where everyone could do their own thing. Homework, however, was essential; after breakfast Jodie showed Ralph how Amy was progressing so that he could take over from her, giving her a much-needed break. She decided to kick back, sitting on the sofa and reading her new book from Jo Thomas, her latest favourite author to read on her Kindle. She loved reading and wished she had more time for it, knowing that one day she would. Her real love of reading had started during lockdown, listening to Fern Britton reading every night for ten minutes an excerpt from her many books; a time to stop and have some me time which Jodie began to look forward to every night. Lockdown became a very mind-, body- and soul-trying time so everyone wanted a highlight to their day. Jodie decided on a tasty chicken dish for Sunday lunch with dauphinoise potatoes, which she had picked up at her last shop, with two slices of lemon cheesecake.

Chapter Twenty-Three

Monday morning soon came around and Ralph started his new job in a nearby industrial estate, working as a carpenter, restoring furniture, and making new items as and when required, which he loved, finding it a very therapeutic experience. It left him little time to get anxious these days as that had been successfully dealt with, leaving him happier than he ever could remember, and now he was back with his love, Jodie, and Amy and their new addition, Rosie. Life was finally looking much better now as they were all reunited as a happy family. Amy started to work for her Rainbow badges which she enjoyed doing after school; Jodie spent many evenings stitching them onto a red sash, showing off the different badges from cooking to sewing and hospitality, to name just a few. Amy and Lottie often worked together, especially with the cooking badge, giving them hours of pleasure. Jodie soon became more practised in her sewing skills as she sewed them on the sash.

They would outgrow Rainbows before their eighth birthday ready to join the Brownies before the all-important Girl Guides during their teenage years, becoming the best of buddies all the way through, supporting one another in the good times and low periods, encouraging one another along the way; enjoying camping in and outdoors, cooking together in their given groups and eating around a bonfire, weather permitting, singing songs together with a few helpers playing the guitar and a drum; making lasting memories along the way. Amy and Lottie would look back on their past, hopefully being able to pass on to their children their skills, if and when they married, assuming they would one day, as Jodie and Ralph and Sam could only hope.

Jodie and Sam continued their friendship with regular

meetups at the local café on their days off, becoming part of the café family as soon as they walked through the door. Neither were ready to move on from their jobs for now, though Jodie had plans to have another child as her biological clock was slowly ticking by; she did not want to have a baby in her forties despite it not being as much of a risk factor as it had been in Jodie's parents' day. Having more technology on offer with regular scanning and checkups, the risks had been eliminated and were now a thing of the past. Life had indeed changed in that respect, giving parents more reassurance and certainty, offering more hope to all expectant mums. This could only come as good news as technology had advanced. A premature baby, born for example at twenty-four weeks, would be placed in an incubator, hooked up to various life-saving devices such as oxygen, this being the most important factor in keeping the brain alive and away from immediate danger. It offered a much higher survival rate than decades in the past where the survival rate had been desperately slim and in many cases non-existent.

Life in the Smith family was definitely moving swiftly forward as they finally became a family again, especially having Rosie; their dog was at the centre, loving all the attention they gave her. She was living her best life, in her new forever home where she belonged. She quickly adjusted to Daisy the guinea pig, ignoring her pretty much once she was in her hutch, both were comfortable in their surroundings. Another year soon flew by and Jodie and Ralph were delighted to be expecting a sibling for Amy. They were all very much looking forward to the new arrival, especially as Jodie was approaching the end of her thirties and would bring another child into the world in the nick of time, just before she turned forty.

The alarm buzzed at 6.30 one sunny Saturday morning, causing a stir as Ralph turned over with blurry eyes, trying to reach out with his index finger to hit the snooze button on his phone, before rolling onto his back to catch another forty winks before it pinged again ten minutes later. He heard the odd stirring noises as Jodie came to; however, all wasn't completely well, as he thought he heard odd groans, indicating to him that she was in slight discomfort, but he dismissed it as he thought she was still in a dream. Ten minutes later she was still groaning as she became more and more distressed, having a few pains and briefly forgetting she was pregnant, till she placed her palm on her tummy.

'Oh heck,' she spoke out loud as she reached out her right arm to Ralph; he quickly came to.

'Are you OK? I know it's a silly question, but is it the baby?'

'Oh my, it's on the way,' she replied in a bit of a panic.

'Just breathe slowly in, then out. OK, what's the next thing to do?' he asked in a slightly lighter tone of voice.

'Listen very carefully,' she started to explain, 'it's all in my phone notes. Go to my contacts and find the midwife's number and ring her now; tell her I've started having contractions and they're about every ten minutes. I'll time them until you need to take over as the pain and frequency increases ...ouch!' she gasped, trying to breathe through each one.

Ralph was now in the swing of things as he jumped out of bed, feeling a bit lightheaded, but needs must.

'Hello, you're through to the midwife. Is everything OK? How far along is Jodie, is she coping for now?'

Ralph started to explain that she was becoming more and more uncomfortable as the contractions were getting closer together.

'OK, Ralph, you need to take her to hospital and I'll meet you outside with a wheelchair to take her into the birthing suite. Ring her friend so that Amy can be looked after. She told me Sam is the one she wants Amy to go to.'

'OK, I will ring her now. She's got a key to the cottage.'

'Perfect,' Sally, the midwife, said before ending the call. Ralph remained as calm as possible for Jodie's sake.

'Give me my phone and ring Sam, I can still talk to her before the pain gets worse.' Ralph passed her the phone as instructed.

'OK, Jodie, don't panic, I'll be over in five. Amy's safe with us for as long as it takes.'

'Thanks, darling, you are the best.' Jodie told her.

Ralph grabbed some clothes to put on before picking up her packed bag to take with them to hospital. Fortunately, Amy was oblivious to all the goings on as it had just turned 7am; she enjoyed her Saturday morning lie-ins. Jodie by this time had managed to go downstairs and was waiting for Sam to come over to take over. She heard two distinct two knocks at the door, followed by, 'It's me, Sam,' before she turned the key. She was greeted by Jodie as she suddenly bent double, having another contraction. They were becoming more frequent and making her increasingly uncomfortable.

'OK, darling, I'm here now.' Sam put a comforting arm on her back, stroking it in circular movements, helping Jodie to feel calmer. Ralph greeted her, rushing downstairs as he saw the increasing urgency to get her to the hospital. The baby was fast approaching and time was of the essence.

'OK, we'd better go, Sam. I'll leave you to muddle through the rest with Amy,' he added, before taking Jodie, linking his arm in hers, supporting her as they walked towards the car outside.

'Good luck!' Sam shouted before Ralph shut the door behind them. Jodie was by this time becoming increasingly uncomfortable as the contractions got stronger every few minutes. She wondered how on earth she was going to endure the car journey to the hospital and sitting down absolutely didn't help. She just screamed her way through till Ralph finally parked up outside the maternity unit, where Sally awaited her with a wheelchair to quickly push her to the labour ward. It was all systems go, as Ralph fortunately found a free parking bay. His inner clock was racing as he was told that the second child could appear much faster than the first, as the body remembered going through this before. Jodie was made as comfortable as can be on the labour bed whilst Sally examined her. She was nearly 10 centimetres dilated, which meant her waters could break at any given moment … and whoosh, like a flowing river it gushed out all over Jodie's maternity book. All she knew was that the baby was clearly desperate to make an appearance, alerting everyone to its arrival. The gender would be a surprise as both had requested not to know at her latest scan. She was offered gas and air, as it was too late to give any other pain relief ; the baby was very much on its way into the world.

Jodie, suddenly remembering the pains, called out, 'Please get her out! I can't stand the pain; the first was bad enough,' she drunkenly told the midwife, who said, 'I remember that one too,' smiling back at Jodie.

Ralph stood by, feeling helpless, grabbing hold of Jodie's hand as she squeezed it tight during the last few contractions, till finally she gently pushed the baby's head out, panting through each breath. Finally with one big almighty effort she pushed the baby out completely. She breathed a big sigh of relief as her day's work had come to a joyous end.

'It's a girl, you have a beautiful baby girl, Jodie,' at which point Ralph leant into Jodie and placed a big kiss on her lips, nearly crying with overwhelming excitement. Sally, meanwhile, had cut the umbilical cord then wrapped the baby in a white towel for now, placing her into Jodie's open arms.

She looked down at her gorgeous blue-eyed girl, who looked directly into her eyes as if to say thank you, I'm here now.

'Have you chosen a name for her, Jodie?' the midwife asked, smiling at her.

'Yes, Isla,' she immediately answered, feeling very proud as emotions ran through her with excitement.

'Perfect.' She wrote that down on a piece of paper and noted the time and date of birth as well. She briefly took the baby to record the necessary height, weight and length before handing her back to her mum. 'She's a perfect weight and all seems fine, congratulations to you both, and I understand a little sister for Amy.'

'Thank you,' Jodie and Ralph said, before Sally continued to explain what was going to happen next. Jodie felt famished after her hard morning's work, so Sally asked for some cereal and toast with a cuppa for them to be brought in by the auxiliary nurse who was bringing the beverage trolley around. Jodie was due to be moved to a ward for further rest and baby checks before hopefully being discharged later that day.

Ralph pulled out his phone to ring Sam, and give her the good news that Isla had safely arrived, weighing 7lbs 5oz. He went into the corridor to ring her, so as not to interfere with the machines on the ward. They would inform everyone else once they got home. After a few hours of rest, and reminding Jodie of the importance of breastfeeding, the midwife discharged her, leaving the bed ready for the next delivery.

*

Jodie finally met up with her long-lost stepbrother, James, who proved to be a very loving additional member to the family and who soon fitted into their busy lives and loved having Amy as his niece. They soon got to know one another over time, with visits to the cottage becoming a regular event, making the most of Amy as she grew up. James, and Dot, Jodie's mum, soon settled their initial differences, leaving all things firmly in the past where they belonged. It required patience and sensible adjustments to make a happy family unit work. Life was too short for anything else, as nothing would ever be perfect, but perfect for them being most important. Amy had ideas of wanting to adopt another small dog but a new brother or sister would definitely be enough for now, as they all adjusted to a new baby, enjoying the addition to the family unit.

Amy climbed the school ladder to a secondary school a few miles away with Lottie. Their relationship deepened through the years, remaining the best of friends, encouraging each other along the way, always there to support each other when needed. Both families often got together, Sam and Jodie keeping their weekly coffee dates in the local café. Sam met a new love in her life who showed his commitment to her and Lottie, making everyone feel happier, when they finally tied the knot in the church which they had started to attend every other week. The enjoyed regular family meetups in the arboretum and meals in one another's houses, making happy memories they could look back on when their children grew up. They compiled family photo albums, adding to them all the time, writing journals together, and they would sit together, remembering the good times they had shared. They could all delve into the albums over a cuppa in future generations.

Jodie and Ralph focused on positivity as they went through their daily lives, going in different directions during the day but spending quality time with one another in the evenings and weekends, supporting their children along their life's adventures. James soon became a regular visitor, enjoying man to man discussions with Ralph over a pint in their local pub, and joining in family meals at weekends, which he had never had as a child: making up for lost time and meeting his new niece, Amy's sister, Isla. She was a picture of health and happiness to all who dropped by on occasions to visit her: chuckling away, showing signs of pure contentment, making everyone jealous yet over the moon for them. Rosie the spaniel also soon became accustomed to her high-pitched giggles as she roared with laughter, especially after having her tummy tickled, especially from those who knew her best: family and close friends. Soon the house became a hive of activity as all and sundry dropped by, often bringing gifts, ranging from toys to baby clothes for baby Isla, and the odd family all-in-one meals, like lasagna, helping Jodie and Ralph, saving them having to cook in the early weeks of having Isla. Jodie felt tired most days from feeding her through the night until Ralph took over with bottle feeding once Isla needed formula milk as she continued to grow, needing more nutrients; doing the night shifts, giving Jodie much-needed rest and forty winks. Jodie was grateful to her friends during the week, who gave Amy lifts to school and her outside activities, which by now had increased as she grew through her teenage years to young adulthood. Ralph became the breadwinner, leaving Jodie to enjoy being a mum again for the last time. That in itself was a frightening thought, knowing that she was getting older each birthday, yet glad since they had only planned on having two children, feeling blessed they had had no problems conceiving. God was indeed looking after them, as she never lost her faith; yes, she had had her doubts when life brought up the odd furball. Everyone believed in something: there was always a higher purpose in life, she would like to think. They found a local church: a more modern, happy clappy family service, where they felt at home, taking great comfort from the weekly singing of choruses, sermons and talks, leaving much food for thought as they went through the week ahead.

Amy became more and more interested in the church and eventually was offered the usual confirmation classes by the female pastor, who had recently joined, the previous male pastor having moved on to his next parish. The classes ran for twelve weeks, up to the big confirmation service one Sunday morning in May, which became a very important day in Amy's life, one that she would never forget. as long as She continued to follow her faith, as she swore her oath on the Holy Bible, for the rest of her life: something that should never be taken lightly, in her parents' opinion. Jodie had hoped that Amy would one day pass on her belief to her sister, Isla, when it was her turn to attend confirmation classes. The confirmation classes were held weekly in Amy's school. Her RE lessons covered not only the Christian faith but also multicultural faiths as they lived in a multicultural society.

The day of the confirmation service was indeed a big event for the whole family and close friends, hopefully all enjoying the day. All that was needed was for the sun to brighten up the day's events, allowing a lovely buffet outside in the cottage garden. Jodie wanted to ask who could provide sandwiches and cakes: she wanted to mark this very special occasion for her loving, caring daughter. She started to spread the word around, by mouth, as you do. Jodie was most grateful to receive a text from her best friend, Sam, who was more than willing to help with the catering on the day.

I'll provide various sandwiches and a Victoria sponge cake and/or carrot cake, some juices, the girls will be happy with that I'm sure. Something for everyone. Hugs S Xx

Jodie fired one back, giving her a thumbs up emoji.

Once she got everything in motion, she started to compile a to-do list on the notes app on her phone, jogging her memory as she ticked them off one by one. She already felt a great sense of pleasure and achievement, knowing that she was going to pull this event off in style. As it was only going to be for the chosen few, to excuse the pun, catering seemed a doddle. Jodie just needed to borrow some outdoor chairs, a trestle table, some crockery and cutlery, buy some flowery paper serviettes and paper plates and the job was a good'un, she reassured herself with a big smile across her face. She also bought a pack of confirmation invitations with silver encrusted lettering for the header, making it a cheaper option than going to a printing company; those days were now in the past. Affordability was always the key. Anyway. it was no comparison to weddings, you just had to pitch your spending budget.

Two weeks later the day of Amy's confirmation arrived; it was held one Sunday morning in May at the church. All had an early night before the morning's service followed by the reception, which was held in the cottage garden as intended. Jodie looked up the weather forecast on her phone, seeing that temperatures were going to be in the 20s, which was very pleasing. Someone was looking after them from above, she concluded. One by one they all started to arrive from the church after the service, where Amy had clearly spoken the words, 'I do,' at the appropriate times in the service, causing both Jodie and Ralph to shed a happy tear, saying, 'Amen,' to conclude the service. Amy made her way slowly back to where her family were sitting, being greeted with hugs and kisses from all around her. Amy felt relief that it was over, yet felt a sense of blessing, a peace within her she couldn't quite put into words. It felt good to be in God's family, which she clearly expressed in her happy smiles as the day went on. The pastor, Grace Woods, shook her hand during the buffet as she walked towards her, saying she had been a diligent student on the course, showing signs of great willingness to take this matter seriously, which Amy seemed chuffed to hear, thanking her for her teachings. She then made her way around, greeting everyone in turn, thanking Amy's parents for their support throughout and the lovely buffet laid before them.

Home to roost and relax after the day's events. They decided to order a takeaway as Jodie was too tired to cook, choosing a Chinese from the JustEat app which Ralph had downloaded earlier, and which filled them up before bed, all needing an early night.

Monday morning came around quickly, though thankfully it was a Bank Holiday, and after yesterday's confirmation they were all relieved to have an extra day off to recover. They were grateful for a lie-in, holding out for as long as possible before Isla started to shuffle about in her carry cot, kicking, making gurgling noises and indicating that she was due for her first bottle of the day. Peace over, they both rolled over, giving one another a morning kiss.

'Here we go again,' they said. Jodie was relieved that her breastfeeding days were coming to an end: she was only feeding to drain her remaining milk. They all took turns holding the bottle to Isla's mouth: seeing her suckle was a picture of pure heaven as she clasped her tiny fingers around her bottle helping to support it. It was in those times that they could not help but feel blessed to have a new life in their world; they were truly one happy family, watching Isla grow by the day as she explored the world around her. They only needed to blink and things changed again, and that precious moment was gone; just happy memories.

Chapter Twenty-Four

Three months had elapsed in the Smith household. Isla was starting to get more active; she lay on a soft blanket on the floor with a play swing frame above her, dangling soft toys to grab hold of and pull on, feeling the different textures, lighting up her sparkling eyes, smiles all over her pretty face as she gurgled away to herself, possibly trying to form words. Only she knew what she was saying; so long as she was happy, they couldn't be happier. They could watch her for hours and Jodie often did, knowing this milestone would soon pass her by as it was her last child. Amy would often babysit while her mum busied herself in the kitchen or just caught up with the mundane chores which had to be done; all mucking in together.

Amy was soon at the end of primary school and was going a final coach trip organised by the headmistress, for Year Five and Six classes, to a water park offering kayaking and canoeing for all abilities and the less physically able; up and down the beautiful scenic lake along the river Wye in mid-Wales. A very exciting end to their primary schooling before entering the big world of secondary school, where their future would start in earnest. Amy was indeed ready for this, as was her still best friend Lottie, whom she had known from the very beginning in school. They were pretty much inseparable, even with their mums meeting weekly at the local café on the high street.

Ralph moved up the career ladder in his new job, with his craftsmanship leading to a floor manager post at his firm. This enabled them as a family to live a more financially comfortable life. Jodie returned to her teaching assistant post after an initial six months' maternity leave, which tied in very nicely with Ralph's promotion, making life in general easier all round.

A residential trip was organised by the school's head for Years Five and Six to an indoor camping retreat along the River Wye, in the idyllic area of mid-Wales. It took a lot of organisation, starting the year before, giving all pupils lots to look forward to as the school year came to a close at the end of July. Teachers and parents volunteered to help that week if needed, depending on many pupils went. This time there were twenty, all girls. They gathered at the school at nine o'clock on a Monday morning to be escorted on a coach to the residential site. It was very exciting as they were paired up with their travel buddies, getting to know one another as they chatted and giggled along the way. Three hours later the coach turned onto a gravel area in front of their home for the week. Miss Thomas made her way to the front, taking the already switched on microphone the driver gave her, to explain to the girls what was happening next.

'Testing, testing,' she said, as it hissed with shrill high-pitched sounds before she moved the mic into the perfect position to start her announcements. 'OK, we've arrived at the holiday site for the week, which I'm sure you will have already noticed.

'Yeah,' shrieks from the rear of the coach broke out in jolly unison.

'As I was saying, or trying to,' she smiled, fully understanding the excitement, 'listen very carefully, I'm only saying this once,' she continued. 'Will everyone start to make their way to the front of the coach, one at a time, saying thank you to our wonderful driver, Dave, for getting us safely here today.' Suddenly loud applause arose from the back as they clapped together. 'Once outside, please form a tidy line. Dave will open the luggage compartment underneath and start unloading your bags, placing them in a pile to one side. Once he gives you the all-clear, he will hand each piece of luggage out whilst you look closely to see if it's yours. This must be done in an orderly manner, or else you'll have me to answer to. Is that clear, girls?'

'Yes, Miss Thomas,' they all shouted out together. Within ten minutes all the luggage had been claimed by the owners and they walked briskly inside the building, a member of staff leading the way, followed by Miss Thomas. A brave receptionist, seeing the numbers, soon calmed them, welcoming them to their residential retreat as she ticked their names off on a list on a clipboard, then pointed them to the dormitories further along the corridor, where they would be staying with their buddies during the week. The rooms were equipped with bunk beds with lightweight bedding. By this stage they were all paired up with the person they had sat next to on the coach, firm friendships having already been made. The girls were laden with rucksacks strapped on their backs, fully equipped and looking all very excited. Fortunately the sun was out and the weather forecast for the week ahead was looking promising, making all the difference. Soon they were all settling in as they unpacked, putting clothes in the various chests of drawers around the dormitory, trying to make a good impression, even if they did just stuff their clothes in and force the drawers to close; it was a learning curve for all. It was possible to tell from how the clothes were folded who had packed: either their mums or the girls. Organisational skills were well and truly put to the test, which was the whole reason behind the trip. It was an introduction to independence before eventually leaving home, following their dreams in life.

Each day started with a rota for sharing bathroom facilities, which they soon got used to, followed by a meal in the dining room, lining up by the serving counter in an orderly fashion. The day then progressed with an itinerary set by the teachers with various outdoor activities. All the girls were put into groups according to their chosen activity, so an element of planning was required regarding suitable clothing before they started the day ahead. It soon became clear as the days unfolded; they didn't want to miss out on anything.

All seemed to be going well until one day Jodie received an unexpected phone call from Amy's head of class, saying she had had a bad fall whilst on her year's trip in mid-Wales. Amy's canoe had capsized, with her friend Lottie being caught up in a downstream current and hitting a large rock nearby. Both girls were out of their depth and received head injuries. They were wearing the orange life jackets given to them before setting off from the water's edge. Amy was the stronger swimmer of the two of them. This was totally unexpected although accidents did happen on the river from time to time. Fortunately, one of the other onboard teachers, two canoes behind them, spotted signs of the girls, as they started to wave their arms up in the air, before their canoe did a somersault upside-down, lingering a few moments underneath the surface of the river. Both teachers had been given walkie talkies by the rescue crew cabin where the canoes were hired out, as a safety precaution if the need arose. Miss Thomas, one of the teachers on the trip, rang through to the rescue crew, alerting them of the immediate incident. After asking initial questions about who was on board, their names and ages and, most importantly, if either of them could swim, they sent out an inflatable red dinghy, with its engine at the stern. Two rescue crew, a male and female on board, were soon whizzing through the river current to help the girls, by which time they had managed to swim out from underneath the capsized canoe. Amy had somehow been able to grab hold of Lottie as she kicked her legs frantically until they reached safety at the water's edge. They were shivering and shaking, holding hands as they noticed a tiny red boat-like shape becoming more and more visible as it came hurtling towards them, much to the girls' sheer delight. Amy waved her arms from side to side up in the air, so that they could be seen. As the dinghy came closer towards the shore, Amy heard shouts from the crew.

'Stay there, we are nearly with you,' a man's voice called out to them, as they sat together embracing one another, shivering and in tears, holding on for dear life as the dinghy slowly floated onto shore with its engine already turned off.

'Hello, you two, we are here now to help you. It's OK, you're safe with us now. The female member of the crew calmly spoke to them, seeing the girls happy to see them yet cold and muddled as to what had just happened.

'OK, my name is Julie, and this is Paul, my assistant. We are going to keep you both safe.' Julie promptly took out two foil blankets to retain the heat, wrapping them around them before helping the girls one by one on board the inflatable dinghy, which was now bedded on a layer of small stones underneath it. Amy held onto Julie's arm as she gently lowered her into the dinghy; she felt safe at last and warm in the foil blanket. Julie quickly carried out some initial important tests. Temperature and breathing all seemed to be OK as they were kept cosy and warm from the foil blanket, acting as insulation. Once back on dry land they were strongly advised to rest back at the camp until the morning, making sure they drank plenty of fluids and ate good food that evening. Once Julie and Paul had handed them over to their teachers, satisfied they were out of any immediate danger, all that was needed was rest and fluids. The team was soon alerted to another rescue call nearby, which proved the point that a lifeboat rescue team was essential around water as danger could strike at any time.

'You had us all so frightened earlier, girls, but we are so glad you're both OK now. We've been in touch with your parents: don't worry, they aren't annoyed or anything, just concerned. You're both good to go now, to enjoy the rest of the week here. They obviously send their love and virtual hugs,' Miss Thomas explained to them, which reassured them once they felt calmer after the initial shock. They were offered hot chocolate with squirty cream, after a change of clothing from the spare clothes box back at the camp area, lifting their mood instantly, especially with a fruity flapjack.

The week moved swiftly by, with evenings by the campfire outside, singing songs accompanied by a guitar which a member of staff had brought, with hot chocolate and cookies, all handmade by the school catering staff for the trip. A baton was passed around, and each girl had to explain what they had enjoyed the most so far, as well as their difficult moments. The canoe overturning was naturally one of them; one they probably wouldn't forget for a long time, if ever, so they had a story to tell their own children one day in the future. Happy days, but the week ended after four days, as they would return to the school late on Friday afternoon. Thursday evening came with mixed feelings as they gathered up all their belongings around the dormitories, making sure that every nook and cranny was searched twice before closer inspection from the duty teachers. Bags packed, ready to go, they formed a sensible line as they walked out of the building towards the waiting coach lined up outside, placing their bags by the bus to be stored underneath in the luggage compartment by the driver. Three hours later, after a few breaks to stretch their legs, they were back at the school, where their parents, grandparents and guardians were eagerly waiting to cheer them as they stepped off the coach to greet them. They had been chatting to one another before the coach finally arrived, then they all said the same thing when they opened up their child's bag, being greeted by dirty, smelly washing, they needed to put on a face mask! However, they all agreed that the main thing was that a good time was had by all. The children soon peeled off, feeling weary, needing to catch up with sleep as they were reunited with their parents and were given hugs and kisses, waving goodbye to their mates before they followed their parents to their cars, to go home to rest and recover.

The teachers breathed a sigh of relief, after the last pupil had been picked up in the car park. As much as they, too, had enjoyed the week away in the idyllic setting away from routine, they couldn't wait to return home to their families. A chill-out weekend, with a fizzy alcoholic drink in hand, sitting in the garden, was much needed to soothe the body, mind and soul. Fortunately, sunshine was forecast, with a light breeze, enough to blow the washing dry on the line.

Chapter Twenty-Five

Meanwhile Jodie, Ralph and baby Isla enjoyed precious time together, making memories along the way, with Rosie keeping them sane, with many walks to the park. Isla was soon enjoying her company as she tried to help Isla crawl along the lounge carpet, imitating her moves, whilst Isla giggled and laughed to herself. She was indeed one very happy, contented baby, amusing visitors when they dropped round. Life was good and for that they were all very grateful. To be healthy was the main thing in life, denied to too many these days, they agreed.

*

Some three months had passed, and Isla was soon up on her feet, wobbly at first as she took her first steps, gaining confidence each day, to the point where she wouldn't stop walking until, due to sheer tiredness, she fell in a heap on the carpet, always bouncing back, as children do. Jodie was relieved when those days came to an end, as she had to watch her like a hawk all the time. Ralph took over when she had to prepare meals, which was a somewhat welcome distraction. She would ask her Google mini to play upbeat tunes in the kitchen, helping her to relax and focus on the job in hand, with the odd dance in between keeping her fit.

Isla started at playgroup in the local church twice weekly, where mums were also offered tea and coffee as they sat and nattered to other mums, forming lasting friendships whilst their little ones played with various toys, donated by others who had long outgrown them. Jodie made the most of these social events, knowing Isla was her last child; she would never get this time back. She was a very dedicated mum, enjoying every stage as they grew up, watching Amy and now Isla reach those all-important milestones. They both progressed through primary school, moving to the same secondary school. Extracurricular activities included the usual Brownies and Girl Guides, with weekends away at camp. Both girls enjoyed working their way through the different badges, especially the nature ones, which they found the most exciting. Jodie's days of chief badge sewer-on soon disappeared after Amy perfected her needle and thread skills, sewing an armful and immersing herself in most crafts; becoming Miss Independent, which naturally stood her in good stead later in life. They couldn't be happier for their girls, something all parents wished.

Time moved swiftly by and those interesting yet challenging teenage years kicked in, where the teenager knows best, well, that's how they saw it, as they each found their individual walks through life, learning more about themselves from the frustrations along the journey. The all-important GCSEs and A level years were the most stressful years to get through. It was all worth it in the end as they each went in a different direction with their career choices. Amy, having always been an outdoor girl, decided to follow a veterinary career, being a great lover of all creatures. She followed in her father's footsteps, as he had grown up on a farm.

Isla, on the other hand, was more a people person, seeing the need for more carers, especially in old people's homes, where anyone might need that extra one on one care someday in the far distant future. Isla regularly volunteered in nearby care homes, earning extra pocket money to help, going away with friends or that must-have a meal out, which she loved. She kept many of her friends from both schools, including Lottie, who was originally Amy's friend.

Other weekend activities included riding; Amy joined a riding school in the countryside, with weekly riding lessons on a lovely rust-coloured horse named, appropriately, Rusty. She attended a hands-on weekend, arriving early in the morning to catch her assigned horse from the field armed with her bridle, which proved difficult on occasion as her horse was quite content eating grass or was just generally stubborn at that hour, something Amy could relate to herself, especially the latter. She wasn't an early riser, but soon snapped out of that one as she found the singing of the birds to be very therapeutic at that hour. Amy was awarded a pink rosette for best grooming skills shown over the weekend, which placed the biggest smile on her face. After many indoor arena lessons, she learned to walk in rhythm with her Rusty, then the art of trotting, using all her muscles and more to keep up with the rest of the horses, then to canter, being the toughest of them all as the pace became faster and faster, which Amy really didn't enjoy, as she had to hold on for dear life! She much preferred a gentle walk through the country roads, until one day the inevitable happened. She fell off, knocking herself out and suffering from concussion. She remembered only waking up at home in her bed, notably confused, asking the same questions time and time again, which was clearly worrying for her mum, dad and Isla. The doctor was called out to check her over and he prescribed lots of bed rest until the initial effects had worn off, when she could resume normal life. Amy fortunately wasn't put off by the misfortune but she took her time mounting a horse again, before going out along the country roads.

Isla took on more jobs in different homes for the elderly, which she thoroughly enjoyed, meeting and chatting with the residents over endless cups of tea and coffee, homemade cakes and cookies, either made on site or by volunteers who donated them regularly. Isla even tried out her skills on them, perfecting them along the way, adding another skill to her CV. It all helped to form a picture which she would use to promote herself in future jobs. As they both reached driving age, Amy and Isla were very keen to learn that skill, which needed all the alertness they had, as the roads got busier in the twenty-first century. Amy passed after two attempts at the practical test, acing the theory test. Life was beginning to get more expensive as Mum and Dad spent their hard-earned money on block lessons. Amy naturally started asking her mates who had already passed for any driving school recommendations and reasonably priced instructors, preferably local to the area. The day eventually arrived with both girls banging on the cottage door, shouting, 'Mum, Dad, we passed!' One of them opened the door to see their certificates held up to prove it, though why would one lie about such a milestone, never to be repeated.

Amy's and Isla's lives were now independent from their parents'. As affording another car was out of the question for now, Ralph initially insured them on Jodie's car, as it was the older of the two. It proved to be a very costly outlay. Jodie and Ralph had to set some ground rules for driving; one important rule was restricting the number of friends who wanted a free lift, possibly leading to driving distractions and unforeseen collisions, which no one wanted. The girls respected their parents' wishes, paying them petrol and doing chores around the cottage, sharing the load equally between them. On a few occasions like birthdays and wedding anniversaries, they pulled out all the stops, cooking them a favourite family meal or a romantic dinner for two, whilst they disappeared, walking to their local pub or café on the high street.

*

Family life continued pretty much as everyone else's, the boring mandatory weekdays with their daily routines, then those magical days out, either in the arboretum or a meal out, meeting their friends with their children, forming lasting friendships along the way. The years flew by quickly after they had completed secondary school. They had to decide about further education, be it at college or university, before entering the often scary, big world of work until retirement, which was obviously decades away. Amy decided to attend an agricultural university, to learn all about creatures great and small, which she thoroughly enjoyed, especially the placements she was offered to gain more hands-on experience. Her first placement was on a dairy farm in the Cotswolds, in beautiful surroundings. Isla didn't fancy going to university, so she embarked on different courses at college for the caring profession, though not entirely sure she would choose this as a lifelong career.

The biggest milestones were when the girls turned eighteen in the summer, Amy first, then Isla a few years later. They each wanted to mark the occasion by celebrating with friends at a local Italian restaurant in the village.

It was party time in the Smith household; balloons, banners, booze, the whole shebang, with no expense spared, although desperately trying to stick within a budget.

'Neither of us earns heaps of money, but we want you to look back on this time with fond memories in later life, where you can tell your children all about your coming of age.'

'Thanks, both of you, we promise to be on our best behaviour. All we want is a meal out at a local Italian restaurant with our friends, possibly a few mocktails at a bar or something. We'll even contribute some money, if that helps.'

After much discussion they decided that the girls would have a meal out at their favourite Italian restaurant, moving on to a dessert bar serving delicious ice creams, with different toppings, and crepes and waffles, alongside mocktails as well as special coffees. Jodie and Ralph realised that their two once-young girls had become grown up, loving their independence yet trusting and sensible by nature. Their job was done, they could finally relax, dropping their guard a little yet always lurking in the background; ready to offer support and advice when asked as the girls made their own way in the world, knowing they had done their best. Now it was over to them as one day they would fly the nest, knowing they could always come back for advice or a shoulder to cry on whenever they wanted. They could only do one thing now, and that was to step back and be proud of how their two girls had turned out.

Acknowledgments

I have thoroughly enjoyed writing this book over the past year, gaining inspiration from other books within the feel-good genre. All the characters are from my own imagination as they have played through my mind, and I also drew on my own childhood memories. I always enjoyed travelling, keeping a diary of events whilst visiting relatives in my teens, flying solo to Germany, which has remained my second home, forming memories I will never forget. My love of animals extended from owning two goldfish won at a fair back in the day, to a hamster, then later on my first German short-haired pointer, featuring on every photo my father ever took whilst I was growing up!

Most importantly I must thank all from The Choir Press in Gloucestershire for all their help and hard work; without their input this book would not have become a dream come true. My heartfelt thanks to you all. Lastly to my family for the ongoing support and love throughout, and to close friends; I love you all.

Milton Keynes UK
Ingram Content Group UK Ltd.
UKHW010631101123
432322UK00006B/368